STORM
ON THE
HORIZON

THE ZONE

PAUL A WINTERS

This is a work of fiction. Names, characters, businesses, places, events and incidents are either the products of the author's imagination or used in a fictitious manner. Any resemblance to actual persons, living or dead, or actual events is purely coincidental.

Cover art by Matt Stawicki

Revised: January 2016

Copyright © 2014 Paul A Winters
All rights reserved.

ISBN: 1480172596
ISBN 13: 9781480172593
Library of Congress Control Number: 2012920443
CreateSpace Independent Publishing Platform
North Charleston, South Carolina

AUTHOR'S NOTE

One winter night many years ago, I had an extraordinary dream. I awoke and jotted down a brief summary of it as the sun peaked over the horizon. Afterwards, the dream left me wondering why the main character was out in the desert trying to locate aliens he couldn't see. To satisfy my curiosity, over the next couple of days I wrote a prologue right up to the point where the dream started. Before I knew it, this alternate reality drew me in further because of so many unanswered questions. Who were these mysterious aliens and where did they come from? How did all the technology they were using come about? With so many possibilities coming to mind, I felt compelled to continue the tale. The journey to complete it has been long and challenging but what matters most is that I never gave up. I'm excited to share with you the answers to the questions I had back then.

As a reader, you deserve the very best! From the beginning, my focus for this story has been on quality not quantity. I wanted it thought provoking, intense, and emotional—the kind of book you can't put down or stop thinking about long after you finish. I hope you enjoy reading *Storm on the Horizon: The Zone* as much as I did writing it.

Thanks to everyone who helped make my dream a reality.

At the start of each chapter, an icon will appear to represent a major shift in the story and the main character(s) involved.

Story Threads		Main characters and the names given to them throughout the book.
1		**Hamrick:** ★ ★General Dave Hamrick
2		**Hopper**: Captain Lucas Phillips
3		**Dell**: Second Lieutenant Annadell Thompson, Eva
4		**Pierce:** ★ ★ ★ ★ General Shadley Pierce, Reformer
5		**O'Connell**: Chief Scientist Kathleen O'Connell
6		**Reckston** and **Ritan**
		Information

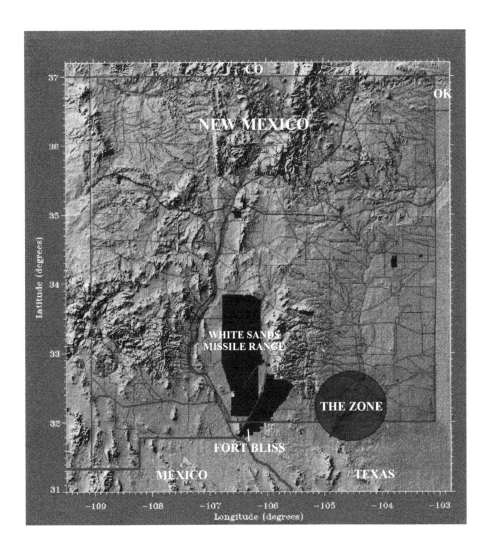

ANNIVERSARY

5/1/2033

Eileen's summer dress and auburn hair flutter in a warm gentle breeze as she sits on a dusty park bench on the outskirts of El Paso, TX. In the distance, the Franklin Mountains begin to cast shadows over the arid desert landscape. Her face expresses sadness as she finishes writing a letter then seals it in a small white envelope. She puts it in her purse then gazes off towards a dozen or so tough-looking soldiers with their wives standing about enjoying time off post after several months of intense training.

Her soft brown eyes search for her husband Captain Lucas Phillips and spots him standing next to a windblown tree amid a group of celebrating men in Green Berets. He looks over at her as if reading her mind and blows her a kiss. She smiles and waves thinking he always had a knack for being in the right place and time. However, her smile slowly fades. Today is a special day in their relationship and she wanted to share her feelings with him.

With the sun long set and rain on the way, they start the hour-long trip back to Fort Bliss. The ride is quiet but Eileen is relieved to be alone with her husband. She looks at his calm, clean-shaven face then breaks the silence. "I've listened to your graduates call you "Hopper" all day but you'll always be Lucas to me." She takes the envelope from her purse. "Do you remember when we met five years ago today?"

Hopper smiles as he takes a hand off the wheel and runs his fingers through her hair. His voice is quiet but confident. "Yes sweetie, how could I forget?" He tries to lay his hand on her knee but she prevents him by gingerly handing him the letter.

Eileen takes a deep breath before speaking again. "Lucas, please pull off to the side of the road for a bit. I have something I want to share with you."

Hopper tenses as he parks the car on an embankment near a creek swollen from recent rains then turns to look at her. Her caring expression reminds him of the first time he met her on the midnight train out of Fayetteville, North Carolina, shortly after his brother's death. It seems like only yesterday when she sat down next to him to kindly lend an ear and shoulder. She was his guardian angel that night, sent to comfort and unlock his hardened heart. He realizes now he wouldn't have had the strength to continue on home without her.

Hopper swallows hard as he looks at her letter in his hand knowing this talk was long overdue. He tries to smile. "I know you've given me the best five years of my life. From the moment we first met you've accepted me for who I am and have given me the chance to love and be loved."

Eileen tenderly touches his cheek then leans over and kisses his lips. "Lucas, you know we have a special relationship. I've never had stronger feelings for you than I do right now."

Hopper gently caresses her hands. "I know what you're about to say. That I've been distant lately." He lowers his eyes. "I'm sorry sweetie, it makes me feel guilty troubling you with all my thoughts. Every day, I'm expected to put my feelings aside to train soldiers for combat situations around the world. When I come home at night, all I want is to see you smiling. I really do love you more than you'll ever know." He looks up and tenderly wipes a tear streaming down her face.

Eileen motions for him to open the letter but pauses when the sky brightens with a brilliant red glow. Off in the distance an angry red, orange, and yellow clouds boil skyward. It looks as if the sun is bursting from the earth itself. Seconds later, a massive shockwave ripples over the desert landscape like a giant tsunami, violently rolling their vehicle into the watery depths of the creek below.

Eileen slowly opens her eyes and as if in a dream, stares out the car window at the glowing water around her. She is startled when Hopper gently nudges her arm but his voice is desperate as he calls her name.

"Eileen...*Eileen!* Are you all right? We don't have much time, the cab is filling with water!" She listlessly shakes her head no and then yes. He quickly turns his attention to the windshield as his survival skills take over.

She tries to shift her legs but realizes they don't move. With water gushing into the cab, she is unable to look down. Panicking, she feels her legs with her hand then realizes she's paralyzed from the waist down. Time slows, sounds fade and a calm spreads throughout her body. In slow motion, she watches the water rise to her shoulders as her husband tries desperately to save her. Intense emotions swell up inside when she realizes she may never see him again. With great effort she reaches over to get his attention. "Lucas, honey...I want you to always remember...I love you."

He quickly glances at her with concern. "Hang in there sweetie! I'll get us out as soon as the water pressure equalizes. Can you swim?"

Eileen doesn't have the heart to tell him the truth but answers in a brave voice. "I'll meet you on the other side." She gives him a sad tender smile amid the chaos.

Hopper realizes something is terribly wrong but with water up to their necks, there is no time to ask. He squeezes her arm tightly as he looks into her caring brown eyes once more. "Try not to worry, when we get to the surface everything will be OK! I'm going to kick the windshield out now, are you ready?" Her eyes open wide then nods. "On three…One! Two! Three!"

Water instantly floods the compartment as the windshield breaks away. Moments later Hopper emerges from the water illuminated by an eerie red glow radiating from the clouds above. He realizes he is still holding the envelope and subconsciously puts it in his upper shirt pocket as he wades to shore.

As the seconds tick by, it becomes clear Eileen is in trouble. He frantically runs back into the water and dives to the car to see her lifeless body still restrained in her seat belt. He tries desperately to free her but the latch is broken. Unable to hold his breath any longer, he reaches out and runs his fingers over her beautiful face one last time then lets the current carry him away.

On shore, Hopper stands motionlessly watching the raging clouds spreading out in the sky above. He drops to his knees as he looks at the water where his wife's body is then raises his head in anguish and cries out, "Why did you have to leave me now? You made my life bearable…you gave me strength…hope…" His body slumps as he leans back on his legs and whispers, "Eileen, what am I going to do without you?" Hopper's body trembles in agony as he rocks himself back and forth.

The sky grows dark overhead as dust and ash fall like snow around him. Numb with shock, he crawls up the embankment to the road and collapses on the pavement.

He will never know how long he sat there or who picked him up— only that he was taken to a makeshift hospital. The days that follow are a blur as he tries to cope with Eileen's death and the massive destruction around him. With no outlet to release his emotions, his heart fills with anger. He slowly recovers as the weeks and months pass by but the wound in his heart never fully heals.

WALL OF FIRE

5/1/2033

Alone at his desk Major General Hamrick rubs his tired eyes then reaches for a cup of coffee only to remember that he finished it moments ago. He frowns then glances through dusty office blinds just as lightning flashes on the horizon. He may be only fifty-three but the stress of his job made him feel much older. He sighs thinking he should have already retired to spend more time enjoying life with his grandkids.

He opens a file labeled "Captain Lucas Phillips" to read his performance evaluation. In the upper right-hand corner is a picture of a muscular man in his early thirties with short black hair and a crooked smile. He nods remembering a time when he was young and fit then continues to read.

Outside, rain splatters against the window as a red light shines through the cracks in the blinds and onto the far wall. The lights go out as he turns the page. Irritated, he opens a drawer for a flashlight but stops as flickering red light catches his attention. *Just my luck, another fire caused by lightning.*

He fumbles over to the window and draws the blinds. A brilliant red glow instantly immerses him. "Oh my God!"

Across the desert, a massive wall of fire boils skyward and quickly spreads out to the horizon. Without thinking, General Hamrick drops to the floor and covers his eyes. Seconds later all the windows in the office shatter into a million pieces as intense heat singes his body and burns his lungs. An eternity goes by for the immense shock wave to subside. However, before he can stand, it returns from the opposite direction like an unleashed tempest.

To keep himself from ejecting out the window, he desperately grabs the radiator as the roof rips violently away. As the wave subsides, he finds himself staring in terror at the sky filled with boiling bright-red clouds streaked with yellow and orange.

Hamrick raises to his knees to peek over the remains of the windowsill to see Fort Bliss, Texas, burning out of control. The horror of it all is soon lost as thick ash and smoke descends from above leaving only distant explosions and screams in the night.

Choking on fumes, he tears a piece of cloth from his tattered uniform and covers his face. He limps through the ruins of the operations building in hopes of reaching the subterranean army base far below.

After traversing through a massive amount of debris, General Hamrick finally stands in front of a heavily fortified door in the basement of the building and puts his hand on a metal plate at its center. A green security light from above immediately scans his body. As the door slides open, he enters a brilliantly lit stairwell and descends but each step causes intense pain to his injured leg.

He finally reaches a level labeled COMMAND CENTER then opens a glass door and enters a large open hall with green plants and white furniture dotting the area along with moving images of landscapes displayed on the walls. Several people in lab coats rush by without looking at him. He follows them and passes several large connecting corridors before arriving at a barricaded entrance guarded by four heavily armed men who salute him as he enters.

Inside, he finds a skeleton crew of officers and technicians frantically running around trying to get the equipment back online. Most of them are still in shock, horrified by scenes displayed on large three-dimensional screens overhead.

Hamrick approaches a sophisticated chair in the center of the room surrounded by several rows of computer terminals normally manned by station operators. Duty officer Master Sergeant Quinn hastily arrives and hands him some damage reports. In a way, he welcomes them to keep his mind occupied and composure intact.

Before he can finish the first page, the Sergeant lowers his head and interrupts. "Sir, I'm sorry to inform you that the plane carrying the Post Commander and Deputy Commander went down during the explosion and are presumed dead! You are now the highest-ranking officer on Post. What are your orders?"

General Hamrick takes a mental step backward. He never wanted to be in command at the loss of his friends. He takes a deep breath then pats the Sergeant on the back before sitting down in the command chair. He looks at a maze of buttons and monitors surrounding him but focuses on one in particular showing a satellite view of a massive, reddish brown cloud spreading out over the Chihuahuan desert in all directions.

Hamrick takes a deep breath then flips a switch on the armchair. "Attention to all personnel. This is General Hamrick. General Adams and General Harding may have died during the explosion. I'm now acting Post Deputy Commander until this crisis is over. As of this moment, we are at DEFCON 1. We must protect this base and our country at all cost. I want all surviving personnel to report to base and get critical systems back online and counter-strike missiles armed and ready, ASAP! I don't know what we are up against so I'm counting on you to make it happen. Hamrick out."

THE ZONE

5/1/2033

A catastrophic explosion encompassing over 120 square kilometers devastates parts of southeast New Mexico and surrounding areas killing an estimated thirty thousand people. Immediately following the explosion, President Andrew Wellington puts the country in a state of emergency.

Four star General Shadley Pierce diverts his flight while en route to Washington DC and hastily arrives at Fort Bliss' underground Command Center, as investigations get underway. Frustrated with General Hamrick's cautious probing of the abnormal storm raging inside the blast zone, he quickly takes command. Without further delay, he orders six assessment teams into the area to look for survivors and survey the damage.

Radio and visual contact is quickly lost as the teams disappear into the mysterious cloud of boiling dust. Six hours pass with no sign of them returning. Angry at the loss of contact with his troops, he orders three heavily armed squads of Special Forces into the same area but they too disappear. General Pierce immediately quarantines the area then orders the construction of hundreds of temporary watchtowers outside the massive storm's stationary outer perimeter.

Meanwhile, back in Washington, DC, scientists from around the world assemble to discuss radical weather changes and random communication blackouts worldwide. Soon, several strange facts begin to emerge.

Less than a minute before the blast in the desert, power outages occurred throughout the southeast New Mexico region, which coincided with a mild earthquake. Other than thermal radiation, no other anomalies such as biological or radioactive emissions were detected before, during, or after the blast. All forms of radio communications have become nonexistent in and around the area. Atmospheric and ground conditions continue to deteriorate as the raging storm intensifies. However, the most disturbing fact of all is the total inability of the military's most advanced satellites called Eagle Eye, to penetrate the storm for topographical scans.

Under extreme pressure to provide additional details about the blast and ongoing storm, President Wellington orders Pierce to increase military operations in and around the Zone. Meanwhile, at an official press release, he reassures the public and world leaders that investigations by the military and top scientists are proceeding as planned and that the situation is already under control. However, it is far from the truth...

5/6/2033

Safe, deep inside Fort Bliss' fortified Command Center, General Pierce orders one hundred and eighty personnel operating fifteen tanks and thirty all-terrain support vehicles into the raging storm to look for survivors in a city known as Carlsbad. Its location is approximately sixteen kilometers inside the perimeter. However, ten minutes into the operation ground sensors record multiple explosions in the vicinity. Pierce immediately orders an additional eight hover jets armed with armor piercing rounds to provide air support for ground troops who may be under attack. Soon as they disappear into the dust, ground sensors record another series of explosions.

As dusk falls over the region, hopes of any hover jets, vehicles or personnel returning to base quickly fade. Personnel at Command soon dub the operation the Bermuda Mission in reference to the Bermuda Triangle where boats and planes have mysteriously vanished without a trace. Nine days pass before another plan is prepared and implemented.

5/15/2033

Angry and frustrated, General Pierce orders a company of eighty soldiers connected by several fiber-optic cables into the storm to record audiovisual data in real-time. The soldiers spaced some five meters apart, form a human chain four hundred meters long. As the last of them march into the raging storm, personnel at Command watch in horror as unseen forces ram the cables throwing the men off their feet then sequentially crushed. Amid the screams of pain and gunfire, some of them cry out about a presence invading their minds just before all fiber-optic cables go offline.

Days later, after a careful review of the data, scientists and experts are still unable to detect the unseen forces that destroyed the troops. The "March of Madness" will never be forgotten.

6/3/2033

Abruptly, the rampant storm inside the Zone dissipates leaving the area basking under an unusually clear blue sky. Eagle Eye satellites immediately transmit the horror of all the preceding battles. The men and women of Command are stunned as hundreds of dead soldiers lie scattered among pieces of fragmented vehicles, tanks, and hover jets. Personnel review the satellite images in vain but find no traces of life or adversary forces.

Adding to the mystery, the town of Carlsbad has completely vanished leaving no trace of any kind. Before a reconnaissance mission can get underway, swirling dust clouds violently erupt from the ground leaving the area once more impervious to communications or visual information.

Armed with data from the brief clearing, General Pierce, his staff, and fellow scientists prepare for their next opportunity. Months later, they finally get their chance to implement their plans.

OPERATION IRON CROSS

8/13/2033

Without warning, an enormous pulse of light erupts from the center of the swirling chaotic storm inside the Zone and spreads out beyond its boundaries like a ripple on a pond. Immediately, the sky clears and electronic communications restore across the region. Within the hour, Operation Iron Cross advances on the Zone like a hungry bird of prey.

Deep under the ruins of Fort Bliss, at the heart of Command, General Pierce directs a large mechanized army as Operation Iron Cross unfolds near the quarantined area. Several large 3D monitors around the room display a moving wedge-shaped formation of ground vehicles and hover jets that kick dust high into the air as they move across open desert. As they near the invisible line of the previous storm boundary, a third of the army at its center suddenly halts as the left and right flanks continue to advance.

Moments later, thousands of weapons come to life and create a massive wall of tracer-round crossfire. High overhead, Eagle Eye satellites map the impact of deflected ammo rounds, while mainframe computers plot dozens of moving objects on a large topographical map at Command.

Finally able to see his enemy, Pierce stands up and points to the screen. "So...you're afraid to show yourselves. Well, I can see you now cowards!" He immediately transmits the enemy positions to the attacking army as well as a retreat order to move outside the perimeter. Seconds later, hundreds of high-impact missiles erupt from the hover jets and streak across the sky as they home in on invisible targets.

Pierce's anticipated feelings of victory vanish as all missiles, ground vehicles, and hover jets residing inside the Zone suddenly explode in rapid succession as if swatted by an invisible hand. Personnel in Command watch in stunned silence as the section of the army left outside the boundary remains mysteriously unscathed as it retreats from the massacre.

Minutes later the Zone is quiet once more. Only rolling black smoke from the burning wreckage drifts lazily across the desert. Pierce gazes wildly around the room then abruptly leaves for a secluded conference room to vent his anger as his staff continues to stare at the horror displayed on the overhead screens.

GENERAL THERAPY

10/31/2033

With autumn leaves turning colors and falling from their branches on the surface, it really didn't matter in the underground facility of Fort Bliss, Texas. Few things change except the flow of personnel coming and going. Lately though, peace and quiet is hard to find amid all the influx of urgent requests and soldiers running about. Only in the dead of night do the planning halls and conference rooms empty along with the food courts in the main dining area.

The few remaining personnel on duty are the cleaning crews in the garden district, a high-vaulted, cathedral-like area where the colors of the lights slowly change from hour to hour. It is one of the largest open places in the underground complex where people can relax and escape the harsh realities of living underground. The air is mostly fresh from all the abundant plants and trees growing throughout. Several paths wind their way through sculptured grassy mounds to a large circular pool at its center bubbling water from an underground spring. Surrounding the pool are several picnic tables and benches with the sound of recorded birds and crickets chirping in the background.

On one of the park benches sits a man in his late fifties wearing a white doctor's coat and reading an e-journal on a tablet about the latest treatment for claustrophobic disorders. He runs his fingers through his gray hair then pulls subconsciously on his beard. He grunts as he takes off his glasses to clean a smudge then puts them back on only to find himself staring at a heavily armed soldier wearing active camouflage only a meter away.

Fear prickles throughout the old man's body as he realizes he is face-to-face with one of General Pierce's deadly elite soldiers called High Guards. The soldier's bushy eyebrows rise and fall as his gaze shifts back and forth then focuses on him. The tablet falls to the ground as the man clutches his chest. "Are you here to kill me?"

The soldier glares at him then gives him a toothy grin. "Come now Dr. Matthews. If I wanted to do that, why would I give you the opportunity to ask?" He takes a cigar out of his pocket and lights it. "My name is Colonel Barland and I'm here to escort you to your quarters where you have an honored guest waiting, General Pierce himself. I'm sure that won't be a problem, will it?"

His right eyebrow rises as he cocks his head to one side and taps the pistol at his waist. "I highly recommend we shouldn't keep the General waiting." He sarcastically swings his arm out and bows. "After you."

As the two men enter a maze of halls displaying colorful outdoor scenes, Dr. Matthews finally breaks his silence. "What's all this about? If the General needs medical attention there's plenty of staff on duty for that."

They stop walking and look at each other. Barland presses his lips together then leans his face in close. "First of all, you'll find out soon enough, and secondly, if you don't follow my orders we're both in trouble. So let me give you some advice: I strongly suggest you lose the attitude. The man you're about to meet isn't in a good mood to say the least. Don't upset him anymore than he already is or you'll have to live with the consequences. Just do whatever he asks and everything should be OK."

Barland squints at the doctor then steps back.

Dr. Matthews nods as he gets the point. The two continue walking towards the base's living sectors in silence. As they approach his private quarters, they see two High Guards standing at the entrance blending with the patterns on the wall. They snap to attention and salute Colonel Barland. He returns the salute then motions the doctor to enter in alone.

Matthews waves his hand over a plate near the door and enters only to discover his living quarters in disarray. An overweight man wearing a highly decorated uniform sits on his couch looking as if he hasn't slept in weeks. Matthews suppresses his anger as he walks in and waits for the door to close then extends his hand. "Welcome to my quarters General, how can I assist you tonight?"

Pierce looks at the hand then grunts. "I've just about reached my limit of bullshit today so let's just get straight to the point, shall we? Confidentially speaking of course, I can't sleep a wink at night and was hoping to get some kind of relaxants from you."

Matthews crosses his arms and strokes his beard. *Jeez, another pill popper on my hands.* "So what you're saying sir is that you want me to secretly supply you with prescription drugs without knowing what your problem is, correct?"

Pierce stands up on wobbly feet and laughs maniacally as he shakes an index finger at him. "Well said Dr. Matthews. That's exactly what I'm saying. Now that we understand each other, I'm sure you have a stash somewhere around here." He looks around the ransacked room. "Go ahead and get it so I can be on my way."

Matthews struggles with his conscience then finally shakes his head. "Sir, there's no guarantee they'll work without knowing what your problem is. Could we sit down and talk first?"

General Pierce stares at him with eyes that have dark rings under them. He puts a finger on the doctor's chest. "Listen up Doc! You're starting to piss me off. I'm not here to play doctor-patient games. If you don't provide me with what I want, I'm going to make you regret it."

Dr. Matthews replies in a calm professional voice. "Hmm, why go through me then? I'm sure there are dozens of ways to get what you want."

Pierce lets out a sigh then whispers, "I was hoping to not involve staff or my High Guards. I cannot share my weaknesses with any of them. The lack of sleep has really put me at wit's end." He stares at the doctor, his voice rising on every word. "I have the President demanding answers that I cannot give. Everything I've tried in the Zone so far has been a complete failure. How can I gain respect when I look like a total fool to my peers? Not knowing what we're up against makes me extremely frustrated. I want results even if I have to kill every damn man, woman, and child."

He points a shaky finger at Matthews again. "You got that?" The big man sinks to his knees in despair. "Not once in my entire adult life have I ever felt so helpless."

Dr. Matthews is shocked to see one of the most powerful men on the planet kneeling at his feet. He awkwardly crouches down to look the General in the eye. "Alright, I'll help you. Let's sit and talk about how to proceed, OK?" He extends his hand once more; this time Pierce takes it and uses it to help himself to the couch.

The General lays his head back then closes his eyes as fatigue takes over. "If you tell a soul about what just happened, it will be the end of you."

Dr. Matthews quietly sits in a chair opposite the couch. "Don't worry sir, what happens here stays here. A doctor-patient relationship is as confidential as a confession to a priest. Now, let us be brutally honest with each other. Are you willing to do that sir?"

Pierce shakes his head back and forth in disbelief. "You're still going to ask me stupid questions? You think you can fiddle with my brain and somehow miraculously solve my issues?"

Dr. Matthews curses under his breath as he looks around then walks over to his bed covered with miscellaneous items Pierce dumped there. *Yes! That's exactly what I'm going to do.* He sifts through his belongings and retrieves two devices, one that looks like a watch and the other resembling a clear elastic band. Pierce squints at the doctor as he returns and hands him the watch device.

Matthews clears his throat before continuing. "Please put this on. I've been doing some advanced testing with this for possible use on our troops to reduce their post-traumatic stress disorders. It's called a BRAVE, short for Biometric Rhythm Adapting Vector Enhancer. This one is custom-made so I can access it for routine checkups if a patient has any ill effects. It works on biorhythmic feedback that takes into account physical, emotional, and intellectual cycles. The device modifies those cycles to enhance how someone thinks and feels. This is probably the fastest and most efficient way to help you tonight sir. Don't you agree?"

Pierce wearily nods. "So this thing can make me sleep...hypnotize me?" He grunts a weak laugh. "What the hell? I'm not trying to quit smoking. Just give me some pills."

Dr. Matthews gives him a stern look. "Do you want to sleep peacefully tonight?"

Pierce reluctantly clamps it over his wrist as the doctor slips the elastic band around the General's ankle.

Dr. Matthews takes Pierce's wrist and turns the device on then reads the display. "The BRAVE also monitors and analyzes body functions like blood pressure, respiration, audio, visual, and thermal stimuli. Depending on the area you want to focus on, it will continually adjust vectors within the brain to meet certain conditions. If used properly, yes, it can help someone quit smoking. It can boost confidence, overcome fears, or even make someone feel like a king for the day."

Pierce's eyebrows rise in interest then looks closer at the device as the doctor continues to explain.

"You can preprogram it for up to three specific things by pressing your thumb on the watch's center and then verbally telling it what you want it to do. When you're done, press one of the buttons on the side like this. Later, when you want to get a good night sleep, press the same button with your thumb on the display. The BRAVE will automatically prepare your mind and put you into a deep REM sleep. The next morning you should awake feeling refreshed. However, before we continue, I need to fine-tune it to your specific metabolism by allowing it to analyze your chemical and hormonal concentrations. I need to prick your finger now and put a drop of blood on the display. Are you OK with that sir?"

Agitated, Pierce nods as Dr. Matthews cleans and pricks his finger then smears a tiny drop of blood on the surface of the device. As the outer rim turns deep orange, it vaporizes. Immediately the rim flashes green then shuts off. "Looks like the device completed its calibration. Ready to give it a test run to see if it puts you to sleep?"

General Pierce stretches. "It's about time." He rubs his fingers together then presses his thumb against the display, immediately the surface turns orange and blinks. Pierce looks up at the doctor hesitantly. "Are you sure this thing's working properly?"

"Absolutely, just remember to say 'BRAVE' first and then give it a simple command. Next, press one of the buttons on the side to lock it in. Please continue."

Pierce holds the device up to his mouth. "BRAVE, I want to sleep then wake feeling refreshed." Pierce looks at the doctor for approval then pushes a button on the side.

Dr. Matthews smiles as he helps Pierce lie down on the couch. "Sweet dreams sir." A minute later Pierce's eyelids flutter close and is soon fast asleep. Matthews carefully reaches over and presses his thumb against the display. A red ring appears on the outer rim. "BRAVE, this is Dr. Matthews, voice command override two one one seven." The device emits a beep as the outer rim begins to alternate between red and green.

Dr. Matthews grabs a pen and notepad off the table in front of him. "Now, let's see what is going on in that brain of yours shall we? BRAVE, bring patient into a daydream trance."

General Pierce's breathing becomes shallow then opens his eyes. Dr. Matthews clears his throat. "Sir, do you know where you are?"

Pierce looks around as if seeing it for the first time. "Yes, I'm in your quarters."

"That's right. I want you to stay relaxed just as you are and think of us as good friends OK?"

Pierce settles on the couch. "OK."

"Now earlier, you were expressing your frustration about failures in the Zone, losing respect, and feeling helpless. Is there anything else keeping you from getting a good night's sleep?"

Pierce's eyes widen as he responds in a subdued voice, "Yes, but I can't tell you."

"I understand it might be painful sir but the more you open up, the better you'll feel later. Whatever you tell me now will become less important and eventually fade from your mind. Do you want these thoughts to go away?"

Pierce dreamily smiles as he thinks about it. "Yes."

"Well then, tell me what's on your mind."

Pierce slowly turns his head to look at Dr. Matthews. "I can say anything?"

"Yes, anything."

Pierce sits up on the couch and looks the doctor in the eye. His face is pale and expressionless. "I ordered my High Guards to poison food shipments which killed thousands of innocent people. I then imprisoned dozens of others to cover it up."

Matthews drops his pen on the floor as he subconsciously backs away from the man. Matthews fumbles for words. "I…ah…what? Are you serious?"

"It's the truth. I was ordered by the President to end the Famine War in a quick and decisive way but that's not what bothers me."

"So…so you mean…there's something else that bothers you?"

"Of course. What I fear most is my secret getting out. It haunts me day and night."

"I see, it's not the killing part that bothers you but being caught. So tell me sir, how does it make you feel knowing so many innocent people died because of you?"

"I couldn't care less. It was a job, just like killing chickens on a farm. It felt good to serve my country and be in charge. Just like it did when I had a thug beat up some bullies when I was younger."

Dr. Matthews' hands begin to tremble as he realizes the man staring at him is a cold-blooded mass murderer. *What the heck was I thinking? This man will kill me in a heartbeat if he realizes what he just told me.* He stands and paces as General Pierce's cold hollow eyes follow his every step. *Must stay calm. He won't remember a thing. Just continue to act normal and finish what you started and pray he doesn't wake up on his own.*

The doctor wipes sweat building on his forehead then sits back down. "OK sir, you've done very well. Please lie back down. I have only a few more questions to ask."

Pierce slowly lies back down on the couch.

"As promised, everything you told me will no longer bother you. Now, I want you to imagine a time, say… a few years in the future where you're happy, productive, and a respected member of society.

In essence, someone greater than you are today. Tell me when you have something in mind."

General Pierce smiles and emits a hoarse laugh. "Well, I've had this lifelong dream for world peace. Do you want me to share how I plan to achieve it?"

Dr. Matthews pauses as he thinks about it. "No need, it sounds like a very noble goal. Now, try to think of some short-term goals to achieve over the next couple of years. Let me know when you're ready to continue."

Pierce is quiet for a few minutes then answers in a dreamy voice. "I'm ready. I realize the things I must do."

"Great, the goals you set today will always be in the back of your mind compelling you to achieve them. Completing a goal will bring abundant joy knowing you are one-step closer to true happiness. Before you know it, your efforts towards world peace may someday be a reality.

Dr. Matthews pauses as he thinks of anything he might have forgotten then continues. "Under no circumstances will you remember having this conversation. Nevertheless, you will continue to follow my suggestions. Is that clear sir?"

Pierce nods obediently. "Clear, Dr. Matthews."

"Oh, and one more thing. I'm going to give you a small container of mints. To you they'll be a powerful drug to help you relax at night. Now, on the count of three, you'll awake feeling happy and refreshed." Dr. Matthews leans over and puts his thumb on the BRAVE display. The alternating lights on the outer rim turn to a solid green and shut off. "One, two, three."

Pierce opens his eyes and stretches. He quickly sits up and looks at Dr. Matthews. "Wow! I feel like a ton of weight has lifted off my shoulders. How long was I out?"

Dr. Matthews watches Pierce's face for any signs of remembering then forces a smile. "Only about ten minutes or so. The benefits of the nap won't last that long though. I suggest using the BRAVE only when you're ready to go to bed. As you can see, it works but be careful where and what you command it to do, OK?"

Pierce stands and gets ready to leave.

"Wait, I have something to give you." Dr. Matthews reaches into his coat pocket and retrieves an unmarked tin then hands it to Pierce. "Here's the medicine you asked for. It is a powerful relaxant only to be taken as a last resort."

Pierce looks inside the tin and smiles. "Well, if I'd known these were in your pocket all along, I would have had Colonel Barland just take them from you." His face changes to a menacing stare. "You've been a big help Doctor. Just keep your mouth shut and everything will be all right. Do you get my point?"

A shiver goes down Dr. Matthews back as he remembers how dangerous this man is. To ensure Pierce's privacy and his own life, he decides to use a Brave device on himself to wipe any memory of their meeting if approached by anyone else. "No need to worry about that sir! I can guarantee you I'll never say anything to anyone…ever!

He nervously escorts the General to the door of his quarters. "Now, if you have any problems, you're welcome to give me a call." The door automatically opens and the soldiers standing outside come to attention.

General Pierce walks out and stops without turning around. "Dr. Matthews, thank you for your cooperation." With that, he continues down the hall with Colonel Barland by his side and the two guards following close behind.

Later that evening Dr. Matthews reviews the Famine War details on his computer and discovers that in the spring of 2029, a shift in the subtropical jet stream over the Atlantic Ocean causes widespread devastation to Latin American croplands. Hardest hit is Mexico where hurricanes pound the country one after another followed by widespread droughts and fires.

By late summer of 2030, Mexican officials, desperate to obtain food by any means possible, threaten to invade the United States by mass migration for fertile cropland north of the boarder. The conflict comes to a head when a militia group of unauthorized immigrants, acting on behalf of starving Mexican citizens, assassinates President Steward approaching mid-term of office. Vice President Wellington accedes to the presidency and immediately gives General Shadley Pierce free reign to end the escalating situation before an all-out war ensues.

Hundreds of Mexican officials and thousands of its citizens mysteriously die over the following weeks forcing Mexico to the brink of civil war. Under General Pierce's recommendation, the United States generously offers substantial food assistance, industrial farming equipment and sustainable farming methods to grow food on their own land until the crisis passes in exchange for key mineral resources and partial government control. With no other viable options, the President of Mexico accepts the offer. In the following days, General Pierce becomes a humanitarian hero and the President's right-hand man.

Dr. Matthews leans back in his chair then pulls on his beard to give himself time to think. Enlightened by Pierce's confession and actual events, he realizes it will be hard to treat his deadly, unremorseful patient. He shakes his head in frustration then turns off his computer. With a long night ahead, he begins the tedious task of cleaning up his quarters.

CONCLUSIONS

11/2/2033

At a secret military underground facility near Groom Lake, Nevada, a courier hastily leaves for Fort Bliss to hand deliver an important message to General Pierce. It is from Chief Scientist Kathleen O'Connell, who sends her most recent conclusions drawn from satellite pictures, ground sensors, scientific tests, and information gleaned from the previously failed military missions.

```
Dear General Pierce,

Considering these extreme circumstances, I apolo-
gize for our inability to provide you with fur-
ther details about the occupational force inside the
Zone, especially in regard to its strength or vul-
nerabilities. Along with knowledge gained from our
own failed experiments, here are our best hypotheses
and observations to date:

1. We are dealing with a technologically advanced
   race that may have telepathic abilities.
2. The enemy has the ability to camouflage itself to
   a transparent state or is transparent itself.
3. To date we are unable to sense the enemy, much
   less record them optically or electronically.
```

4. All forms of radio communications in and around the Zone are effectively being jammed during the dust storms.
5. Current conventional weapons are ineffective.

We believe our only chance to understand the enemy is to capture or collect samples of its technology to study and analyze. Without such information, we will continue to face defeat.

Kathleen O'Connell
Kathleen O'Connell, Chief Scientist
Bunker 24 Facility, NV

PRESIDENT WELLINGTON

11/12/2033

President Wellington gazes out the window at the Washington Monument, trying to remember a less troublesome time. He turns and glares at General Pierce who stands quietly in front of his desk, then shakes a finger at him.

"Your inability to collect data regarding these...these *aliens* is intolerable. Your failed missions have destroyed billions of dollars' worth of equipment and sent close to a thousand men to their deaths. We're running out of time and options here. The press and my political rivals are using this to destroy my chance of re-election in 2036. You understand I want to be the first President to serve more than two terms since Franklin D. Roosevelt?" He shakes his head. "Honestly General, I'm very disappointed that you don't have any concrete information to give me. What do you have to say for yourself?"

Pierce calmly pulls out a cigar from his uniform and puts one end in his mouth. He slowly walks to the window before speaking in a cold calculated voice. "Mr. President, the reason I've failed is because you want a quick solution. If you'd taken the time to read O'Connell's report, you would know she suggested capturing one of these aliens, or at least some of their equipment to analyze. Only then, will we have a chance to develop technology to combat them but it's going to take an out-of-the-box strategy." Pierce puffs on his cigar as if it was lit waiting for the President to respond.

A look of resolve slowly spreads across the President's face as he ponders Pierce's words then raises an eyebrow. "Hmm, ever watch football?" He sees Pierce nod then continues. "Back in my college days at Michigan State University, our team went up against the University of Southern California who were the National Champions at the time. At the end of the fourth quarter, we were down by four with no time-outs remaining and only seconds left on the clock. Our only chance to win was to throw a Hail Mary pass and hope one of our receivers would catch the ball in the end zone.

The President pauses as he reflects. "I guess there's no victory without taking risks." He looks at the General with growing excitement in his voice. "I do agree we need an outside-the-box solution. I'll contact the Prism Institute in Virginia later today; I think they're the best think tank we have. I'm sure they can come up with an effective capture plan if you motivate them enough. I also want you working with the research teams to make our equipment undetectable while finding a way to see our enemy. I expect you to be as effective with this project as you were during the Famine War. Is that clear?"

General Pierce bestows him a toothy grin then gives a sharp salute. "Yes sir! It will be my pleasure." Pierce turns to leave then asks, "Mr. President, did your team win the game?"

The President answers in a distant voice. "Yes. I threw the ball as best I could and one of our receivers caught it for the winning touchdown. We were lucky, but lately our luck is getting us nowhere. I didn't promote you to be my Chief Military Adviser to keep losing battles. Take the time and resources you need to ensure victory." He shakes Pierce's hand and motions him to leave then turns to gaze out the window once more.

Cohesive Plan

In an effort to test theories, accelerate data collection on prototype equipment and to prevent a rebellion of troops unwilling to risk their lives inside the Zone, the President and leading scientists finally agree to General Pierce's radical plan to use volunteer death row inmates.

During the brief clearing periods when the violent, raging storm inside the Zone subsides, volunteers who accomplish their tasks within the storm's boundary will receive full pardons. Up to now, there have been no survivors. Even after a great loss of life, scientists are still no closer to understanding what resides within.

Meanwhile, the best minds in the world work on a cohesive plan for capturing an alien. They finally agree on five areas of focus: communications, defense, a secure containment area, mobility, and a viable strategy to tie the other four together.

Over the next couple of years, several military technologies are created and enhanced around a master plan code-named Hail Mary. By August 2035, three of the projects are completed. New communications systems are developed, unconventional antimatter weapons designed and tested, and an energy containment area built at the Bunker 24 facility in Nevada. Finally, in early November 2035, a revolutionary breakthrough in quark technology allows for bilateral phasing—an instantaneous, point-to-point mode of travel considered key to mission success. Soon after creating the first prototype phasing bands, a select group of men begins training on the new equipment while it's refined and adapted for the upcoming mission.

VOLUNTEERS

11/18/2035

Deep underground in one of Bunker 24's labs, Hopper adjusts his prototype metallic jump vest as he steps through a reinforced concrete door into a large semi-lit chamber. The room glows from control panels making it possible to see a transparent barrier surrounding one side of a raised circular platform at its center. Next to him stands a muscular man with sandy-blond hair wearing a vest similar to his own. He realizes they will be doing their first training jump together.

Two armed guards approach and escort them to the platform as the smell of ozone intensifies from buzzing transformers. They briefly scrutinize the muscular man before leaving to reposition themselves near the entrance. A moment later, a stocky man in a white lab coat approaches the platform and adjusts his glasses. "Ah, Captain Phillips and Specialist Greenwood. I'm Chief Scientist McCloud. It's good to see you both prepped and ready. I hate nothing more than when someone is late or unprepared. My time is precious, so let's get started."

McCloud walks over to a workbench and picks up a thick metal armband with a row of four buttons above and below a curved 3D display. "This is a multi-functional, portable quark phasing band and is a working prototype so *please* take care of it." He clamps it over Hopper's lower arm then turns him around to attach body sensors to the back of his vest. "This technology has been instrumental in discovering an invisible shield approximately six kilometers inside the Zone boundary that prevents phased objects from going any further." Puzzled, he shakes his head as he turns Hopper around once more to apply sensors to his chest.

The comment peeks Hopper's curiosity. "Excuse me Chief, so how is it possible to phase things from one point to another? Wouldn't it take a tremendous amount of energy for something like that?"

McCloud answers without looking up. "Do you know how the first laser worked?" He glances up briefly. "No? They did it by shining light through a synthetic ruby rod with a reflective surface on one end and a partially reflective surface on the other. Through a process called light amplification, photon energy built up inside until an intense beam shot out. Easy enough, right?

"To achieve the energy output to phase people and equipment to other locations, we essentially use the same process, except we use quark particles. And instead of a ruby rod, we generate a containment field that uses a relatively small amount of energy that amplifies upon itself until it reaches critical mass and tears a hole in subspace. This hole can be positive or negative in nature. Either way, the energy looks for a place to discharge. By introducing an equal tear in subspace with the opposite charge, we can temporarily short the two locations together and in essence, fold space. The problem is, outside this lab, it's too dangerous to generate these fields close to our test subjects." He pushes his glasses to his forehead as he discovers a problem. "Hmm, now let me finish here."

Hopper notices Greenwood looking at him intently; he puts out his right hand. "Hi, my name is Lucas Phillips but you can call me Hopper if you like." Greenwood shakes his head and looks away. Hopper's instincts tell him to keep talking. "I'd say you look around twenty-two, twenty-three years old? I just turned thirty-four last month. You know, I'm told this phasing process is pretty safe now."

McCloud looks up from his inspection and frowns. "Hmm, you mean relatively speaking of course." He moves over to Greenwood and clamps an identical armband on his arm then starts applying sensors.

Hopper smiles then continues. "I think the ones in charge are teaming us up, looks like we'll be working together from now on." Greenwood doesn't respond and they stand in silence for a few moments.

McCloud finishes applying sensors then gives the two of them the thumbs-up. "OK gentlemen, everything's ready. In a couple of minutes I'll activate the platform." He taps Hopper's phasing band. "Now, when you two reach your destination, wait a few minutes before activating the portal by pressing the four top buttons in sequence from left to right. Then, on the bottom row, press the first and last buttons simultaneously, OK?"

He steps back to address them both. "It's critical to jump through the portal when you enter it. If you do as I say, you'll return safe and sound to this platform. Got it?"

They both nod in unison.

"Now, in a dire emergency you can active your own portal by accessing this panel marked ECO, which stands for Emergency Control Override. If both of you use one portal to jump, due to some inherent limitations, you must jump together." He nods to them then rubs his forehead as he walks off the platform to a nearby control panel.

Hopper begins to inspect the phasing band but is startled when Greenwood blurts out, "Twenty-five! I'm twenty-five years old." He continues a few seconds later. "I don't know who you are or what your crime was, but we're not friends. If you have plans of being friends, forget it! Just do as you're ordered and maybe we can survive long enough to be free again."

The two guards near the entrance stop talking to observe them. One of them starts to approach but Hopper waves him off and turns back to Greenwood. "You know, I appreciate your openness. We don't have to be friends. However, your goal to be free is the same as mine but for a different reason. I'm here for revenge." A lump forms in Hopper's throat as he continues. "Whatever's out there, it killed my wife. So all I ask is that we work together to increase our chances of success in the upcoming mission." Hopper stops talking as memories of Eileen flood his mind.

Greenwood's defensiveness evaporates. "Man, sorry I misjudged you. I didn't realize a person from the free world would volunteer for a suicide mission." He extends his hand to expose a tattoo on his arm of an old time pocket watch with no dials. "It would be an honor to be your friend." As the two shake hands, the platform briefly activates sending a pulse of energy tingling through their bodies. They release hands feeling like they just made some sort of pact.

McCloud's voice breaks the spell. "Alright gentlemen. You have nothing to worry about, all readings look normal. Training jump one will commence in thirty seconds."

Hopper and Greenwood look nervously at each other as the seconds tick by. When the countdown reaches zero, a massive surge of energy passes through their bodies. The room winks out of existence and a white light briefly surrounds them as they fall through space.

HAIL MARY MISSION

4/7/2036

Hopper scans the scorched plain of the Zone as he drives an all-terrain vehicle. Hot desert air blows across his face as he glances at two men in an identical vehicle paralleling their course. He adjusts his headset then activates the mic. "Monty, report!"

The driver of the other vehicle waves to the Captain and replies, "Nothing to report! We haven't seen any damn aliens yet! It still peeves me Command sent us in without weapons. They're all a bunch of—"

"Save it Monty! I want you to stop on the plateau up ahead and scan the area with binoculars." Hopper glances at Specialist Greenwood in the passenger seat next to him. After months of training together, he considers him a close friend but always wondered why he was on death row. When asked about it, he only replied he was sorry and regretted what happened in the past.

Hopper turns his attention back to the horizon as he drives their vehicle to the crest of a small hill and applies the brakes. He addresses Greenwood as the engine winds down. "I don't get it, were a kilometer into the Zone and still haven't made contact. What do you think they're up to?"

Greenwood wipes sweat off his face and shrugs. "Well, maybe they're observing us to find out why anyone would be so stupid as to drive two un-armed vehicles *straight* into a death zone!"

Hopper's tension eases up a bit. "When you put it that way, you're probably right." He picks up his binoculars and scans the horizon to the base of another low-lying hill searching for aliens no one has ever seen. Subconsciously, he puts his right hand over his left shirt pocket where he keeps Eileen's unread letter confirming his decision to volunteer for this mission.

Eileen, Command's confidence in our ability to succeed is unfounded. Our equipment isn't even fully tested. Still, these three men believe they have a chance of surviving. I guess anything is better than death row. On days like this, I wonder who's in charge when they tell us to make contact with an invisible alien! What kind of order is that? Eileen, since you've been gone, this world hasn't been the same. If we fail today, at least we'll be together again..."

A communication from Command blares in Hopper's ear. "Foxtrot One, this is Delta Four Tango. Over."

Hopper lowers his binoculars to adjust the volume. "This is Foxtrot One. Go ahead. Over."

"Foxtrot One, Eagle Eye reports no unusual ground activity in your vicinity. Currently tracking you on a northeasterly route. Have you made any kind of contact? Over."

"Delta Four Tango, this is Foxtrot One. Negative. Proceeding as ordered. Over."

"Foxtrot One, this is Delta Four Tango. Roger. Out."

As the conversation ends, Hopper finds himself gazing at a sparse growth of crushed vegetation in the distance. Curious, he looks closer and sees an extremely faint haze covering the area. A chill prickles down his back and neck as a cold probing sensation enters his mind. Without knowing how, Hopper realizes the aliens are finally making their move.

He glances over at Monty in Rover 2 and keys his mic. "Did you guys feel something just now?" He doesn't wait for a response as he swings his body around and quickly scans the entire area again.

Greenwood looks nervously at Hopper. "I felt it!"

Hopper snaps out of his surprise and notifies Command. "Delta Four Tango, this is Foxtrot One. I believe contact has been initiated!" He quickly addresses his men. "Time to earn your freedom guys! I have a hunch the enemy is at two o'clock, sixty meters out over a patch of crushed vegetation. Initiate the battle plan—now!" Hopper immediately presses a button on the dashboard to initiate a large misty portal on the front of their vehicle as Greenwood activates a new multi-weapon jamming system.

Hopper floors the accelerator of his vehicle kicking dirt and rocks high into the air then makes a beeline straight towards the crushed vegetation. Rover Two peals away in an attempt to ram the invisible enemy on its flank. Hopper struggles to keep the vehicle in a straight line as he tries to contact Command once more. "Delta Four Tango, this is Foxtrot One." He hears nothing and tries again. "Delta Four Tango, this is Foxtrot One!" He looks nervously at Greenwood who gives him a thumbs-down.

Seconds later, an alarm blares as sensors confirm an incoming energy signature directly ahead. Hopper curses under his breath as he realizes they won't reach their alien target in time. With no time to bring the vehicle to a stop, he grabs his backpack then motions Greenwood to do the same and leaps from the vehicle. Before their bodies have a chance to stop rolling forward from momentum, their vehicle explodes into a thousand jagged fragments. The intense shockwave sends them sprawling backwards across the barren ground. The fate of Rover 2 is unknown as Hopper hears a second explosion in the distance. Miraculously Hopper and Greenwood are unharmed as they look at the mangled remains of their vehicle.

Greenwood gets up first and helps Hopper to his feet. With a cold presence continuing to grow in their minds, they don their packs and run. Hopper presses a button on his portable phasing band to activate a subspace communication uplink to Command and is relieved to see the display flashing green. Through ragged gasps of breath, he gives an update. "Not much time...Aliens in pursuit...Two survivors...Condition critical! He tries to catch his breath then continues. "Request immediate extraction!"

Moments later the sophisticated device on Hopper's arm grows hot as a dim milky portal materializes fifty meters to the south of them. With no time to spare, they run toward it trying not to think of the unknown presence at their backs. They safely reach it and dive through together only to find themselves lying on muddy ground in a heavy downpour.

Lightning briefly illuminates the area for them to see that they are in a small valley surrounded by sheer rock walls. Both men look around confused as they slowly get to their feet. They had expected to arrive at Bunker 24's main phasing platform, not in some mountainous region. Hopper checks his band to see the words: DANGER— BREACH IN PROGRESS. He shows it to Greenwood as he tries to suppress his growing anger. "This place is not in the original plan. I'm not sure what we're supposed to do now." He points to the high cliffs surrounding them. "We have no weapons or a place to run."

The band emits a sharp three-tone warning followed by a feminine voice. "Unauthorized portal activation. An unidentified object will materialize at this location. Vacate vicinity immediately."

Greenwood runs both hands through his hair as he looks at Hopper's grim face. "I think whatever destroyed our vehicle is following us! I don't know what's going on but let's get the hell out of here!" Greenwood grabs Hopper's phasing band and presses his thumb on the curved display causing a small panel to eject from the top labeled ECO. "I'm not the one in charge here, but I suggest you activate the emergency control override before that thing arrives!"

The device beeps and begins a thirty-second count down.

Hopper cocks his head to one side and gives Greenwood a sarcastic smile. "You think *now*...is a good time?" He pushes the button without waiting for a response. The phasing band grows hot again as it creates another portal fifty meters out, only this time it is smaller and dimmer than the first. They immediately run to it and jump safely through. Unknown to them, the ground they just left flattens as if crushed by a great weight. The portal's energy field magnifies in size and intensity then disappears with a loud thunderclap.

Hopper and Greenwood find themselves lying in bright sunlight on a large metal platform surrounded by a flat desolate landscape in every direction. Hopper immediately pushes the ECO button creating a new portal out on the desert where it shimmers in the heat. A few seconds later, a wave of nausea overcomes them as a massive light flashes right behind them. They see nothing but start to feel a cold presence enter their minds once more.

Greenwood looks at Hopper with fear clearly visible on his face. "Damn, it's already here! How is that possible?"

Hopper doesn't answer; his mind only fills with rage toward the alien chasing them.

The two men immediately scramble to their feet and run for the portal knowing each step could be their last. Beyond the bounds of possibility, they somehow reach it alive and jump through.

Dire Predicament

Hopper slowly opens his eyes to see a clear blue sky above. Confused, he turns his head to one side. In the distance are white sand dunes, blasted rock, sparse vegetation, and low-lying mountains. He raises his arm to look at the display on his multifunctional phasing band to discover he is roughly six kilometers inside the Zone, just west of the Guadalupe Mountains.

A gurgling sound startles him. He turns his head to the other side to see Greenwood's scorched, tattered body with his legs severed below his knees. The veins in his forehead bulge as he tries to speak but no sound comes out.

Hopper crawls toward him but stops when his phasing band emits a sharp piercing tone that grows louder by the second indicating it will soon self-destruct. He quickly unlatches it from his arm then looks for cover but finds none.

He locks eyes with Greenwood, in that moment time slows. A brief exchange of facial expressions allows them to communicate clearly with each other.

Greenwood's eyes grow large then nods ever so slightly. *My friend, it's time for me to atone for my sins. Save yourself.*

Hopper's eyebrows furl then moves his head back and forth. *It wasn't supposed to be this way.* He throws the band as far as he can over Greenwood's body. His heart pounds loudly in his chest as he nods and tries to smile. *Thank you. Peace be with you my friend.*

Greenwood tries to smile back. *Same to you.*

The band flashes in the air as the sun reflects off its display. It explodes as it touches the ground sending out a powerful shock wave in all directions. Hopper tumbles backwards as metal fragments and rocks slice into his flesh. Intense pain courses through his body as he loses consciousness.

Hopper wakes with his eyes stinging in intense pain and is unable to open them. He carefully touches his eyelids then the hot ground to realize he is blind. His heart races as he tries to grasp how dire his predicament has become. *If being blind is not bad enough, I'm back inside the Zone, no means to communicate with Command and have zero chance of at rescued at my current location. To make matters worse, if the aliens don't get me first, I will surely die when the raging storm returns.*

His body begins to shake with rage until he lets out a hoarse scream. He forces himself to stop then raises a clenched fist to the air. "How could you guys at Command do this to me? I was here to help! If I get out of here alive, the person responsible is going to pay! You hear that?"

Hopper stops to catch his breath. *You said the plan was simple. Make contact, activate the portal on the front of the vehicle then ram it into an alien to send it to the containment area. You forgot to mention a chase would ensue through multiple portals then be abandoned inside the Zone!*

Hopper's anger finally runs out but it soon turns to worry as he ponders what to do next. *The only thing I know for sure is my location. If I can somehow make it to the outer perimeter, it's possible a border patrol could rescue me then.*

A bead of sweat runs off his forehead and down his cheek as he tries to think of a way to do it. A smile forms on his lips as he speaks out loud. "Yes, it's a long shot for sure, but maybe…it's possible to use the heat of the sun to guide me west!"

Encouraged, he sits up causing pain to shoot through his entire body. It quickly passes then carefully pats his limbs to check for broken bones but only finds bleeding lacerations. As far as he can tell, they're nothing serious. Next, he touches his utility belt and knife then searches his backpack only to discover the canteen missing. He groans but immediately realizes Greenwood's may still be intact.

He runs a hand through his hair trying to figure out a way to locate him then removes his knife and pushes the blade deep into the ground. He opens a pouch on his utility belt and removes a ten-meter length of cord then ties one end to the handle. He turns away and crawls on his hands and knees while dispensing cord out behind him until he reaches its end then executes a circular search pattern. Midway through, he feels the cord hit an obstruction then crawls inward to discover Greenwood's mangled body.

Grief swells inside him as he moves broken limbs out of the way then turns the body over to search the backpack. He finds the canteen intact and removes it to discover it still full of water.

Relieved, Hopper lays a hand on Greenwood's back. "You've saved my life twice now. I'm sure God has granted you forgiveness. Rest in peace my friend."

He twists off the cap then takes a drink before putting it on his pack. He pulls on the cord to draw his knife towards him then secures it on his utility belt. Satisfied, he carefully searches the ground with his hands for a shrub and finds one. He yanks it out and breaks off the root to help guide him on his journey.

He slowly stands then mumbles to himself. "Eileen, even though I'm going to walk through this desolate, hostile place, I will fear no evil knowing you are here by my side." He reaches out as if to hold her hand then turns his head skyward and slowly rotates his body in a circle. A sad smile briefly crosses his lips before stumbling forward towards the setting sun.

Hours later, he stops when he can no longer feel any radiant heat. He feels the stubble on his face and figures it must be around dusk. Exhausted, he removes the mat from his backpack and spreads it out on the ground. He lies down on it and quickly falls asleep only to wake during the night thirsty, in pain, and shivering from the cold.

Hopper drinks the remaining water from the canteen and discards it then dozes on and off until he finally feels the warmth of the sun as it breaks over the Guadalupe Mountains. With effort, he gets his aching body to stand then turns around. With the sun at his back, he continues his difficult trek west.

Countless hours later, Hopper finds he is unable to determine his direction any longer. He sits on the sunbaked ground then unrolls his mat and covers himself with it. Unable to cool himself adequately, he becomes delirious and passes out. When he finally comes to, he feels the sun on his face but bleeding wounds, fever, and dehydration have taken a heavy toll on him. He stores his mat on his pack, and then with a fierce determination to reach the perimeter, he stands once more.

Dizzy and confused, a shimmering image of his wife Eileen appears in front of him wearing a summer dress looking exactly as she did the day the alien blast took her away. Her body and auburn hair glow brightly as she gives him a kind, warm smile. Hopper licks his dry lips and whispers to her.

"I've been waiting for you…when you said you'd meet me on the other side, I didn't think twice…I wouldn't have left you in the car if I knew what would happen…please forgive me…"

Hopper's mind tingles as he feels a presence enter his mind. He fights the sensation only to find himself lying facedown on the ground. He struggles to stand up again but doesn't have the strength. Instead, he crawls on his hands and knees but stops as a woman's soft voice fills his mind.

I am here to help you.

Hopper sits back on his legs as his emotions flare. "Eileen, my angel…they wanted me dead. It's alright now…we'll be together soon." His lips split and bleed as a smile spreads across his face. He extends his hand but she only turns and walks further away.

All will be OK. Don't worry my love. I'll guide you to safety. You're almost home. Let me be your eyes and follow me.

Despairing that Eileen will leave him, he staggers to his feet and stumbles forward.

She turns around and smiles again. *Yes, you're doing great! Keep going. I'm here waiting for you.*

Hopper continues, determined to keep up but his legs have no more strength and abruptly falls to his knees.

Eileen's expression changes to worry as she faces him with open arms. *You're almost home. Run to me...Run to me now! Don't hold back. You have to make it my love. Let me save you!*

Realizing he is dying, Hopper reaches out one last time. Eileen's face is solemn as she stands before him and touches his outstretched hand. Her aura brightens even more as she melts inside him. Peace fills Hopper's soul but it quickly turns to terror as he loses control of his limbs.

He feels his body stand up and run towards unintelligible voices in the distance while a horrendous screeching sound begins to blare. Have the vicious aliens somehow tricked him and taken over his body? He simply doesn't have the strength to care anymore as countless phantom hands grab and force him to the ground. The trauma is too much to bear. Welcoming death, he plummets into unconsciousness.

COMMAND CENTER

4/7/2036

With the Hail Mary Mission fully underway, Command's Operation room bustles with activity as men and women sit at their computer terminals surrounding a large central chair loaded with monitors and buttons. Cradled within, Pierce hears the voice of Staff Sergeant Carver from his communications terminal. "Sir! Captain Phillips just reported they made contact with the enemy."

Pierce's heart beats loudly in his ears as activity in Command comes to a halt. The only sound in the room comes from the cooling vents.

Captain Madison from tactics finally breaks the spell. "3D video from Eagle Eye Six shows both rover teams are on offensive maneuvers. Switching output to main screen."

A desert landscape appears showing two vehicles traveling at a high rate of speed, one heading northeast across the Zone and the other moving on a southerly trajectory.

Pierce nervously looks at Sergeant Carver then asks a question. "Are we in contact with either rover?"

"No sir. It appears we lost that ability the moment they activated their jamming system."

Pierce's frustration grows as he receives another report from Captain Madison. "Sir! Both rovers now appear to be switching over to evasive maneuvers!"

General Pierce looks up in disbelief as the images of Rovers 1 and 2 suddenly disappear from the screen indicating their destruction. Pierce grinds his teeth as victory slips through his fingers once again.

Pathetic fools, I shouldn't have used Captain Phillips or his gang of convicts for this mission. They messed up somehow. Now I have another failure to explain.

The General's face turns red from anger as he swivels in his chair and points to Staff Sergeant Carver sitting in shock at his terminal. "You! Get the President on the line now!"

A small green dot appears on the main screen indicating team one's position via a phasing band uplink. Pierce glances at it then holds up his hand to cancel the order. Sergeant Carver hastily gives him an update. "Sir, Eagle Eye Seven is receiving a weak subspace communication uplink from Captain Phillips' auxiliary phasing band."

Several cheers go up around the room but it quickly fades as everyone strains to hear the message. Out of the roar of static, they finally hear the desperate voice of Captain Philips as he runs for his life.

"Not much time…Aliens in pursuit…Two survivors…Condition critical!" Several seconds pass as his breathing intensifies and becomes more ragged. "Request immediate extraction!"

Acting like a man redeemed, General Pierce signals Captain Madison to activate the portal. Seconds later, it energizes and appears as a white dot fifty meters west of the green one.

Tension increases as the screen zooms in until they see two men running towards a murky white mist. Someone in the background shouts, "Don't let us down. You can make it!" A thunderous cheer erupts around the room as the two men disappear inside the mist.

Pierce's heart pounds loudly in his chest as he addresses the room. "This isn't some high school football game! Everyone stay focused and keep that portal active at all costs! There's a chance we can collect valuable data about them just by being in this vicinity!" Pierce holds his breath as he subconsciously taps his fingers.

Captain Madison quickly reads a flow of data from his terminal and exclaims excitedly. "Sir! A second phase is now in progress! An alien actually entered the portal on its own and appears determined to chase those two men!"

Surprised, General Pierce lets out his breath and glances at the men and women frantically collecting data. A red light on one of his displays starts flashing rapidly. He taps it to see Command's resident Chief Scientist McCloud standing next to a huge crystal sphere with flowing streams of light pulsating inside.

McCloud speaks as soon as he sees Pierce. "Sir, I put the alien's phase field in partial stasis! We have roughly two minutes to glean data before the reentry sequence completes!"

Captain Madison interrupts McCloud's conversation. "Sir! Sensors at Mountain Retreat, Colorado indicate something is interfering with the men's auxiliary phasing band!"

Frustrated, Pierce pushes another button on his chair. Dark clouds and flashes of light fill the display. Pierce unconsciously takes out a cigar from his pocket and chews on it as he scans supplemental information at the bottom of the display. "Do you think weather conditions are affecting it?"

"It's possible sir, but it only started after the alien entered the portal. One moment." He quickly types in a sequence of commands on his keyboard. "Running a local rerouting program…uplink has been fully restored."

General Pierce glances at McCloud on one of his displays then squints at data scrolling down on the right side. "Time's running out Chief, what have you discovered?"

McCloud looks up perplexed. "Preliminary subatomic particle scans indicate an object with no substance. Magnetic imaging indicates a large amount of unknown metal but cannot locate where it is. Thermal readings show a biomass inside but there's not enough data to determine what it is. Spectral analysis indicates several other anomalies that will need further investigating." He looks at Pierce on his screen. "Intriguing, isn't it? I'm sending the data over to O'Connell as we speak. Hopefully she can make use of it for final adjustments to Bunker 24's containment area."

Exasperated by the lack of concrete data, Pierce rudely interrupts. "I don't want to hear about what you *don't* know. Report back when you have something useful to tell me!" Pierce is about to disconnect when an alarm goes off throughout the room.

Captain Madison looks up from his station and reports in a panic-stricken voice. "Sir, I can't explain it but for some reason the uplink is becoming unstable again. It looks like we'll lose the connection in about thirty seconds. If that happens, the phasing band and exit portal for the alien will self-destruct."

General Pierce glances around the room. His voice wavers with uncertainty. "Suggestions anyone?"

McCloud quickly answers. "Sir, I suggest you send the authorization code to allow Captain Phillips' phasing band to function independently. We still don't have enough data and we can't afford to lose the alien!"

General Pierce looks angrily from McCloud to Captain Madison. The Captain's face breaks into a cold sweat as Pierce stares at him. "Do you have a better solution?"

Madison nervously shakes his head back and forth. "I don't sir, and it's probably our only alternative right now." He stops to clear his throat then continues. "McCloud, can you delay the alien in transit a few more seconds to give the men more time to activate the ECO button?"

McCloud gives him a hesitant nod.

General Pierce starts to swear but Sergeant Carver interrupts him. "Sir, uplink will fail in ten seconds."

Pierce swallows his anger then turns to Captain Madison: "Send the authorization code now! Sergeant Carver, contact O'Connell and tell her to be ready to capture that damn thing! McCloud, activate all ground sensors at Groom Lake and have Eagle Eye Sixteen updated with any new modifications before the next phasing sequence completes!" He sits back in his chair and shakes his head. *Get your act together fools. These aliens have already kicked my ass one too many times.*

A female computer-generated voice makes an announcement over the intercom. "Link to Mountain Retreat severed. Quark phasing band running in independent mode."

The Command Center grows silent as everyone watches a detailed topographical map of Mountain Retreat, waiting for Captain Phillips to activate another portal.

McCloud breaks the tense silence. "General, I can't contain the alien in stasis any longer. I must rematerialize it—" He stops as another screen catches his attention. "Sensors are reporting a portal activated fifty meters southeast of the men's current location. Let's hope the chase continues."

General Pierce nods as he watches the men safely enter the portal only to rematerialize on a large metal platform out on the desert of Groom Lake Nevada. Everyone's attention returns to the portal at Mountain Retreat but what happens next, stuns everyone. The alien signature appears directly over the portal and instantly phases through.

Sergeant Carver frantically reports. "O'Connell says she needs more time to make the modifications!"

Infuriated, Pierce's face flushes red as he looks at Sergeant Carver and yells. "Tell O'Connell she doesn't have any more time!

The damn alien is already at the designated capture point! Never mind…I'll tell that woman myself!" Fuming, he actives his own mic. "O'Connell, this is General Pierce! I'm ordering you to spring the trap at once!" He anxiously watches a red dot representing the alien position at the center of the platform as the two men continue to run towards a misty portal in the desert.

Captain Madison's voice borders on panic as he reports again. "Sir! The men's portal is destabilizing and will deactivate within a few seconds!"

General Pierce glares at him. "I don't care about that! Those men were going back inside the Zone anyway." Angry stares converge on him as the men reach the portal and disappear. The dot representing the alien also vanishes as the platform collapses beneath it. An intense white light immediately erupts from the depths of a large hole revealed underneath as their prey falls into the containment area. The men and women at Command stare in disbelief at successfully springing the trap but remain quiet as they wait for word from Bunker 24.

Moments later, they hear the shaken voice of Chief Scientist Kathleen O'Connell over the loud speakers. "Alien…con…contained sir! Stasis field holding at …eighty percent!"

Celebrations finally break out as General Pierce takes a deep breath then leans back in his chair and laughs, ecstatic to capture an alien. *Whatever you are, I've played by your rules. Now play by mine.*

BUNKER 24'S CONTAINMENT AREA

4/7/2036

Deep inside the Bunker 24 facility, scientists and armed soldiers scramble to take positions near a large circular transparent wall surrounded by a multitude of protruding instruments. Chief Scientist O'Connell stands nervously at a massive control panel waiting to collapse the metal platform forty meters overhead. Perspiration runs down her face as she watches a screen showing two men running away from the alien position. She glances down at a row of red lights slowly changing to green. In her ear, she listens to the tense conversations occurring at Fort Bliss' Command Center. Her heart skips a beat as the alien position begins to move. A growling, angry voice comes over her headset. "O'Connell, this is General Pierce! I'm ordering you to spring the trap at once!"

O'Connell looks once more at the row of lights and screams at it. "Hurry! *Hurry!*" Unable to wait any longer, she pounds a large red button on the control panel. Immediately, sirens go off as smoke erupts from burning insulation and sparking circuits all around the facility.

Suddenly the ground ripples under her feet followed by a gut-wrenching shockwave that throws her against the control panel. Dazed, she turns around to see the distorted outline of an extremely large object encased in a glowing web of pulsating blue energy. The light shines brightly on her limp body as she listens to a computer-simulated voice issuing a report. "Stasis field deployed. Object neutralized."

O'Connell wipes blood from her face then looks at the damaged headset lying on the floor. She reaches into her lab coat for a small computer tablet and initializes a data link to Command. Her voice is weak as she gives Pierce an update. "Alien...con...contained sir! Stasis field holding at ...eighty percent!"

Several soldiers rush to her side as she collapses to the ground. Around her, scientists and technicians frantically continue to adjust the containment field as they take her to the post infirmary for medical attention.

Telepathic Investigation

Later that day in a nearby laboratory, a middle-aged woman in an orange bodysuit is strapped to a table with dozens of wires connected directly to her head. Her gaze darts wildly around the room as three technicians monitor her brain waves. A clean-cut man wearing a white collared shirt enters her field of vision and examines her pupils.

"Hi Alicia, my name is Dr. Foster. I feel honored. You are our first female volunteer to attempt contact. I'm sure you're aware of the risks though. I've been told you've signed the waiver in exchange for your freedom, right?"

The woman nods nervously as he prepares a syringe.

"I know you're scared but I'll do my best to take care of you. I'm going to put you under now. In a little while, you should become aware of your surroundings again as we increase activity to different parts of your brain. If everything goes according to plan, I'll ask you to perform a series of tasks, OK?"

Her voice trembles slightly as she looks deep into his eyes. "OK...I can see you're a good man."

The doctor's face-hardens then forces a smile. "You have nothing to worry about Alicia. I'll be with you all the way. Just relax now."

He gently turns her head to the side and injects a mind-altering drug straight into her jugular vein. Immediately she starts shaking violently on the table. Desperate minutes pass before he can adjust her brain waves enough to settle her down.

He looks up to find his technicians staring at him in shame. "I know this isn't easy for any of us but we're not evil people. We're following orders from General Pierce to find a way to make contact with whatever's inside the containment field, figure out what it is, and where it came from. But just like you, I don't want to lose any more volunteers, so let's give Alicia our full attention alright?"

They nod halfheartedly as they turn their attention back to the brain-scanning equipment. Dr. Foster looks at his watch then presses a button on a computer screen to start the recording session.

"Time is thirteen hundred hours. Experimental batch four has already been injected into test subject"—he pauses to look at a clipboard—"number nine." He puts it down and attaches a handmade metal hoop lined with bulky sensors to his head. A cord on the back runs to the machine connected to Alicia. He lies down on a recliner next to her and whispers. "You say I'm a good man…" He shakes his head then closes his eyes. "I promise to do everything I can to keep you alive."

Alicia grows cold as a tingling sensation spreads throughout her body. The room around her quickly dissolves only to find herself floating in a sea of darkness with what sounds like crashing waves on a beach. As time goes on, she starts to grow impatient but it finally lifts and stars begin appearing all around. A sphere close to her radiates a warm light giving her a sense of peace. She cannot define how big or small it is; only that it is beautiful. She touches it and is surprised to sense it is Dr. Foster. The sounds of waves recede to the background as his thoughts enter her mind.

Alicia...Alicia, are you there? Where are you? Open up to me. Please don't die. Damn it Pierce! You're such a heartless man...I must stay focused. Alicia, can you hear me? Let me know if you can hear me. Say something...anything...

I'm here Doctor! I can you hear you.

What's with Pierce anyway? At least I have a conscience.

Don't you hear me Dr. Foster? I'm right here.

It's possible she's brain dead just like the rest. Damn it Alicia please say something! I don't have the heart to euthanize you too.

Shocked by his revelation, Alicia tries harder to communicate. As the minutes pass, Dr. Foster's voice becomes less clear and focused.

Alicia...Alicia, I'm such a weak man. How could I agree to this? She deserves better than this. I'm a murderer. Alicia, we tried everything to make this work. I hope your spirit body rests in peace. I'm sorry but my time is up.

Alicia realizes she has no spirit body, only a sense of where it should be. *Is that what's missing? Do I need a spirit body to channel my thoughts?*

She imagines her body lying on the table but nothing happens.

Good-bye Alicia. May you find true happiness in the afterlife.

Out of sheer desperation, she plunges her whole presence into the warm star of Dr. Foster and sees her naked spirit body materialize around her. It glows brightly from the light surrounding her.

Stop! Please stop! I'm here. Don't kill me!

Alicia? You're alive? Oh my God. I can't believe what I was about to do!

I heard all your thoughts but couldn't get through to you until now. I don't blame you. Just tell me what I need to do then promise me to bring me back alive.

I promise you I'll do my best but we need to hurry. If my consciousness doesn't return soon, it may be forever lost inside the machine. Quickly now...tell me what you see.

It looks like I'm at the center of the universe surrounded by bright stars. Most of them are moving but the ones farther out just fade from view. Your mind is like a sun with my spirit body residing inside.

That's very interesting. Now tell me, out of all the suns and stars, are there any that look different somehow? Look closely.

Alicia rotates her spirit body to search the black sky. Off in the far distance beyond many stars, she sees an incredibly intense blue one. It's so bright that she almost doesn't see a smaller one near it.

Yes. There are two blue stars but one is so intense it looks like it went supernova. I can barely see the other. What do you want me to do?

Make contact with the bright-blue star but be careful. It may be the captured alien. If possible, try to hide your presence while you gather information.

I'll try, but it's so intense. I'm scared!

Try not to worry about it Alicia. Just keep me around you. Please hurry though my mind is already trying to disengage.

Determined to make contact, Alicia turns her body and bravely faces the bright-blue star. *OK, I'll try.*

She extends her arm causing the star to enlarge until it dwarfs her presence. Its rays are so extreme they numb her body. With a pale delicate hand, she reaches out and touches its glass-like surface. Pain explodes within her mind causing her body to tumble backwards. When Alicia finally comes to her senses she discovers the light surrounding her has dimmed dramatically and panics. *Hey! Dr. Foster! Are you still with me? Dr. Foster, please say something!*

Out of the sounds of breaking waves, she hears a weak and distant voice.

I'm still here Alicia. I'm not giving up, don't you give up either. Remember, we are in this together. I've instructed my technicians to keep me connected no matter what. Do you realize what I'm saying?

Oh my God! You're dying.

And so are you...but this may be our last opportunity to get information. Go to the faint blue star this time and try something different. Hurry!

Alicia thinks for a moment then reaches out once more until the blue stars fill her vision. She keeps the small, dimmer one between her and the one going supernova. *Ah... Doctor?*

Yes Alicia?

I don't know if this is going to work, but I'm going to plunge us both deep inside the small one and absorb as much information as I can. Take us home if the alien becomes aware of our presence. OK?

It's a good plan; I like it. Alicia...I can see you're a good woman.

Alicia can feel and hear his thoughts and knows he means it. It gives her strength as she readies her spirit body. Empowered, she accelerates toward the dim star and pierces its clear-blue skin. The sound of a crashing waterfall assaults her as she floats inside the mind of an unknown creature she can't comprehend. The light surrounding her dims even further but stays intact. Outside Dr. Foster's protective sphere, colors shift and fade like flowing water. Her senses expand into the alien mind and receives a response almost instantaneously as flowing currents become rivers of ice and converge on her presence blocking her view in every direction.

An icy cold fluid enters the sphere and stings her entire body. As the pain becomes unbearable, she ceases to move as an overwhelming presence fills her mind. A blurry vision of a pedestal rising from the floor opens to expose an octagon container with a dark, oval object floating inside. The scene suddenly freezes. Out of the deafening sound of crashing water, she hears one word that makes her heart almost stop...*Hell.* A long hissing sound follows a few seconds later.

Minutes pass as if waiting for her response. Without warning, all her memories, thoughts, and feelings are exposed and analyzed. She begins to lose herself as she sees her spirit body as if through the eyes of the alien. Somewhere in the back of her mind, she hears Dr. Foster scream. In that moment, something phenomenal happens. The ice water quickly recedes. Both Alicia and Dr. Foster discover their spirit bodies floating in the blackness of space. They look at each other then towards a large planet floating in front of them covered with volatile, rusty-brown clouds. Another word enters their minds… *Home.* An intense feeling of sorrow quickly follows it.

The rusty-brown planet fades from view as other stars appear and shift around them as they travel to two that are almost touching. Their vision goes blank before reaching them.

Alicia wakes on the table with someone desperately calling her name. She slowly opens her eyes to see Dr. Foster shaking her gently. His face is haggard, eyes bloodshot and on the verge of collapse. One of his technicians removes the metal hoop from around his head as the other two support him. "Thank God you're alive Alicia! I didn't think we were going to make it." He lays his head on her chest making her shirt wet from tears.

Alicia gently puts a hand on his head and strokes his hair. She smiles as emotions swell up inside her. She's seen a hidden world and been reborn. From this day forward, the world will never be the same for her. The technicians carefully remove the wires attached to her head and place her in a wheelchair. Dr. Foster follows as they take her to the staff's living quarters.

After the technicians lay her in bed, Dr. Foster checks her vitals then they all quietly leave. With the effects of the drugs still coursing through her body, she can sense Dr. Foster's thoughts as he stands outside the door wishing he could stay and watch over her. Comforted, she closes her eyes for a long-deserved rest.

After a good night's sleep, Dr. Foster and Alicia meet in a spacious conference room to discuss what they saw and experienced together.

Alicia is dressed in casual street clothes for the exit interview. She leans forward to grab a coffee cup off the table as Dr. Foster prepares to take notes. He finally looks up and gives her a genuine heartfelt smile. "I hope you slept well and don't have any ill side effects from yesterday's experience."

Alicia looks around then winks. "If I did, I wouldn't call it an ill side effect."

Dr. Foster smirks. "That's good to hear." He lowers his head and clears his throat. "Now, for the record, I have to ask you some questions." He pauses to take a deep breath then continues. "What do you think the aliens are?"

Alicia contemplates the question as she sips her coffee and then answers. "So, what do I think the aliens are? To be honest, I really don't know. There were so many chaotic sounds and images fading in and out of my mind at the time. However, a few things stand out. For instance, when I first made contact I saw a pedestal rising from the floor that opened up to reveal a container with a dark oval object inside."

She cocks her head to one side as she ponders. "Who knows? Maybe the aliens developed from eggs or cocoons of some sort. Shortly after seeing that, I heard the word *hell* followed by a long hissing sound similar to what a snake or reptile would make. I get an overall feeling that they may be a reptilian race of some sort. Especially after it found us in its mind and tried to absorb our thoughts to kill us. You were there. Don't you agree?"

Dr. Foster nods. "Yes, that's exactly what I felt too. It's just that I need to hear it from you for a report I'm writing. So please continue. What else did you learn about the aliens?"

Alicia puts her cup on the table and creates a circle with her fingers. "Before we returned to our bodies, I saw a world covered in rusty-brown clouds as if seen from orbit. Then, I felt a wave of sadness and heard the word *home*. So what does that all mean?

She shakes her head. "Who knows? It could be they miss their home world. Maybe their planet can no longer support life and are looking for a new one. Or… they need new hunting grounds." She laughs then leans back in her chair. "You felt and saw some of what I described, but that's pretty much all I can tell you."

Dr. Foster nods then stands. "Well, thank you for volunteering to get us this information. You've been a tremendous help to our country and the world. It's been a pleasure and an honor working with you Alicia. I know you're itching to go so I hope you have a good life out there. Be safe and if possible, give me a call from time to time. I've already approved your exit documents and arranged transportation to take you wherever you want to go. Although it's not much, I've even added some funds to your account. It should tide you over for a month or so. As of now, you are a free woman. Please take care of yourself OK?" His emotions are in turmoil as he extends his hand.

Alicia hears Dr. Foster's voice in her mind. *I wish we could be together but I don't see how that's possible. I hope you do well out there.*

She stands and pushes his hand aside to give him a big hug. "Dr. Foster, you've shown me what true commitment is and made me realize that deep down; I'm still a good woman. I will never forget you as long as I live. Even though I'm leaving today, let's not say goodbye, because who knows, maybe we'll meet again someday." She releases him then points to his chest. "And don't you forget that you're a good man too. She kisses him lightly on the cheek then turns and leaves. She pauses briefly at the door to wave then exits the room.

Dr. Foster's smile changes to a frown as he realizes he will truly miss her.

Dear General Pierce,

As per your request, we finally made contact with the being inside the craft but were only able to collect bits and pieces. It's possible our form of telepathy is incompatible with theirs and it may not be possible to gather any real, meaningful information. However, after discussing the situation with test subject number nine, we concluded that the creature might belong to a hostile, reptilian race that developed from eggs or cocoons. We also believe they have traveled from a distant rusty-brown, cloud-covered planet to reach ours. Without a doubt, they have the ability to read and see through the minds of others. After detecting our presence, the creature sifted through our minds with ease. Unfortunately, we have not been able to duplicate our results since the alien closed its mind to us. On a side note, test subject number nine fulfilled the terms of her agreement. She was processed from our facility and released.

I will provide a full report as soon as we can finish analyzing our data.

Regards,

Dr. Johnathan Foster
Dr. Johnathan Foster,
Bunker 24 Facility, NV, Telepathic Investigation Division

Over the next two days, other teams of scientists and engineers feverishly perform a multitude of tests and experiments on the invisible, impenetrable object in the containment area. They compile their data and immediately send it to other research facilities for further analysis.

O'Connell's Retreat
4/8/2036

O'Connell wakes to the smell of antiseptic and a throbbing headache. Her vision is blurry as she looks around but realizes she is in Bunker 24's infirmary. She looks down at her body to discover she is wearing a hospital gown with her hands and arms covered in bandages. *How ironic, one of the most crucial times in the history of mankind and I'm lying in bed. That bonehead McCloud—I told him we needed to double buffer for potential energy surges.*

She pushes a button on her bed. Minutes later a nurse arrives carrying a cup of water and some pills. O'Connell looks at her nameplate. "Nurse Riley, can you tell me what's going on in the lab?"

"I'm sorry Ms. O'Connell I don't have clearance for that information. I'll let Dr. Matthews know you're awake. Please, take these. They'll help you relax and deal with any pain you might have."

Nurse Riley leaves without another word. A half hour later Dr. Matthews arrives looking like he just awoke from a hard night.

O'Connell is irritated because it took him so long and struggles to be polite. "I'm glad you could fit me into your busy schedule Doc."

The doctor looks at her as he bites his lower lip. "Ms. O'Connell, I'm a busy man so let me do my job and keep quiet for now." O'Connell fumes as he takes her vitals. "You sustained a minor concussion, some second-degree burns to your arms, and a few cuts here and there."

O'Connell is unable to contain her feelings any longer. "Well Doc, let me quit being an inconvenience and send me back to work."

Dr. Matthews runs a hand through his hair as he chooses his words carefully. "I'm sorry. I have orders to keep you under observation for the next forty-eight hours."

Clenching her blankets, O'Connell sits up in bed and struggling to keep her voice calm. "You've got to be kidding. I have a department to run."

Dr. Matthew rubs stubble on his chin and steps to her side. "I don't have time to kid around. If you don't stay in bed, I will post guards outside your door. Is that clear?" He turns his back on her and leaves without waiting for her to reply.

She suddenly feels groggy and lies back down realizing the pills just kicked in. She struggles to keep her eyes open but drifts off to sleep anyways.

Later that night she wakes with a pounding headache and voices in the hall. Her name is mentioned a couple of times and decides to eavesdrop. She quietly creeps to the door and listens to a man with a raspy voice.

"I tell you, I wouldn't want to be in her shoes. I hear McCloud resents the fact that O'Connell outranks him. He wanted to be the one in charge at Bunker 24 during the capture instead of being stuck at Fort Bliss."

A second voice, a little deeper than the first responds. "You mean McCloud is using her injuries to get her out of the lab so he can come back and take over the alien investigation?"

The man with the raspy voice chuckles. "Yeah…something like that. Apparently, he convinced General Pierce not to release her for the rest of the week, maybe even longer. Life sucks for O'Connell doesn't it?" Both men chuckle this time.

"I thought McCloud was a nice guy."

"Yeah when he wants something, but he can be downright mean if you're late or in the way." There is a brief pause before he continues again. "This woman isn't going anywhere. Let's say we get some beers and call it a night?"

"Now you're talking. Let me check on her first though."

O'Connell shakes her head in disgust then quickly slips back into her bed. Seconds later, the door to her room opens briefly then closes. She pretends to be asleep but anger rises inside her as she hears their footsteps fade down the hall. *If they don't want me here, fine! I'll leave.* O'Connell nods to herself as she decides to depart for the Ryedale Research Center in Houston, Texas, in the morning.

Sometime in the early morning hours, she awakes and immediately searches the room for her clothes but doesn't find them. She sneaks across the hall and enters a linen closet where she finds a lab coat, shirt, and pants then returns to her room. Footsteps echo down the hall and stop in front of her door. She quickly puts the clothes under a blanket then jumps on top of the bed as Nurse Riley opens the door.

She looks at O'Connell suspiciously, "What are you doing up at this hour? Have you been out of bed?"

O'Connell scans the room for a diversion then picks up a glass of water from the nightstand. "I was thirsty." She smiles innocently as she takes a sip. "Oh! It's so warm. Can you get me some cold water?"

The nurse reaches for the cup as O'Connell spills it down the front of the woman's uniform. "Oops! How clumsy of me! Let me help you with that."

Nurse Riley takes a deep breath and counts to herself but stops as O'Connell dabs the front of her shirt with a blanket. "Please don't touch me. Why, you did that on purpose! I'll be glad when they discharge you from here!" She turns and leaves.

O'Connell breathes a sigh of relief and mumbles under her breath, "Yeah, you and me both."

She waits until the nurse's footsteps fade away then retrieves the clothes and puts them on. She gets out of bed then quietly opens the door and heads to the nearest stairwell marked LEVEL 17. Emotion and tension build within her as she descends sixteen levels. Her head is pounding again by the time she reaches level thirty-three. She enters a password on a security panel near a large metal door with faded lettering: SECURED AREA - DO NOT ENTER WITHOUT PROPER AUTHORIZATION.

A cold shiver runs through her body and settles in her head. The pounding recedes as she opens the door and walks down a dimly lit corridor and into a large room with a raised circular platform at its center. On one of the control panels is a dusty bronze plaque that reads, PROTO PLATFORM #1.

Thank God, they decided to keep this place intact when they moved the main lab to the upper level. She turns on several computers then enters another password. After a series of equipment checks, she switches on a bank of large power generators that begin to hum in the background. Satisfied that everything is working properly, O'Connell makes one final adjustment and inputs the coordinates for the Ryedale Research Center.

She rubs her temples as her vision begins to blur then carefully walks onto the platform. She gestures in the air with her middle finger. "Hey McCloud! This one's for you! A moment later, a circular metal tube rises from the floor and surrounds the platform engulfing her body in a ball of white light."

As O'Connell disappears from the lab, sparks erupt from the control panel causing the lights to flicker and the generators to shut down. The room becomes quiet with only wisps of white smoke drifting in the air. Moments later the underground facility shakes violently from a massive explosion.

~ALIEN CAPTURE~
INSIDE BUNKER 24'S
CONTAINMENT FIELD

4/7/2036

Mentally exhausted, Reckston leans back from the immersion display then closes his eyes to get his bearings. Using his limited telepathic abilities, he discovers the Crawler materialized on a large metal platform located on a desert lakebed with the two men already running towards another portal in the distance. The stress of the jumps are overwhelming him. No one has ever phased a Crawler multiple times using such archaic technology while simultaneously adjusting for variances.

Tired of the chase and unable to go any faster, Reckston changes his goal of catching the men to shutting down their escape route. He quickly sits up and immerses his hands back into the liquid display to orient the Crawler towards the portal then launches a deactivation sequence. He finishes and is surprised as the first man enters. Frustrated by his miscalculation, he quickly opens his fingers then pans his hands apart but the second man also vanishes. He instantly loses mental contact to find himself staring out across his command bridge. Without warning, alarms blare throughout the compartment as the metal platform collapses below him.

Reckston's restraining harness keeps him firmly seated as his Crawler tumbles wildly down the throat of a dark vertical tunnel lined with metallic netting. He tries desperately to activate a distress beacon but centrifugal force prevents him.

The Crawler crashes to a halt upside down in a swirling pool of energy. Internal alarms go off as smoke appears beneath several destroyed control consoles. Disoriented, he disengages his harness and falls several meters to the ceiling. Unharmed, he quickly inspects the damage but is distracted as the phase field stabilizers begin to crackle and hum.

Seconds later a massive ball of energy builds outside his vehicle and bursts with an earsplitting explosion. The shock wave sends him reeling headlong into the bulkheads. Sprawled out on the ceiling, Reckston's blue-flecked eyes tear as thoughts of his wife and daughter flash through his mind. *I was...I was trying to make a difference.* His lips press together as he passes out.

Reckston groggily comes to amid electrical sparks and warning lights. Smoke burns his eyes and lungs as he looks around and is surprised to be alive in null state. He crawls to the rear cargo hold and opens an emergency panel containing his biosuit. As the door swings open, a bulky black suit falls on top of him. He quickly puts it on and locks the helmet in place. He takes a deep breath as fresh air flows into his helmet.

He turns on the suit's onboard computer as he walks underneath the command chair to examine the monitors up above and activates a diagnostic program. The results are depressing as he turns on some backup equipment and the distress beacon. His tension remains high as outside particle scans continue to destabilize his phase fields.

Feelings of claustrophobia and isolation overcome him as he realizes the only other time in his life he lost contact with Breeding Tube Command or BTC, was during the first few minutes after arriving at this desolate place.

Reckston searches the wall and finds an emergency hatch marked CRY-COMM then presses his hands against a circular scanning plate. Seconds later, a large multi-cylinder tube emerges from the floor, which not too long ago was his ceiling. Immediately a green light starts flashing as an outer cylinder slowly sinks to expose an octagon container with an oval shape inside. He stares at it a moment then carefully removes the container and inserts it into a slot on the main control panel. He never did like the idea putting the brains of BTC females in cryostasis but thankful for it now.

The lights dim briefly as the Cry-Comm integrates with the onboard computer. After a brief pause, a woman's voice breaks the silence. "Speech mode activated. BTC neural-link failure. Backup power...forty-nine percent. Wait...compensating for external field fluctuations...Hello Reckston."

The man clears his throat trying hard to remember how to speak. He moves his lips slowly. "Hell...hellooo?"

The woman's voice continues. "My name is Ritan. Records indicate you have been in the field two years, eleven months, and seven days. Are you having difficulty speaking? Say yes or no now."

Reckston tries hard to form his word carefully. "Yessssss."

"Understood. Beneath my cradle is a compartment that contains several neural serum cartridges. Retrieve all of them and inject one into your suit's onboard medical kit. The serum will allow you to communicate with me telepathically."

Reckston completes the task then sits down as the serum enters his bloodstream. He feels his mind expand, then expand again as a new world opens to him. Huge amounts of audiovisual data flood his brain. With difficulty, his mind slowly masters the flow and begins analyzing his surroundings.

Immediately he is able to see through the eyes of his captors as well as two individuals trying to read his mind. Sadness fills him as the woman named Alicia reminds him of his wife Anna living in a rusty-brown planet, both struggling to survive in desperate times.

He senses that the man named Foster is only there to observe and support Alicia then bring her mind safely back but senses he is too weak even to help himself. With effort, he carefully extracts the two from his mind and sends them safely to their bodies in a distant lab. He closes his mind from further intrusions then focuses his awareness on the here and now.

With Ritan's assistance, he realizes how desperate his situation is and quickly turns his attention to his only escape route. He moves to the center of the cramped bridge and inspects two circular disks. They are one meter in diameter, one on the floor and the other on the ceiling directly opposite each other.

Ritan, run a full diagnostic on the Dynalink Converter to see if it's operational.

Seconds later lights on a control panel turn on then shut off.

Ritan's voice enters his mind tinged with disappointment.

Activation failure. I am unable to locate external pulse waves. Without them, we don't have enough power to complete a phase. Sensors also indicate an outside dampening field is still in effect.

Frustrated, Reckston sits down and stares at red flashing displays showing the dire state of his crawler and fuel cells. He checks his biosuit's computer once more to verify it is synchronizing with the Crawler's mainframe. *Ritan, turn off all nonessential systems. Maybe we can survive long enough for the BTC to attempt a rescue.*

After a brief pause, Ritan replies. *All nonessential systems shutting down. Since we are no longer receiving pulse waves, the Crawler will destabilize and phase out of null state in less than thirty-two hours. Given the fact that we are unable to establish contact with the*

BTC, they will assume our phase fields have already destabilized. I'm sorry Reckston no rescue will be forthcoming.

Over the next twelve hours, Reckston tries desperately and fails to reestablish a link to the BTC or lock onto pulse waves necessary to recharge the fuel cells of his Crawler. Feelings of despair overwhelm him as he sits against the wall to wait for the inevitable to happen.

Unable to do anything else, Reckston and Ritan take turns asking each other questions, enjoying the fact that for the first time in their lives they are free to think independently from BTC's manipulation and contrary actions.

Reckston stands up and begins to pace as he thinks up his next question. *OK Ritan, I have one. Tell me something interesting before you became part of the BTC neural network.*

That was such a long time ago. Well...hmm. When I was seven, my class visited the Arcadian Space Station, the only place left unaffected by Radiantnine. I didn't know at the time the station was, in essence, a giant gyroscope. Part of our training there was to get to know how big and desolate our world had become. Our class was the last trained to keep the remnant populations united until the transport centers were complete. I remember crying that day wondering how we let our world become so utterly devastated and devoid of life.

She stops as she relives that distressing moment.

Reckston feels her discomfort and decides to change the subject. *I think now is a good time to ask me a question.*

Ritan's lights blink on her container. *I know you are in direct violation of BTC's directives. What made you decide to help these people?*

Reckston heart skips a beat. He tried hard to keep his thoughts a secret but realizes she must already know everything. He pauses before answering.

It didn't happen all at once. It formed over the years of patrolling the outer perimeter. I've always questioned Command's motive of slaughtering innocent people in the name of secrecy. I became a scientist to solve problems, not to become a killer. We are the ones in the wrong, not the men and women outside our cage who wish to discover who we are and then eventually exterminate us.

Yes, I disobeyed direct orders to kill those two men in the Zone. I wanted to explain to them that the problems we created upon our arrival involve them soon. I hoped they might even be willing to help us somehow. I can't even blame Alicia or the doctor for trying to read my mind. They were following orders like everyone else in this pointless, escalating war. Honestly, I believe the only way to stop this imminent world-ending crisis is to combine technologies from these people and ours in hopes of a hybrid solution.

He stops, frustrated that he is powerless to do anything about it now.

Ritan remains quiet as she lets him settle down and eventually he dozes off to sleep. Hours pass before Reckston reawakens. When he opens his mind to see what is happening outside the Crawler, he discovers hundreds of people still determined to discover their secrets. He expands his mind to its limit and focuses on a distraught individual with the same goal as himself: to escape. How could this be? He quickly reads her thoughts, which gives him an idea. In a leap of intuition, he decides to gamble on a very improbable escape.

Ritan! I need your help fast. Can you to get the precise destination coordinates from the woman preparing to activate a phasing platform on level thirty-three?

Ritan examines Reckston's thoughts then enters the mind of the woman named O'Connell to discover she is suffering from a mild concussion and eliminates her discomfort.

Reckston doesn't wait for a response as he grabs a felt bag and stuffs it with neural serum, a Dynalink phasing band, and several other supplies.

Coordinates acquired, computing a trilateral phase now.

Reckston rushes to the bridge and uses several command overrides to disable all built-in safety features hoping to generate enough power to attempt an escape. He hesitates then decides to enter the Crawler's self-destruct code as well. *Ritan, this is a one-way ticket. So give the Dynalink Converter everything you got!*

Working on it. Maximum power reaching apex! Fields aligning! It's going to be close... Nineteen seconds for dual portal activation!

Calmness overcomes Reckston as energy-starved equipment comes back online. He realizes if his plan doesn't work, he'll at least die by his own hands. Ritan interrupts his thoughts.

Reckston, please don't leave me here to die! I believe in your cause and can help you make a difference!

Embarrassed, Reckston quickly pushes several buttons to put her back in cryostasis then ejects her from the control panel. He stuffs her container into his bag then positions himself between two circular disks opposite each other. He nervously watches control panels erupt into showers of sparks one after another. As the two disks turn blue, the cabin distorts around him then fades to black...

DELL'S GIFT

4/8/2036

The time is 1800 hours. Sergeant Jacob and Corporal Casey are in a watchtower on the outer edge of the perimeter of the Zone. Corporal Casey enjoys the brief, unexplained period of clear weather as he looks at the shadow of the guard tower extending out into the desolate landscape.

His heart begins to pound when he notices movement where there was none before. He quickly picks up a pair of binoculars to get a better look and sees a man wearing a standard-issue military backpack, camo pants, and a bloodstained shirt staggering over a sand dune. "Sir, I think…"

Sergeant Jacob jerks awake dropping the duty roster on the floor. He looks at Corporal Casey sharply and points to the rank on his shoulder. "Are you still some sort of newbie Corporal? Look at these stripes. I work for a living."

He notices the Corporal's strange expression and follows his stare then grabs the binoculars from the young man and scans the vicinity for himself. Sergeant Jacob's face changes from annoyance to disbelief as he fumbles for the phone. Corporal Casey continues to watch as if hypnotized by the man struggling blindly toward their position.

While en route to the Ryedale Research Center, General Pierce receives word of sector seven's alert status. In minutes, he is talking to the outpost commander. "Like I said Colonel, I'm not going authorize any rescue mission inside the Zone. Period! Is that clear?"

Colonel Max's face turns red with anger but he is able to control the tone of his voice. "Very clear sir."

Pierce continues, "Good, report to me if the man reaches the outer perimeter or if current conditions change. That is all." He hangs up without waiting for a response.

Fuming, Colonel Max disconnects the speakerphone and looks at the First Sergeant standing quietly nearby. "Well, he didn't say we couldn't use civilian intervention. Have the company day runner locate Ms. Thompson and send her to watchtower one-eight-one ASAP."

The First Sergeant nods then walks out. Colonel Max immediately dons his cap and leaves his office to find a driver. He arrives twenty minutes later at the watchtower in an all-terrain vehicle ready to observe for himself, the unexpected visitor in no-man's-land.

Ten minutes later Ms. Thompson, also known as Dell, arrives and enters the tower wearing jeans and a loose T-shirt. She runs a hand through brown windblown hair and gazes at the Colonel with intense deep-blue eyes. "Hi Colonel Max. What's going on?"

He notices her nervously touching a worn silver medallion with a blue center as he guides her over to the observation window facing the blasted desert landscape. "I need your expertise to identify a man inside the Zone boundary and help him get out if possible." Corporal Casey hands her a set of binoculars and points east.

Dell subconsciously touches her medallion again then follows the shadow of the watchtower out into the desert. "I don't see…" Her lower lip quivers as she spots a seriously injured man struggling to stay on his feet.

Sergeant Jacob and Colonel Max guide Dell to a chair as she projects her mind out into the desert. Instantly, her spirit body materializes over the blind man and is amazed to see he is still alive considering his dire state. Raw emotions overwhelm her senses as she probes his mind. Immediately, the man shakes his head and crumples to the ground but rolls over and starts crawling on his hands and knees.

Dell realizes he doesn't have much time to live without immediate medical attention. Gathering up her courage she gently touches him on the forehead and reacts as if lightning pierced her chest. A feeling of abandonment overwhelms her thoughts as she sees a bald-headed, blue-eyed toddler looking out a window at a bizarre, multi ringed ship rotating in a field of black. The image instantly changes to her first terrifying out-of-body experience caused in part to save her injured father. It is so unexpected she almost loses contact with the man but regains her senses as he crawls farther away. Feelings of guilt and despair build up inside her as she resolves to redeem herself for her past failure.

I won't let you die. I promise to guide you to safety.

From a great distance, she feels hands shaking her body. With difficulty, she spans the gulf back to the watchtower to hear Colonel Max's frantic voice in her ear.

"Dell, can you hear me? Tell me what's wrong! You grabbed your chest and started shaking. What do you want me to do?"

She pushes him away and struggles to respond, "I'm…OK. He's injured…blind…close to death…sound the tower siren…he needs me!"

Colonel Max anxiously motions the Sergeant to activate the siren but he signals back that it's broken. He points a finger at the Sergeant and mouths the words, *"Fix it!"* He turns his attention back to Dell and in a calm voice responds. "OK, we'll do that as soon as possible. I have a medical team on its way. Hang in there and bring that man home."

Dell nods then allows her spirit body to materialize near the crawling man again. Without hesitation, she touches his forehead—this time experiencing only a mild tingling sensation. In a gentle voice, she sends him a message with her mind.

I am here to help you.

The man immediately sits back on his legs and extends a hand as if reaching out to her. With effort he finally speaks. "Eileen, my angel…they wanted me dead. It's alright now…we'll be together soon."

Feelings of pure love and hope saturate Dell's mind as she senses a renewed strength inside him. She realizes Eileen must be someone he loved without bounds.

He must think I am this person. The sound of my voice has brought him temporarily out of his plight. To save him, I must continue to let him think I'm this woman.

The man's intense love continues to build inside her, finally its strength and devotion overwhelms her spirit. She has craved this kind of emotion her whole life and fully absorbs it, so much so, that it will forever be part of her soul. Her life of solitude and loss will be too much to bear without him now. In that moment, she vows to save his life even if it means losing her own.

The tingling sensation in her chest intensifies as her real body begins to tremble. She is so determined to save him that her telepathic powers increase and accepts them for what they are. She looks down at the man with a renewed sense of wonder. If given the chance, maybe he could love her the same way he loves this woman named Eileen.

She floats away, hoping to draw him in the right direction.

All will be OK. Don't worry my love. I'll guide you to safety. You're almost home. Let me be your eyes and follow me.

A dazed smile spreads across his blood-cracked lips as he staggers to his feet and begins walking toward her.

Yes, you're doing great! Keep going. I'm here waiting for you.

About a dozen soldiers line up near the perimeter to watch the man staggering toward their position wondering how he could still be alive inside the storm boundary of the Zone. They cheer him onward with each passing step but his pace is painfully slow. Oblivious to everyone else, Dell feels the presence of several aliens closing in fast on their position. With no more time to spare, she realizes the man won't make it but gives him one last desperate plea.

You're almost home. Run to me...Run to me now! Don't hold back. You have to make it my love. Let me save you!

Compelled by spiritual intimacy and his powerful emotions, she performs the ultimate act of love by drawing all her life energy from her physical body then floats toward him with her spirit arms open wide. She melts inside his body just as the tower siren begins to blare.

The men at the perimeter watch as if witnessing a miracle as the man stands erect and runs straight toward them as if guided by the hand of God. Locked in a battle to save his life, Dell is dying inside the watchtower as her body violently convulses on the floor. A scream escapes her lips as the last of her energy fades away.

Outside, the waiting soldiers catch the running man in their arms. Sounds of cheers fill the air but inside the watchtower, a frantic struggle to save Dell's life begins. Colonel Max and Sergeant Jacob frantically perform CPR to keep her alive. They are relieved to hear the sound of a hover jet landing over the wail of the tower siren. Eventually two medics burst inside the room and quickly take over. Desperate minutes go by before they restore her pulse and get her breathing on her own. In a corner of the tower, Colonel Max and Sergeant Jacob sit in numb silence realizing how close they came to losing her.

As dusk falls across the desert, Colonel Max watches with concern as an army hover jet takes off into the clear night sky. Its twin turbine engines whine loudly as it rushes the two unconscious individuals to the William Beaumont Army Medical Center at Fort Bliss.

GENERAL DARKNESS

4/9/2036

Deep in thought, Pierce stands alone as he looks at the sleeping figure of Hopper through a small observation window. *So...it is you. I should be happy to see you alive but I hate how everyone is praising you. It's as if you redirected all my success for your glory. It was supposed to be my turn to be the hero again. Now, you're the man people are willing to follow to hell and back, not me. Hmm...I wonder what you did differently than the thousand or so men and women who died in the Zone. Ah, it doesn't matter...I still think I would have preferred you dead.*

The General hears a noise behind him and turns around to see a doctor with a clipboard passing by.

"Doctor...Dr. Himes! What is the current condition of Captain Phillips?"

The doctor looks up agitated then notices his rank. "Sir, shrapnel in the eyes have temporarily blinded our patient. He is also suffering from extreme dehydration and has multiple lacerations that are infected. Frankly sir, I'm surprised he's alive."

General Pierce steps closer to the doctor. "Will he live?"

Dr. Himes tenses. "Sir, it's too soon to tell. We won't know for a couple of days at least."

General Pierce slowly turns and walks away as his mind desperately tries to figure out how to turn this situation to his advantage.

General Therapy II
4/10/2036

Dr. Matthews is awaken by an alarm coming from his computer in the living room. He rolls over to see it is three o'clock in the morning. He stares at the ceiling as his anger rises. "Who is crazy enough to call me at this hour? Don't people know I work the day shift? This is outrageous!"

He fumbles for his glasses then turns on the light and squints. He quickly gets out of bed and enters the living room. On the display terminal is General Pierce's unshaven face with dark circles under his eyes.

The General immediately starts speaking as soon as he activates the call. "Thank you for getting your ass out of bed. Since you're not doing anything important at the moment, I hope you don't mind having a little chat with me. I've had a rough night."

Dr. Matthews shakes off his sleepiness and swallows hard. "Ah... not a problem sir. What can I do for you?"

The General holds up an empty tin and shakes it. "Remember this?"

"Oh yes. If you're out, just come by in the morning and I'll give you a refill."

"That won't be possible. I'm at the airport heading to DC shortly. Lately the BRAVE device doesn't seem to be working as well and I've run out of these tasty little pills you gave me. I'm meeting the President later today and need to be focused, confident and alert. Is there anything in your bag of tricks to help me?"

Dr. Matthews pulls on his beard for a moment as he thinks. "It's possible the BRAVE is still functioning properly but needs to be recalibrated to a higher output. At its current level, your body probably adjusted to the stimuli it can give. It's something like drinking beer every day. Eventually you won't feel a buzz anymore. Now let's say I switched you to hard alcohol…yes! I can adjust the vectors to increase the amplitude of your biometric rhythms, but it would mean overriding its built-in safeguards. If not done properly, there could be some adverse effects and my professional code of ethics would prevent me from allowing you to do that to yourself."

General Pierce grunts. "I don't care about the safeguards or your bullshit code of ethics. Just do it!"

"Sir, the only thing I can do from my location is to transfer complete control over to you and let you set it yourself but I strongly disagree with that. When you get back to Command I'll fill your tin full of relaxants, OK?"

Pierce's face contorts into pure anger. "I'm not screwing around here, Doc! If you don't cooperate, I'll have my High Guards in your quarters in less than two minutes and they're extremely proficient at getting information. I'm not going to ask you again, so the next words out of your mouth better be how I can take control of the BRAVE!"

Sweat breaks out over Dr. Matthews' body as his heart races in his chest. The room spins as he looks at the door of his quarters then back at the computer terminal. He takes some deep breaths to focus.

"Alright sir, just relax. No need to do anything rash, OK? I'll tell you what you need to know. First things first. Put your thumb on the display and repeat after me…"

General Assignment
4/10/2036

After adjusting his BRAVE device, General Pierce is able to sleep for a few hours on a military transport heading to DC. He wakes feeling refreshed and reads the daily status reports coming out of Bunker 24. He finishes them then goes to the lavatory to shave before landing. An hour later, he arrives at the White House and enters the Oval Office where President Wellington meets him at the door.

"Welcome General, you seem to be in especially good spirits today."

Pierce smiles as he salutes then shakes the President's hand. "Thank you Mr. President. Things are proceeding quickly now that we've captured an alien. Just this morning Dr. Foster from our telepathic division reported what the aliens could possibly be and gave clues on how Captain Phillips may have survived inside the Zone undetected. I also have several interesting reports from McCloud about a newly discovered energy source emanating from within the Zone and a few expense reports that'll need your signature."

President Wellington gestures to his desk. "We might as well sit down then. Shall I have my secretary bring us some tea?"

Pierce nods. "That sounds good Mr. President."

Mid-way through their meeting, a man in a simple military uniform enters and approaches the President. He salutes then hands him a sealed envelope. He immediately does an about face and leaves without saying a word.

Wellington glances at Pierce. "This doesn't look good." He removes the letter inside and reads it to himself, immediately his face turns pale. The President clears his throat as he stares at the words. "Bunker 24's containment area has been completely destroyed by some sort of antimatter explosion. We've failed…"

General Pierce sits in shock as he realizes he just lost half his staff of scientists and the alien prisoner. As his mind races for a solution, he slumps his shoulders and frowns in defeat, then draws his lips taut while clenching a fist to the ceiling. A moment later he rubs his chin and ponders before a large grin grows on his face. He finally smiles as he consoles the President like a child.

"No Mr. President, we didn't fail."

The President looks up as Pierce continues.

"Mainframe computers at Fort Bliss' Command Center and at the Ryedale Research Center in Texas were directly linked to Bunker 24's. It's possible we have enough data already stored to allow R & D to create the weapons and devices we need to defeat the aliens. Let me explain."

The President listens with interest, gaining hope on every passing word. An hour later, the President dismisses the General to carry out his new special assignment.

As Pierce walks out of the Oval Office, he rubs his hands together and chuckles.

The Famine War won't even compare to this new mission. If I accomplish my objectives, my dream of world peace will be one-step closer to reality. His chuckle turns into a haunting laugh as he enters the main corridor of the White House.

TRUE NIGHTMARES

4/8/2036

Hopper's thoughts drift as he wakes to darkness, the sounds of machines, and unintelligible voices. Suddenly, he concludes the aliens have captured him. His heart begins to race as he struggles to sit up only to feel tubes and wires restraining him. Alarms go off all around as his panic continues to escalate. Nearby, he hears the sound of a metal door slam open and heavy steps rush towards him. He screams in terror until there is no air left in his lungs.

Phantom hands grab him and force him down against his will. He struggles in vain until a sharp pain enters his arm. Seconds later a warm sensation spreads throughout his body and fades once more into unconsciousness.

4/11/2036

Hopper groggily comes to with the sound of a woman humming to herself as she holds his wrist. Her soft, smooth hand gently feels for his pulse. "Good morning Captain Phillips. I'm relieved to see you are finally awake. How do you feel?"

Hopper tries to open his eyes but is unsuccessful. He licks his lips and struggles to even whisper, "Where am I?"

"You're in the William Beaumont Army Medical Center at Fort Bliss."

He clears his voice and forms his words carefully. "How…did I get here?"

The nurse pats his hand. "A hover jet flew you here three days ago. Everyone made a big fuss over you too. I know you have many questions but please try not to worry about anything. You're safe now."

Hopper puts his other hand to his face and feel bandages covering his eyes. The nurse looks nervously at red warning lights flickering on the life-support system then to the door. "The doctor will arrive here shortly, in the meantime would you like some water to drink?"

Hopper starts to answer as he hears someone walk into the room.

"Well, well, I see you've met Holly already. My name is Dr. Gilbert." The doctor leans over Hopper and starts inspecting his dressings. "So tell me Captain Phillips, how do you feel today?"

Hopper's voice cracks as he starts to speak. "I feel—" He abruptly stops as nightmare images of death and survival flash through his mind. "I feel blind!"

Raw emotions course through his veins as the life-support machine begins to buzz loudly. He hears the two whispering then feels his IV tubes move on his arm. A moment later the buzzing sound fades away as Hopper drifts off to sleep.

4/13/2036

Days pass before a disturbance in the hall wakes Hopper. He can hear a man with a harsh voice asking a question. "Dr. Gilbert, is *sleeping beauty* awake yet?" Intense whispers follow, a minute later a group of people noisily burst into the room.

A man approaches his bed and he hears the same harsh voice again. "You see, he is awake! Ah…Captain Phillips, my name is General Pierce and I am the Chief Commander for Operation Hail

Mary. With me is General Hamrick and members of my staff. The doctor tells me you've had a rough time over the last five days so I'll be brief. I've come to congratulate you on a job well done. Due to your quick thinking and ingenuity, the Hail Mary Mission was a complete success. Thanks to you, we were able to capture an alien and have gained a tremendous amount of information from it."

Hopper's anger rises wondering why they sent him back to the Zone to die. He takes a deep breath but keeps his voice calm. "Thank you sir."

A beeping sound emanates from Hopper's right in response to his rising blood pressure. Dr. Gilbert's soothing voice interrupts, "Now just relax Hopper."

General Pierce motions for Colonel Barland to escort the doctor out then continues. "You're a lucky man in many ways. I hear you will regain most or all of your vision soon, which reminds me...we believe being blind may have saved your life."

Hopper struggles to sit up as the General leans forward to help. Hopper senses him and irately grabs the front of his uniform and pulls him close. "Who was responsible for phasing me and Specialist Greenwood *back* into the Zone?"

Hopper feels Pierce's body tense as he tries to back away. General Hamrick hastily intervenes and pulls the two apart. "Sir, I really think Captain Phillips has had enough for one day."

"No! I don't think so! I think the Captain here deserves an answer." Pierce's tone is level but Hopper can hear the distaste in it. "Due to unusual atmospheric conditions at Mountain Retreat, we lost the ability to access your phasing band. After you activated the ECO button, the unit followed *preset* destinations just in case our attempt to capture the alien failed. The final destination was inside the Zone to prevent an alien running loose in populated areas."

Everyone remains quiet, though Hopper can hear feet shifting. Satisfied with the answer for now, Hopper falls back on the bed exhausted.

Pierce fights to keep his composure in front of his staff after the assault. He steps away from the bed as a young woman in desert fatigues walks into the room.

General Pierce clears his throat. "Captain Phillips, now that I've answered your question, let me introduce you to Annadell Thompson." He waves the woman closer.

She approaches Hopper and nervously takes his hand in hers. She speaks softly as she closes her eyes. "You can call me Dell. We have not formally met but I helped save your life the day you escaped the Zone." She opens her eyes and releases his hand. "It's an honor to meet you Captain Phillips. I must say, your inner strength is stronger than anyone I've ever met."

A lump grows in Hopper's throat as he realizes this is the first time since his wife's death that anyone has expressed compassion for him. With effort he whispers, "Call me Hopper. I hope to repay you someday for saving my life."

General Pierce interrupts sarcastically, "Well now, this is very touching and all Captain Phillips but repaying is the very reason we're all here. We need you to *volunteer* for another mission inside the Zone when you're feeling better."

Even in his weakened state, Hopper finds the energy to laugh. "Go to *hell*, sir!"

Such an insubordinate response makes General Pierce's anger boil inside him. His voice turns deadly as he responds. "Captain Phillips, I'm not afraid of hell. And even if I was, my conscious is clear. However, you should be worrying more about yourself right now." A deep grunting laugh escapes his mouth.

Pierce's face twists into an impudent sneer as he visualizes having Hopper shot by a firing squad. A tap on his shoulder from General Hamrick interrupts Pierce's dark fantasy.

Hamrick whispers in his ear, "Sir, let me remind you that Captain Phillips is the reason the Hail Mary Mission was a success. Please control yourself, we need—"

General Pierce hastily gestures Hamrick to tell it to the Captain.

Hamrick clears his throat then speaks in a loud voice. "Excuse me Captain. My name is General Hamrick. We've met before; I'm here to compliment you on the success of your mission. You've earned all of our respect..." He glances at General Pierce doubtfully then looks back at the Captain. "...and know you have served our country *far* beyond the call of duty."

Hopper tries to sit up but falls back on the bed, his breath ragged from the effort. "But General, I was left for dead!"

General Hamrick's face flushes as he looks again toward General Pierce. He hesitates before continuing in a reassuring voice.

"Well, what's important at the moment is national security. News of your success has already spread through all branches of the military. You have become a national hero and an inspiration for our troops. You proved the aliens have an Achilles' heel.

"Dozens of soldiers have already volunteered to go on the next mission...if *you* will lead them. They have confidence in you. *We* have confidence in you. Please reconsider and think about what's at stake. Don't let personal feelings get in the way. We are assembling a special squad and Dell here will be a part of it. Right now though, you need to recuperate but by the end of next month, we hope you will lead them."

General Pierce gives Hamrick a nod of approval and steps up to the bed but out of harm's way. "Captain Phillips, it's been a...a pleasure to meet you. Let us know what you decide as soon as possible."

Dr. Gilbert re-enters the room then politely motions everyone to leave.

"Looks like our time is up. If you have any more questions Captain, contact General Hamrick later." Pierce nods at the doctor then promptly turns and leaves with his staff following close behind.

Dell finds herself alone with Hopper and senses his feelings of contempt for Pierce's tactless request and his sense of duty to the nation.

"You know, they're not the enemy. I'll be back tomorrow when you're feeling better." She lightly touches his hand and leaves.

R·EFLECTION

4/13/2036

Dell's irritation grows as she waits impatiently for the bartender to finish flirting with a woman at the end of the bar. Normally things like that wouldn't bother her but today has been extremely upsetting. She subconsciously rubs her silver medallion.

Quit flirting you oaf and bring me a Bloody Mary.

The bartender abruptly ends his conversation and looks at her in shock.

Oh no! I did it again.

The bartender anxiously approaches. "Ah…I'm sorry miss. Bloody Mary, yes?" His hands tremble as he pours tomato juice and vodka into a glass. She gives him a guilty smile as he brings her the drink then hastily retreats to the other end of the bar.

She leaves money on the counter then moves to a booth near a window contemplating how she seems to make people fear or hate her. In her mother's case, both. Since she was fourteen, her mother blamed her for father's death. She picks up her drink and savors its aroma. *Well Mom, I would have traded places with him if I could.*

The memories of leaving her injured father in the desert to find help sends shivers down her spine. *How could I know that day would make the rest of my life a living hell?*

She takes a big swallow as General Hamrick enters the bar still wearing his uniform. She senses his frustration as she waves him over to her booth. "It looks like you had a rough day too."

The General tries to smile. "After the hospital visit today, Pierce and I had a falling out over his handling of Captain Phillips. I don't understand his attitude toward the man but I do know we can't afford to lose the Captain or his following. Anyway, Pierce put me in charge of training for Hail Mary 2.

He gives her a real smile this time then changes the subject. "Normally I don't invite individuals off post but I wanted to thank you personally for helping save the Captain." He leans over and looks into her deep blue eyes. "You did a very courageous thing by putting your life on the line like that."

She struggles for words as she looks into her half-empty glass. "I know you read my personal files so I'll be frank. It was for personal reasons. I felt I was given a chance to redeem myself for my father's death and to...find love."

Her voice trembles as she continues. "If Hopper died that day, I think my will to survive would have ceased to exist. She looks at Hamrick for a moment then speaks with conviction. "Captain Phillips is so full of love and regret. Somehow, I'm deeply connected to him now."

Hamrick gives her a warm smile then reaches out and touches her hand. "You didn't have to tell me that. I can see it by the way you look at him, but be careful Dell. His feelings are still wrapped up with Eileen."

Dell's heart throbs with passion as she recalls Hopper's devotion to his deceased wife.

Hamrick pauses as Dell diverts her eyes. "I just don't want you to get hurt emotionally anymore." They sit in awkward silence for a moment. "Well, let's talk about something else shall we?" Hamrick looks around the bar then back at Dell. "Now that I think about it, it's been a while since I've been off post. Let me buy a couple of rounds for the both of us." He spots the bartender eyeing them then waves him over.

The bartender approaches reluctantly, careful to keep his distance from Dell. Hamrick looks at the man's nameplate. "Gracias Martin, a couple of rounds of drinks for the young lady and myself."

Martin looks at Dell then clears his throat. "The same miss?"

She nods as Hamrick puts up two fingers to indicate the same. Martin promptly departs visibly relieved to attend the task.

Hamrick watches him go, puzzled by his behavior. "You know that fellow seemed a little uptight wouldn't you say? I wonder—" Hamrick looks over to see his driver standing at the door tapping his wrist frantically. "Sorry Dell, looks like duty calls. Let's plan another time to chat. Thanks again for saving Hopper and for volunteering for the upcoming mission. You're going to make a great contribution to the team." He lays some money on the table. "Take care of yourself, I'll see you soon."

Dell waves good-bye as he gets up and rushes out the door. Martin returns to find her deep in thought. He leaves the beverages on the table, picks up the cash, and quickly leaves.

Dell continues to drink well into the evening as she reflects on Hopper's internal struggles as well as her own irrational attraction to him.

Dell arrives at the hospital the next morning with a hangover. After passing several sets of guards, she enters Hopper's room to find him sleeping restlessly. She gently caresses his forehead as she contemplates her emotions once more.

I wish you would love me someday as much as you do Eileen.

Hopper turns over on his side and mumbles Eileen's name. Dell pulls her hand away and leaves the room crying.

Over the next couple of days, Hopper's mental and physical health improves dramatically. With his life signs finally stable, eye surgeons perform several surgeries to repair his damaged corneas.

Three weeks after Hopper's arrival, Dr. Gilbert returns to remove the final set of bandages covering his eyes. As the last set of them falls away, Hopper breathes a sigh of relief as he focuses on the doctor's kind leathery face. After a series of tests, the doctor gives him a nod of approval.

"Well Captain, I see we've been successful at reconstructing your damaged corneas. However, your eyes will be somewhat sensitive to light for a while."

Hopper smiles. "That's alright. It's a blessing just to see again."

Dr. Gilbert smirks as he becomes serious. "There's a young lady in the hall who wants to know how you're doing. Do you want me to send her in?"

Hopper subconsciously runs a hand though his hair realizing it will be the first time he'll see Dell. He motions for the doctor to come closer then whispers, "How do I look?" The doctor laughs then leaves amused.

Dell enters the room a moment later to find Hopper on the bed with his eyes shut. She approaches quietly. "Hopper?" Concerned, she presses her lips together and opens her mind to sense his emotions. She smiles then nudges his shoulder. "Hey! Don't you know you can't fool me?"

Hopper opens his eyes. Dell's deep-blue eyes, warm smile and shapely figure stun him. "I was um…I mean…"

Dell holds a finger up to her lips motioning him to be quiet. "I look forward to getting to know you too."

As the days pass, Dell and Hopper's friendship continues to grow. During one of their first walks around the restored hospital grounds,

Hopper asks a question that has bothered him since they officially met. "Dell, you seem to know exactly how I'm feeling. Can you read my mind?"

She motions for him to sit on a bench next to a bubbling fountain and gazes toward the Franklin Mountains in the distance. Her voice is tense as she begins. "The best way to explain it is that I can use my spirit to be present with someone, to sense their feelings or even send messages...but no, I've never been able to read minds."

Hopper is relieved but curious to learn more. "So when did you realize you had this special ability?"

Dell swallows hard to keep her voice from cracking. "It all started when my father broke his leg during a hiking trip in the Nevada desert when I was fourteen. After he passed out, I went looking for help but panicked and got lost. Without realizing how, something changed inside me. I had some sort of out-of-body experience and was able to sense a man and woman in my vicinity. By the time I arrived at their camp, I instinctively knew where my father was."

Dell looks at Hopper with tears in her eyes. "I soon learned they were Native American Indians. After the man went to look for my father, I told his wife about my experience and she wasn't even surprised. She said Indians have always dwelled in the spirit world and if I wanted too, I could develop my ability through meditation and practice. Even before her husband returned, I already knew my father passed away. His death had a devastating effect on me. To make matters worse, my mother blamed and hated me ever since. At one point, she even denied I was her daughter."

Seeing her pain, Hopper reaches out to comfort her but pulls back as Dell continues bitterly. "I was never close to her anyway. To bring love into my life, I honed my abilities to feel it from others but couldn't tell people about it because of how they would react afterwards. On my eighteenth birthday, I enlisted in the US Army to get away from my mother but they discharged me a year later saying I was mentally unfit for duty. You see, during a training mission an officer wanted to rape me. I could sense his intention and it terrified me. I accidently spoke with my mind and it scared the living daylights out of him. Eventually he pulled enough strings, spread enough rumors..."

Hopper empathizes with her but wants to know one last thing. "So what made you want to help the military this time?"

Dell sniffles then forces a sad smile. "A couple of months after the explosion in the desert, I was drawn to this area. Even from a distance, I could feel something *alive* in there. Eventually I explained it to my ex-commander who took my name and number. A couple of weeks later, General Hamrick called and invited me to Fort Bliss. After discussing how to best use my abilities, he sent me to see Colonel Max in charge of monitoring the outer edge of the perimeter of the Zone. I've been collecting data for him ever since."

She takes a deep breath, clearly disturbed by her memories then stands up abruptly. "I hope you don't mind, but that's enough questions for now. Let's continue our walk, shall we?"

RESEARCH AND DEVELOPMENT

5/30/2036

Drawn towards Dell's supportive caring attitude, Hopper cannot help but think of his late wife Eileen. As the end of the month arrives, he is unwilling to sever his growing friendship and agrees to go on the mission for no other reason than to keep her out of harm's way.

With orders in hand, they board a military transport bound for the Ryedale Research Center to receive updates on the prototype equipment under development. During the flight, Hopper swears Dell in as a Second Lieutenant. Due to abnormal weather conditions, their plane arrives late and have to rush to make their appointment.

Wearing a white lab coat and glasses, Chief Scientist McCloud tries hard to keep irritation from his voice as he greets them at the door. "Ah…Congratulations Captain Phillips on your last mission, I really didn't expect to see you alive again; but thanks to you, my research has advanced tenfold."

He glances at Dell and frowns then speaks sarcastically. "I hope you two enjoyed yourself over the last couple of months while I've been running around preparing your equipment." He looks at both of them then shakes his head in frustration. "Next time, don't be late. I've cancelled several experiments because of your tardiness. Now, *please* follow me."

He turns around abruptly and walks briskly away leading them through a maze of corridors then to a guarded elevator door. After clearing security, they enter it and descend dozens of levels. When the doors finally open, they find themselves in a brightly lit laboratory full of strange-looking equipment placed on thick granite tables.

McCloud looks at them with satisfaction as he waves a hand around the room. "The devices in front of you are powered by a new cold fusion process, so far undetected by the aliens. Conventional power sources have proven fatal for our...ah...volunteers." Wasting no time, he picks up a small device resembling an elastic hoop. "We call this a PSI band. The wearer becomes virtually invisible on the telepathic plane." He inspects a stamp-sized circuit board on its back. "We've had some minor problems with these recently but there's nothing to worry about now."

He notices Dell's look of concern then addresses her specifically. "Each band will be tuned specifically to your telepathic wavelength and block out all others so it won't affect your ability to communicate with team members." He turns back to the table and continues. "The next two devices I have here might look like contact lenses, but I assure you they work quite differently. We call them Nimbus Vision version nine or NV9. The lenses stimulate the cornea to allow you to see distortion fields created by the aliens and will appear as a milky white mist to the wearer. Unfortunately, they don't work in tandem with other optical devices, such as binoculars or night goggles.

McCloud's forehead wrinkles in thought as he looks at Hopper. "It seems glass filters out the distortion fields. Preliminary tests with these devices indicate close to a hundred alien patrols just inside the perimeter—which brings me to these."

He walks to another table and removes a cloth to reveal two high-tech looking rifles with orange and purple tipped rounds lying next to them. "These rifles shoot a form of antimatter created by short-lived Kaon particles which are encased in what we call grains. The antimatter releases when the grains disintegrate on impact and react with an unstable titanium pellet inside. The result is a small nucleonic explosion that atomizes everything within a ten-centimeter circumference."

He picks up the longer of the two rifles and shows them a slim, elongated magazine attached to the underside of the barrel. "We appropriately call this a Hornet; it's specifically designed for long-range fighting." He lays it down and picks up the other one. "As you can see, this one is similar to the first but notice the shorter, fatter barrel and the circular magazines imbedded in the stock. This one is a Wasp and is for close range fighting. It can fire a single shot or three round bursts if necessary."

He sets the Wasp down and browses another table then picks up a small device the size and shape of a large coin with a hole in its center. "This little guy is called a delta-wave emitter or D-wave. It duplicates certain human brain waves the aliens seem to sense. If you find yourselves in a difficult situation, this emitter may create enough telepathic confusion to give you time to escape. To activate it, all you need to do is rotate the outer ring to the desired delay then press the sides together.

He puts it down and picks up what looks like a glorified tuning fork with two amber-colored spheres slowly rotating at the end of a metal arm. On the front of it is a small red button in the center of an eight-centimeter circular display. "Can either of you guess the purpose of this? No? It's a homing device to help guide you to a newly discovered power source deep within the Zone.

Hopper starts to ask a question but McCloud quickly lifts up his hand. "I was told General Hamrick will brief you when you return to the Fort Bliss area. So please, save your questions for him. I don't have all day to chitchat. Now, let's move on to my pride and joy." He motions the two to stay put as he walks towards a raised black pillar with a 3D display projecting from its surface. As he nears it, the display flashes the word DANGER then morphs into a picture of skull and crossbones. A red light immediately immerses his body as several laser turrets lock on to him. He quickly presses his palms into outlines of a human hand on both sides of the pillar. A few seconds later the words ACCESS GRANTED displays along with a smiley face. McCloud removes his hands as a tray ejects from the side containing a dark-green device the size and shape of an aerosol can. McCloud carefully grabs it and holds it out for them to see.

"Now, this one is the most destructive weapon ever made. We call it Thumper. When activated, this antimatter bomb will vaporize everything within a two-hundred-meter circumference. Let me tell you the destruction it causes is a magnificent sight to see."

He holds it to his cheek and grins before remembering about Dell's special abilities. He quickly composes himself then puts it back in its cradle. It automatically retracts, sealing the device once more inside. He approaches them again. "Well, that's all I have to share with you today." He extends his hand to Hopper, "I wish you and your squad the best of luck on the up-coming mission."

Surprised, Hopper shakes his hand. "Ah…Thank you Chief, the items you've created here will definitely give us a fighting chance."

McCloud turns to Dell then rubs his chin as he scrutinizes her. "Hmm…as for you, you are one unique individual. I wish I could clone an army of you." He frowns then addresses both of them. "Anyway, I need to get back to work now." He catches the attention of a passing soldier. After a brief conversation with him, Hopper and Dell soon find themselves escorted out the building and into a waiting vehicle.

Mission Training
6/1/2036

With no time to spare, Hopper and Dell soon find themselves back on a military transport headed towards the White Sand Military

Reservation just north of Fort Bliss to inspect an elite group of combat ready candidates for their squad. They are able to sleep a few hours before arriving on a deserted airstrip around 0700 in the morning. They disembark and immediately enter an all-terrain vehicle waiting to take them to an undisclosed bunker facility. They see General Hamrick quietly watching them with dark circles under his eyes. As soon as they settle down, he motions the driver to go but continues to remain silent until Hopper can no longer contain his curiosity.

"Are you alright sir?"

General Hamrick is startled then finally speaks in a tired voice. "Ah…well, let me begin by telling you how proud I am of both of you for volunteering for this dangerous mission. Our country, even the world may depend on its success so we don't have room for errors. However, one has already occurred. Five days ago, we lost most of our handpicked candidates during a preliminary full-scale test of the PSI bands. Afterwards, McCloud informed me certain brain waves working in tandem, created a form of feedback that ended up frying the minds of everyone.

General Hamrick pauses with a sour expression on his face. "He said they were unable to detect the problem earlier because it depends on how each individual's brain waves interacts with others. I'm told they've been re-engineered to prevent it from happening again. We'll see.

"If that isn't bad enough, the next clearing period is calculated to occur in less than two months. This gives you roughly eight weeks to train an alternate group of men with little to no combat experience into an elite fighting force. I've picked out the best from the remaining pool of volunteers. But first things first." He reaches under his seat and hands them loaded pistols in holsters. "These are being issued to you for self-defense. Believe it or not, world leaders consider both of you the two most important people on the planet right now.

His comment surprises and shocks them, bringing to light the magnitude of the mission ahead. Hopper instinctively takes out his pistol and inspects it. Dell does the same but is more hesitant. Hamrick waits for them to put them on then opens a satchel on the seat and hands them a stack of folders to study.

"Here are your new candidates to choose from. I'm told some of them are already in conflict with each other. We have about an hour or so of driving ahead so look them over before we reach our destination." General Hamrick yawns then leans back in his seat. "If you don't mind, I really need to get a few minutes of sleep."

He turns his attention to the dim bleak landscape outside and is soon fast asleep.

Realizing their predicament, Hopper and Dell shake off their weariness and begin reading the files in the pale morning light. The vehicle finally comes to a stop in front of a small weathered house overrun by tumbleweeds in the middle of nowhere.

General Hamrick slowly wakes then squints at them. "Are we already here?" He glances outside to see an armed soldier in sun-bleached fatigues approaching. "Looks like it, grab your gear and follow me." Fighting drowsiness, he opens the door and steps out. The guard salutes then ushers them inside the house. It takes a moment for their eyes to adjust to find themselves in a poorly lit room with few furnishings. Hamrick immediately walks to the far wall and lays a hand against a black square. The lights flicker as a rusty metal door opens near his feet. He enjoys their look of surprise as they peer down a dimly lit stairwell then beckons them to follow. "Don't worry. This is one of many secret entrances to your new home for the next couple of months."

A door closes behind them as they exit the stairs only to find themselves inside a large metal cage. A soldier at a desk stands and points a gun in their general direction as a green light scans their bodies. He looks at the results then salutes. "Welcome back sir. You may all proceed." The bars at the back of the cage lift to reveal an elevator door.

Hopper notices the man's unit patch on his shoulder then gives the General an inquiring look. Hamrick only smiles as the elevator doors open then motions them inside. He turns to face them as it starts to descend. "The patch you saw was created for everyone working on the upcoming mission. The two squares, one inside the other, represent the inner and outer perimeters of the Zone. The twelve sections on the outside edge signify our major outposts. The circle in the middle is the alien sector and of course, the top missing corner represents the missing link." He points at both of them. "That's going to be you and your squad."

The General turns back to face the door as it opens. They step out and find they are in a spacious cavern with several natural tunnels leading off in different directions. The area is brightly lit and bustling with work crews constructing a shooting range and prepping for equipment to arrive. General Hamrick guides them down a side passage to a door simply labeled BARRACKS.

"I know you two had a long night but I want you to inspect and assess the squad as soon as possible. Currently, Sergeant Holloway and Sergeant Blix have the men out for their morning exercises. The officer in charge should arrive here shortly to introduce himself and show you around." He yawns, "I wish I could stay here longer but I need to leave for Washington, DC." He gives them a tired smile, "I believe in you and in the equipment we developed to allow this mission to succeed. I expect both of you to train the squad to the best of their abilities. Make sure they're mentally and physically ready for the difficult task ahead. Now, if either of you need anything, don't hesitate to call. Due to the importance of this mission, I have virtually unlimited resources at my disposal." With a genuine look of respect on his face, he salutes. "Do well my friends."

Hopper and Dell feel honored and proudly return the salute as he turns and limps away.

Dell frowns as she watches him go while Hopper opens the door in front of them and enters. She follows him inside and finds herself in another brightly lit chamber lined with beds and lockers. On the far rock wall is a large open gate labeled SUBTERRANEAN SECTOR. Dell's frown changes to worry as she addresses Hopper. "If the General keeps up at this pace, it will be the death of him."

Hopper sits down on a bed and shakes his head in frustration. "If it comes to that, I guess we'll be joining him if we don't get this squad to solidify. After reading their personnel files, I think we're going to need a miracle."

Dell lays a hand on his back but removes it as her emotions intensify. She decides to sit on a bed across from him. "I've been thinking about that. If we can demonstrate unquestioning trust and teamwork, I think we can train the squad faster and maximize their full potential. It's risky, but if you're up to it, we can show them what they're capable of."

Hopper raises an eyebrow. "I'm interested, what do you have in mind?"

Dell grins as she explains her plan.

Twenty minutes later a clean-cut man with sandy blond hair enters from the opposite side of the barracks. Hopper recognizes him as Lieutenant Sanders, a twenty-five-year-old officer fresh out of the academy and the only member to survive the previous training accident due to his PSI band being out of sync with the others.

He approaches and salutes. "Lieutenant Sanders reporting as ordered sir." They return the salute as he continues. "It's a pleasure to finally meet you both. Captain, I hear you're great at training Army Special Forces. Hope you have better results training these men than I did."

Hopper smiles and nods. "Good to meet you too Lieutenant." He looks at Dell. "We've just been discussing some ideas on how to do just that. By the way, any idea when our candidates will arrive?" As if on cue, forty men arraigned in four columns enter the barracks from the subterranean sector. They are all wearing brown T-shirts and desert fatigues.

The men come to a halt in the middle of the room as Sergeant Holloway salutes the Lieutenant. "Alpha and Beta squad reporting as ordered sir!"

Lieutenant Sanders returns the salute. "Stand at ease! Listen up men; I have the honor of introducing you to Captain Phillips and his adviser, Second Lieutenant Thompson. As of this moment, the Captain is now taking command of Operation Hail Mary 2. I hope you give him the trust and respect he deserves. Prepare for inspection. Group, Atten…tion!"

Hopper looks at the men with a critical eye. "At ease! I've read most of your personnel files and what concerned me most is the lack of combat experience. However, it looks like you make it up with individual skills."

Hopper walks up to Sergeant Blix and eyes the man's rugged face. "I've read you're already qualified on the new backup radios. Keep up the good work." He turns and begins inspecting the others. "Corporal Bennet...Corporal Beckett...Specialist Myers...Corporal Fernandez. He pauses in front of a soldier who recently had a pair of wings tattooed on his arm. "Congratulations Sergeant Mills on completing your Army Airborne training."

Hopper looks at Dell for a sign then continues the inspection. He stops in front of a hefty man named Corporal Blake then looks him up and down. "I think some of you believe you have a chance of surviving because I escaped the Zone."

Hopper shakes his head then continues down the third row of men and stops to inspect a man with stubble on his face who twitches under his intense gaze. "Well, I'm here to tell you that you don't have a chance in hell of making it out alive if you don't start working as a team. Is that clear?" Hopper is exasperated when they all remain quiet. "I said, *is that clear?*"

The men nervously shout out in unison, "Clear, sir!"

Hopper continues walking then halts suddenly when Dell finally nods and closes her eyes. He turns and faces a young man named Private Parker.

Hopper pulls out his pistol and chambers a round for all to see. "I'm going to show you all how the impossible can be achieved if you're willing to trust and work as a team. Are you capable of following my orders, Private?"

Private Parker's eyes bulge as Hopper hands him the pistol. Hopper calmly asks him again. "Can you follow my orders Private?"

Private Parker looks up nervously then answers in a shaky voice. "Yes sir!"

"Good, fall out and stand fifteen paces behind me."

Parker falls out and begins counting steps as Hopper continues to explain.

"Two things lacking in this outfit are trust and teamwork. Why is that? Is it because you failed to qualify for the original squad?" Hopper receives his confirmation as he watches the men's faces harden around him. "You're not a bunch of misfits. All you need is confidence in yourselves and in your leader. I want all of you to know—and I mean *all* of you—that if you're willing to believe in me, we can defeat any foe who stands in our way."

Without turning around, Hopper raises his voice to get Parker's attention. "Private Parker, are you fifteen paces behind me?"

Parker, still wondering what he's supposed to be doing answers in an anxious voice. "Yes sir!"

"Parker, do you trust me? If you have any doubts, tell me now."

Parker begins to feel light headed as fellow soldiers look at him with curiosity. He answers nervously. "No doubts, sir!"

"That's very reassuring. Now, the rest of you quickly fall out to my left and right." The men break rank leaving only Hopper and Parker in the center of the barracks. "Now I've picked Parker here not because he's the youngest or an expert shot but because he's a medic and knows better than the rest of you how to kill a man." With his back still toward Parker he continues. "Private, pick a place on my body and shoot to kill."

Lieutenant Sanders' voice breaks through the uproar that follows. "Captain Phillips! I've stood by and quietly watched, but isn't this demonstration going a little too far? What if something goes wrong and you really get hurt or worse? If you continue with this course of action, I will report you to General Hamrick at once!"

Hopper remains motionless as he answers Sanders firmly. "Lieutenant, trust and teamwork is what this outfit lacks. If it doesn't start with us, we're dooming ourselves to die in the Zone. Now...if anyone else interferes with this demonstration or doesn't follow my orders, I will personally court-martial you. Is that clear?"

A chant from Sergeant Blix slowly spreads throughout the barracks. "Teams trust...Teams trust!" In moments, the barracks is echoing.

Hopper holds up his hands to quiet them down. In a calm, reassuring voice he asks Sanders the same question he asked Parker earlier. "Do you trust me Lieutenant?"

Lieutenant Sanders clears his throat then answers in a tight, dry voice. "I trust you Captain!"

Hopper holds up his hands to prevent any more chanting. "Glad to hear that. OK Private Parker, are you ready to continue?"

Parker affirms once more as Hopper closes his eyes.

"Good, let us begin."

The room becomes deathly silent as Parker takes a deep breath then removes the slide lock release then pulls the slide all the way back then lets go. He watches a bullet load into the chamber. *It's real alright. Trust him he said. God, I hope he knows what he's doing.*

The soldiers watch Parker as he moves to Hopper's right then kneels down on one knee. He carefully sights the barrel at Hopper's back then slowly moves it up to his head.

If something goes wrong this is going to be cold-blooded murder!

A probing sensation fills his mind as his vision blurs briefly. He ignores the distraction and focuses on the base of Hopper's skull visualizing the center of the cerebellum, a location between the spinal cord and brain. Sweat builds on his face as he slowly squeezes the trigger.

I trust you Captain but please do something...now!

Lieutenant Sanders struggles to remain quiet as he digs his fingernails into his palms. *That Captain is an idiot! He's going to kill himself with a stunt like this. I don't see what he's trying to prove or how he'll survive. Parker's an expert shot and can't miss at this range. Confound it! I have no choice but to trust the Captain…*

Even though time seems to slow when Parker pulls the trigger, the Captain's head quickly shifts down and to the left. At the same time, a puff of blue smoke erupts from the barrel as a spent cartridge ejects from the chamber. Miraculously, Hopper turns around unharmed. The Lieutenant glances to a new gaping hole above the latrine door in utter disbelief. *That's impossible! How could the Captain have known where Parker was aiming, when he was going to fire, or how to move in such a way as to dodge the bullet?*

The men in the room burst into uncontrolled jubilation. Hopper's face is flustered as he holds up his hands. It takes almost a minute for everyone to settle down again. "Before I tell you how this was done, I want you to realize that the youngest man among you believed I could somehow come out unscathed even though he pulled the trigger."

Hopper walks over to Parker who is still kneeling on the floor in shock and takes back his pistol. "If all of you trust me like Private Parker here, we can achieve the impossible. However, trust alone is not enough without teamwork. I have just put my life on the line to prove to you it works."

The men's expressions are mixed with amazement and questioning looks. Heads begin to nod as they realize the truth of Hopper's words. Soon the barracks is buzzing with conversation.

Hopper raises his arms to get their attention once more. "Let me introduce you to Lieutenant Thompson. She has the unique ability to sense feelings and send messages to another person with her mind. She informed me where Private Parker was aiming and when he would fire. It was a simple matter of moving my head out of the way at the last moment. If I can dodge a bullet, imagine how powerful our team can be by adding training and special equipment. Over the last two years, Lieutenant Thompson has been gathering valuable data by sensing alien troop movement inside the Zone and reporting it to Command. She is familiar with our enemy and will guide us through enemy territory, at the same time, relay messages for our squad during the upcoming mission."

Dell steps forward and joins Hopper in the middle of the barracks. She gives everyone a warm smile. "Hello, my name is Annadell but you can call me Dell. I look forward to working with all of you. As you can see from our little demonstration, *anything* is possible."

Hopper speaks to them in a confident commanding voice. "With our new equipment, trust in your fellow soldiers and the willingness to work together as a team, our enemy will not prevent us from achieving our goals!" The men cheer again as their confidence rises. Even Lieutenant Sanders is reassured as he nods in agreement.

Over the following weeks, training is intense for the men as they follow a strict regimen of physical activities to get into shape and to perfect the technique of subterranean close combat tactics. They also perform mental exercises to familiarize themselves with the modified PSI bands and for Dell to communicate with them efficiently. As more equipment arrives from Ryedale, the team becomes familiar with the new Kaon rifles and other equipment. The last to arrive is the antimatter bomb designed to vaporize everything within a two-hundred-meter circumference.

Near the end of the eight-week training period, the group of forty candidates has shrunk to twelve. Those remaining have now become members of the squad, chosen for being the most telepathically acclimated, physically fit, combat ready, and having valuable individual skills. With only one day remaining before the predicted clearing period is to arrive, Hopper contacts General Hamrick to inform him that the squad is an efficient fighting force, fully prepared for the dangerous mission ahead.

GAME PLAN

8/2/2036

During a visit to Washington, DC, General Pierce explains to President Wellington his strategies for the upcoming Hail Mary 2 Mission. He continues with a smug look on his face as he struts around the Oval Office. "Mr. President, I assure you our mortar rockets and remote control drones will create more than enough confusion for the aliens so Captain Phillips and his squad can infiltrate their outer defenses. If necessary, we can even deploy some of the D-wave emitters from our geo-synchronized orbital launch platforms."

Wellington looks up from his desk in surprise. "I thought their onboard guidance systems were detectable."

Pierce smiles reassuringly. "No need to worry about that, my team has figured out an alternative way to get them into the designated target area. What we really need to talk about is what to do after the squad reaches ground zero and detonates Thumper. With the enemy's power grid destroyed, I'm confident it will seriously affect their defenses. I'll have a large combat force on standby ready for when that happens. With McCloud's new Kaon particle weapons, I estimate that it should take less than a week to wrap up any loose ends. When we reach that milestone, our only concern will be what to do with the aliens and their technology?" General Pierce grins then stops to adjust his collar in a mirror. "You know, I have a feeling world peace is just around the corner."

President Wellington marvels at Pierce's confidence and resourcefulness but gives him the evil eye. "I hope for everyone's sake General, your strategy proceeds as planned."

After the meeting, President Wellington decides to boost his reelection chances by addressing the nation and the world regarding the Zone. In front of a podium inside the Oval Office, he stands with Pierce by his side.

"Fellow Americans and people of the world, for over three years now, I've had the world's best minds working nonstop to understand the explosion that occurred in the southeast New Mexico area. They've concluded that an unknown enemy force is the root cause of it and for the drastic weather changes occurring around the world. Under my orders, General Pierce, the *hero* of the Famine War, has contained them inside an area we call…The Zone. Every day that passes, we are one-step closer to understanding who they are and how to bring them to justice. I have a plan to end this standoff and to prevent an all-out war if you support me in the polls and reelect me for one more term. I promise you freedom and justice for our children, our nation and the world!"

Both Wellington and Pierce raise their fists in victory as dozens of cameras flash in front of them. Over the next half hour, the President proceeds to discuss the budget, the state of the economy, recent congressional developments and the return of Mexico's independence.

FINAL BRIEFING
FORT BLISS STAGING GROUNDS

8/3/2036

As the fierce storm inside the Zone suddenly dissipates, it leaves behind pristine weather conditions for the mission ahead. Hopper's team sits nervously around a large sophisticated conference table while General Pierce and General Hamrick quietly whisper to each other near the entrance to the room.

Hamrick shakes his head at Pierce. "I appreciate your concern but my men have already inspected their equipment countless times and I'm sure it's working perfectly. If you want, you can inspect it yourself, it's just outside the door."

Pierce raises his eyebrows then glances at the back of Hopper's head. "Ah…no. That shouldn't be necessary. I just stopped by to ensure everything was running smoothly. I'm heading back to Command now to prepare for the diversion. Good luck General."

Hamrick nods. "Thank you sir, I hope you give the aliens one hell of a show tonight." He salutes Pierce then turns around and limps to the front of the room. Pierce waits until Hamrick begins the briefing before removing a phasing band from his coat pocket and quietly exits the building.

Hamrick looks around the room before speaking to the assembled squad. "I'm honored to stand in front of you. You've all worked hard to prepare for this mission, and with the world's most advanced weapons and technologies custom made for your enemy, I feel confident you *will* succeed but it won't be easy. In the next few hours, General Pierce will conduct a large-scale diversion to provide your initial cover. After that, you'll be on your own.

General Hamrick's face turns grim as he puts on an electronic glove and points to the center of the table. Instantly, a large 3D topographical map of the Zone appears. As he moves his hand around, it's represented within. "We believe the aliens are using the extensive underground system of caves and tunnels in the Carlsbad Caverns National Park area as their base. Your objective will be to infiltrate it and destroy a power source emanating from a cave called the Hall of Giants. We believe it's powering their equipment and a defense grid, which keeps us from phasing a bomb directly there. By crippling its use, there is a chance we can break through the patrols guarding the outer perimeter and finally end this war once and for all.

General Hamrick pauses to glance at his notes then continues. "You won't have much time to reach your destination because the clearing isn't expected to last more than three or four days. If you can't reach the caverns within this time, you probably never will. Visibility and communications will be nonexistent with sustained winds speeds reaching hurricane proportions.

General Hamrick pauses to give Captain Phillips a serious gaze trying to emphasize the point of not too long then turns his attention back to the map. "The Hail Mary 2 Mission—or HM2, for short—will begin here." He points to where Lake Avalon used to be, just outside the City of Carlsbad. "You will need to use submersible sleds to get past the alien patrols here and here. Eagle Eye satellites report that the ruins of the dam shouldn't be an obstacle.

He glances around the table. "I believe the canal trip to Carlsbad will be uneventful. However, if it does prove risky, I suggest leaving the canal somewhere along the west side…around this area here. At that point, your best bet is to travel northwest across the open desert to give you better luck dodging aliens in the rocky foothills of the Guadalupe Mountains. It's highly possible you will run into alien patrols along the way but unfortunately, we haven't a clue as to how many."

General Hamrick straightens his back then smiles at each member briefly. "All fourteen of you will need to rely on your ingenuity, instincts, and each other to survive and locate the power source. Once there, deploy and activate Thumper within one-hundred-meters to insure its destruction. You can escape the explosion by using the quark-phasing band Captain Phillips will be wearing. It can only activate once, so make it count. The portal will remain open for only a minute. This should be long enough for everyone to enter or until the Captain makes it through."

He pauses to look at his watch. "Two hover jets will arrive shortly to take you to your rendezvous point near the old shoreline of Lake Avalon. I suggest you use that time to prepare yourself mentally. Godspeed on your journey ahead!" General Hamrick's expression is sincere as he comes to attention and proudly salutes them.

HAIL MARY 2

8/3/2036

As the last rays of the sun sink behind the horizon, the squad waits outside for the hover jets to arrive in an open courtyard between two buildings. Hopper decides to use the time to encourage and calm the nerves of his soldiers. He approaches Corporal Blake sitting on the ground looking at a picture of a woman holding a baby. He crouches down next to him for a better look. "May I?"

The Corporal nervously hands him the picture then asks a question. "I've heard how you survived the Zone but I always wondered why you did it."

Hopper looks up puzzled. "Did what?"

"Went on the first Hail Mary Mission. You're not a convict, so why did you go?"

Hopper's eyes go out of focus as he feels for the letter in his upper-left shirt pocket then decides to share a side of him he struggles to forget.

"Corporal, your picture reminds me of my deceased wife Eileen." He passes the photo back and takes a deep breath. "She died during the initial explosion of the Zone. After her death, life didn't seem that important to me. For a while, I was put on medical leave and probably wouldn't have come back but one night General Hamrick found me in a bar and offered me a chance to avenge her."

Corporal Blake nods to reassure Hopper. "I'm really sorry to hear about your wife, but I can understand why he wanted you. It's rumored you're one of the best Special Forces trainers we have."

Hopper chuckles. "Don't believe everything you hear, Hamrick selected me because I seem to have the ability to find a way out of a bad situation. To be honest, it's luck more than anything."

The Corporal puts the photo in his front pocket as two large hover jets quietly descend from the sky and land. He stands up then reaches down to help Hopper to his feet. "Well, let's hope I'm as lucky as you are sir." Blake's nervousness diminishes, comforted knowing Hopper will be there to keep him alive.

Hopper tries to smile then strolls between two adjacent buildings to pray as the men start loading their equipment on the jets. He pauses to look at the starry sky and shivers. He can feel the burden of responsibility already mounting inside him. He takes a deep breath and whispers, "Oh Lord, may your spirit guide us safely through this hell on earth we call the Zone. Please give me the strength to protect... to protect—" He suddenly stops as memories of Eileen, Specialist Greenwood, Monty and the many others who passed away under his care.

Hopper shakes his head trying to clear his mind of negative thoughts then turns to go back to the squad when Dell emerges from the night to stand by his side. She breaks the silence. "I know you have a lot on your mind but I might not have another chance to tell you this."

A chill goes down his back as he waits for her to continue.

She takes a deep breath then turns to face him. "After saving your life in the desert, I just wanted you to know...I love you."

Hopper is stunned as he remembers his wife telling him those exact three words just before drowning in the car. *She needs to tell me this now? I've been having a hard enough time keeping myself together without having to deal with this.*

Overwhelmed by her revelation, he grasps for words. He gently puts a hand on her shoulder and tries hard to keep his voice calm but his feelings are in turmoil. "I...what do you expect me to say Dell? Don't you understand? I can't love you..."

Dell steps back hurt. "I thought that if I died during the mission...I just wanted you to know..." Tears form in her eyes as she abruptly leaves.

Hopper watches her disappear into the night as irrational thoughts of Eileen and Dell race through his mind. *If I open my heart right now then see you die, it will be too much for me to bear...I'll die too.*

He looks once more at the stars as his heart yearns for intimacy then heads back to the squad already waiting in the hover jets. Before boarding the lead jet, he orders everyone to activate their PSI bands and insert their NV9s into their eyes.

After flying an hour or so over rough desert terrain, they finally land close to the Zone's outer perimeter next to a channel of water where Lake Avalon used to be. Their bodies appear pale and lifeless in the bright moonlight as they unload their equipment.

Hopper checks the time then signals the squad into the water as thousands of bombs begin to burst across the diversion area dozens of kilometers away. Each member tows a semi buoyant, submersible sled barely a shoulder's width across and only ten centimeters thick. On the front is a large intake with pipes running down both sides ending in nozzles. Behind the intake are two steering handles, a little shelf to lock the operator's arms and elbows in, and a small visor to route water over their heads.

The squad mount the sleds then assemble into groups of two as the water deepens around them. Hopper and Dell take point and are the first to propel through the water towards the remains of the earthen dam. Water turbulence suddenly increases as they pass through a narrow channel created from the breach and emerge safely on the other side.

Within minutes, the shoreline changes from shrubs to barren earth as they skim the main canal downstream.

Forty-five minutes later, Hopper holds up a fist to halt the squad as his NV9 lenses display several misty spheres of light at the water's edge. He whispers to Dell, "I think it's too dangerous to pass so close to them. It looks like they know something's up. Tell the squad to ditch the sleds to their right then assemble thirty meters inland around the three of us."

Dell wipes a wet strand of hair from her face then closes her eyes. In unison, the squad turns toward shore and emerge from the water like turtles on a beach. As they prepare to move farther inland, Dell gives them an unexpected warning.

Everyone freeze! I sense an alien presence fifteen meters to the left of us, which is not registering on our NV9s.

Tense minutes pass before she gives them the all clear. Thirty meters inland, the soldiers reassemble into a circular defense position facing outward around Hopper, Lieutenant Sanders, and Dell.

Hopper takes out his map then equips his night goggles causing the landscape to turn an eerie green. He scans the horizon and is surprised to see the lights from one of the perimeter watchtowers twinkling in the distance. He looks at his map then glances at Dell and others shivering from the water. With the desert unusually cold tonight, he realizes they must get moving before hypothermia sets in.

He points at the map then whispers to Dell and Sanders. "Looks like our best option now is to flank the canal until we reach the outskirts of Carlsbad. You guys agree?" He sees them nod then continues. "Good. Dell, any idea why the NV9s didn't pick up the alien signature?"

Her teeth chatter slightly as she answers. "I'm not sure why, only that its presence felt different and is weaker even though it was right on top of us. Maybe there are different kinds of creatures or maybe they are using a different type of technology we're not aware of."

Lieutenant Sanders groans then whispers, "That would suck, we could be walking straight into a nest of them without even knowing it."

Hopper nods this time. "I agree and we still have a long way to go." He notices Dell's lips turning blue. "Alright, let's move out before we all freeze to death. Lieutenant, I want you to take point."

Sanders gives him a wink. "Aye, Captain." He taps the boot of Sergeant Blix, then whispers. "We're going to flank the canal then travel inland, everyone follow me." He stands up and moves out with the squad following close behind.

Near daybreak, they reach what should have been the outskirts of Carlsbad but find no trace of it. Hopper scans the barren blasted desert with binoculars but there is nothing to see in the hazy morning light. He shakes his head then orders the squad to rest in a shallow gully.

8/4/2036

Around mid-morning, Hopper sends out Sergeant Claxton and Specialist Myers to scout the area. They return an hour later to report seeing several alien distortion fields where the Cavern City Airport should be. Hopper listens carefully then draws a circle on his map and inserts a question mark. With the squad rested, Hopper leads the men northwest towards the direction of the power source as General Hamrick suggested. After a strenuous two-hour march, traveling approximately ten kilometers, they arrive on the edge of a broad ravine.

Out of breath, Lieutenant Sanders approaches Hopper to give him a report. "Hey Cap... I've been talking to Dell, she says it may be nothing, but something doesn't feel right to her. Maybe we should do some recon of the area before continuing further."

"Good idea. Pick Corporal Blake and tell him to be extra careful."

The Lieutenant nods then leaves as Dell arrives and sits next to him. He notices her anxiety and decides to keep quiet. It only increases as Blake disappears over the ridge.

A moment later Dell's body stiffens as the squad hears her voice in their mind. *Blake's in trouble!*

Hopper immediately stands and signals the squad to move out but stops as a brief round of gunfire erupts down below followed by an intense explosion that ripples through the air. Everyone quickly crouches and prepares for battle but there is no sign of an attack. He notices Dell shaking her head violently as if trying to rid herself of the horror she just witnessed. Hopper kneels and holds her tightly trying to understand the pain she must be going through. He gives her a moment then forces her to look into his eyes. In a soft and commanding voice, he tries to get her attention. "Hang in there Dell! I think you'll be OK, just try to clear your mind right now and focus on what I'm about to say." Her eyes slowly focus and relaxes. "Now...I need you to explain to me what happened down there before I send anyone else?"

Dell forces her words out. "He's dead. I think he encountered some sort of energy trap."

Dread overcomes Hopper but his voice remains calm. "Is the squad in imminent danger right now? Do you sense any aliens in the general vicinity?"

She closes her eyes for a moment then hesitantly shakes her head.

Hopper breathes a sigh of relief then signals Sergeant Holloway, Sergeant Mills, and Lieutenant Sanders to come closer. They hastily arrive and huddle. "OK guys, here's the plan. Holloway, take Beta team along with Sanders and Dell and set setup a defense perimeter here as quickly as possible. He turns to Sergeant Mills. "I'll be joining you on Alpha team and enter the ravine to investigate. The area may still be booby-trapped so tell everyone to keep on the lookout for anything unusual. We'll take only our weapons and extra ammo." He looks at the Lieutenant. "Now, if anything goes wrong, you'll be in charge of continuing this mission." He waits for each of them to nod. "Alright then, let's move out!"

With weapons off safety, Hopper and the five remaining members of Alpha team slowly shuffle down the ravine ready for all-out combat. On the opposite side of the ravine, they find Blake's body lying face down near a large circular depression. As Alpha team carefully searches the area for distortion fields and detonation devices, Hopper rolls the body over to find Blake's skin burnt beyond all recognition but his clothes remain untouched. The picture of Blake's wife and kid sticks out of his shirt pocket. He reaches for the photo and stops as their previous conversation plays in his mind. Guilt and suffering quickly overwhelms his senses, suddenly he is unable to move. He is shocked back to reality when Dell issues a warning in his mind.

Big troubles heading our way. Multiple aliens converging on our location. ETA in about five minutes.

Hopper struggles to bury his feelings as he rolls the body and photo into the pit then shouts to everyone. "Code red! Everyone return to the top of the ravine and prepare for combat!" He glances at the body again and wonders if Corporal Blake's fate awaits them all.

Spurred by the danger of the situation, Alpha team quickly ascends to the top of the ravine. Sergeant Holloway approaches Hopper and Sergeant Mills as they try to catch their breath. Holloway points to his team. "Sir, the ground was too hard to dig defense positions so I've spread them out amongst the rocks. Do you have any idea what we can expect?"

Hopper shrugs. "Not yet. We'll have to see how things develop." He pulls out his binoculars and scans the rock formations on the other side of the ravine then glances at the two men. "Tell your squads to hold their fire and wait for further orders."

They nod and scramble off to spread the word.

Hopper spots Dell with her eyes shut lying next to Lieutenant Sanders near a pile of rocks on his left. He joins them and whispers in Dell's ear to avoid startling her. "Can you tell me what you see?"

Her expression turns to horror as she reports. "They're coming in fast—two from the east, two from the west, one each from the north and south. The one behind us though is much slower and is farther out. Maybe they want us to believe it's an escape route. I really don't know, but I can sense they are systematically sweeping the area."

Hopper quickly glances at the Lieutenant then back to Dell. "Do they know we're here?"

She shakes her head with confidence.

He squeezes her shoulder. "You are by far the most valuable member of this team."

Lieutenant Sanders' apprehension is clearly audible in his voice as he peers through his binoculars at the surrounding terrain. "Damn NV9s, why can't they make them work with optics?" He lowers the field glasses then looks at Hopper. "Don't you think we should be heading for the hills right about now?"

Hopper shakes his head. "I've thought about it. We don't have enough time to escape their trap. As soon as they find the body down there, they won't stop scouring the area until they find the rest of us. I think this is the best location to do something about it."

Dell struggles to speak while retaining a link to the alien positions. "I disagree, they don't know we're here…or how many there are of us."

Hopper looks at Lieutenant Sanders then takes a deep breath. "Well, if that's the case, then my decision still stands. If they can't locate us, they'll assume we're not here and move on. Dell, inform the squad we're staying put for the time being." She frowns as she sends the message.

Anxious minutes pass as the squad's NV9 finally allows them to see four misty distortion fields appear and converge on the crater inside the ravine. The hair on their bodies stand on end as charged air drifts across their position. The squad's tension increases even more as another misty distortion appears across the way.

Dell tugs on Hopper's sleeve and whispers in his ear, "I think they've discovered the body and are communicating with something or someone farther away. For all I know, they could be calling in reinforcements. Staying here any longer may prove too dangerous."

Lieutenant Sanders curses under his breath.

Hopper rubs his temple to suppress a growing headache then removes his binoculars from its case and re-inspects the area.

Lieutenant Sanders gives him an inquiring look. "Do you have an idea?"

Irritation grows inside Hopper as he struggles to formulate a plan. "Can you just give me a minute?"

Lieutenant Sanders bites his lip to keep quiet. Moments later Hopper looks at him then points across the ravine. "Check out those rocks to the right."

Puzzled, Lieutenant Sanders picks up his binoculars and zooms in on the area. "Yes, I see them. What am I looking for?"

"If we can dislodge that big rock under the outcrop, I think we can create a landslide and bury those aliens down below and the one across the way at the same time."

Lieutenant Sanders smiles, "Yeah! Nice plan. Ah…but what about the one behind us?"

With no answer to give, Hopper's frustration only grows. "Give me a break Lieutenant. We need to take this one-step at a time." He turns to Dell, "Have the men set their Wasps to shoot semi-automatic, and then fire on my command at the base of the outcrop on my right, focusing specifically under the big rock to dislodge it. We're going to bury our enemy alive."

Dell nods in approval then sends the message.

Hopper waits for the squad to reposition themselves and take aim. Satisfied, he opens a small tube hanging around his neck and takes out one D-wave emitter. He rotates its outer ring for a thirty-second delay then presses it between his fingers. Hopper's irritation fades as he notices the Lieutenant's anxious expression. "Sorry for being abrupt, if this works we'll flank the alien as it comes in to investigate. I hope we will be long gone by then. Now, let's kick some alien butt."

Hopper quietly stands then throws the emitter to the far side of the ravine near the base of the outcrop. As the four distortion fields converge on the device he raises and lowers his arm. "Now!"

The ravine instantly dissolves under a wave of earsplitting explosions. The alien signature across the way disappears as a mountain of moving rock sweeps it away. Seconds later five huge shockwaves erupt from below sending the squad sprawling to the ground.

As the dust settles, some of the men quietly rejoice but Hopper remains quiet as he anxiously waits for Dell to report. She moves her head from side to side then takes a deep breathe.

"I don't feel their presence anymore. From what I can tell, the distortion fields are coming from crafts or vessels that protect the aliens inside." She looks over her shoulder and immediately becomes apprehensive again. "Looks like we don't have much time to ponder. The alien behind us is closing in fast. I'll take point and lead us around it."

All three stand up as Hopper shouts to the squad. "Everyone on your feet. We're moving out, hostile arriving from the south. Dell's taking point."

The squad quickly assembles behind Dell as she guides them away from the ravine. Hopper scans the horizon one last time then follows Sergeant Holloway bringing up the rear.

Minutes later, Dell sends them a warning. *Enemy is now to the southeast. No visible distortion field and it's fighting mad!*

Without warning, near the center of the line of marching men, Corporal Beckett and Specialist Meyers vaporize in an ear-shattering flash of light. The force of it causes the rest of the squad to hurl through the air and tumble to the ground. Everyone struggles to prepare for battle as other explosions continue to pound the ground around them. The sky quickly darkens as small rocks and dirt rain down on them.

During a brief pause, Lieutenant Sanders staggers to his feet and signals the squad to take cover in the newly created craters. Hopper uses the opportunity to run to the front of the line and jump inside a crater with Dell. He is relieved to see she is unharmed but disoriented. He has to yell for her to hear him. "Are you OK?"

Dell's eyes focus on him then visibly relaxes. "Yes, I'm OK now!"

"Thank God! For some reason the alien knows we're here! It's possible someone's PSI band malfunctioned! We can't see its distortion field so tell the men to use their Wasps and if possible, direct their fire!"

She closes her eyes and concentrates, determined to protect the man she loves and the squad who depend on her. Immediately, her body relaxes as if resting on a sunny beach.

Her courage and determination moves Hopper. In that moment, he realizes he should have told her how he felt earlier. His attention however, switches to the east horizon as the squad immediately shifts positions and take aim at a knoll in the distance.

The air fills with the sound of hundreds of rounds discharging but they fall harmlessly to the ground in front of it. Seconds later, a fresh round of explosions pound the squad.

Hopper realizes the alien position is out of reach for the Wasps. He yells to the men, "It's too far away! Everyone, use your Hornets… *Now!*"

He brings up his own and fires it randomly across the knoll, sending rock and dust skyward. The squad quickly follows suit.

Dell opens her eyes, as if in a trance and for the first time in the mission, removes her Hornet from her shoulder and carefully takes aim downrange. Knots form in her stomach as she removes the safety and steadies her finger on the trigger. As if seeing a bull's-eye on the knoll, she fires a single round. In the distance, an arc of light flares skyward.

She shudders as she loses contact with the dying creature inside and struggles with a surge of emotions afterward. Unable to speak or relay a message with her mind, she stands up and notifies the squad of the alien's demise with a cutting motion to her neck. As the sky clears and all becomes quiet, she finds everyone looking at her in amazement. She can feel their gratitude for saving them as it radiates from their hearts and minds.

Hopper takes out his binoculars and focuses on a light shining on the knoll. After weighing the risks, he decides to investigate it in hopes of learning more about his enemy.

Ten minutes later, the squad arrives to see a light emitting from an area about three meters off the ground.

They form a large circle around it as Hopper carefully puts his hands out and advances until he touches a warm, smooth surface. His fingers distinguish the outline of large octagon plating separated by small gaps. He then uses the gaps to climb the invisible vehicle and appears to float in the air.

He finally reaches the shaft of light and carefully moves his hand across it but feels nothing then slowly moves his face into its path. Down below he sees a mangled, blood splattered body lying across a sophisticated control panel. A beeping sound from within catches his attention as it becomes faster and louder with each passing second.

Realizing the danger, he shouts to the squad. "Everyone take cover! I think this thing is about to explode!" Electrical sparks form around the base of the light as the vehicle starts to shake violently.

Wasting no time, Hopper jumps from the vehicle and dives behind rocks just before a powerful implosion rocks the area causing his body to feel like it just got sunburnt. He slowly stands then does a quick head count and is relieved to find no one hurt or injured. The squad reassembles and quickly searches the knoll but can find no trace of a vehicle or debris.

Lieutenant Sanders scratches his head as he approaches Hopper. "Sir, whatever was out here is gone. I think we should get as far from this place while we still can."

Hopper nods. "I agree I'll take point this time." He motions everyone to fall in behind him and moves out.

With the knoll far behind, Hopper lets the squad rest in a gully on the bleak open desert. Most sit in silence as they eat their rations. Between bites of food, Private Parker is the first to speak.

"What a shitty day. It started with Blake's death, now Beckett and Meyers." Several men look up but continue eating. Parker lifts his head up to peek over the rim of the gully to view the horizon, his voice borders on panic. "What are we doing out here in the middle of nowhere?" He turns around and begins to unbutton his shirt collar as his breathing intensifies. "Don't you guys get it? We could be next! This is bad!"

Sergeant Blix stands up and grabs Parker by the shoulders. "Look at me Private." His voice grows loud then shakes him. "I said, look at me! We're all in the same boat right now and we knew the risks from the beginning. I have one word of advice for you Private Parker—just one: Trust!"

He points toward Hopper and Dell sitting at the other end of the gully. "Do you *trust* the Captain, Private?" He brings his face close to his ear, his voice softer this time. "Do you trust him? You have to believe Private Parker. You've done it before."

Parker takes a deep breathe then slowly nods. His voice becomes steady and confident this time. "Yes, I do trust the Captain."

Sergeant Blix releases the young man. Everyone is looking at them as Blix reaches down and hands Parker his food then raises his arms to the sky. "It's a good day to be alive don't you think?" He begins to laugh heartily, soon other men begin to talk and laugh amongst themselves.

Hopper and Dell smile at each other as their spirits also rise. Dell finishes eating and checks her equipment while Hopper unbuckles a nylon pouch on his utility belt and removes the homing device. He pushes a small red button in the center of the circular display, immediately a metal arm, tipped with amber-colored spheres eject from the top and slowly spins. Hopper stands and rotates his body as the device seeks the alien power source. Finally, a green arrow appears and points the way.

He looks up to find himself facing a range of low-lying hills about eight kilometers in the distance. After a quick check of the time, he turns the device off and puts it away. He looks at the squad wishing he could give them more time but realizes their location is not defendable.

He speaks in a loud clear voice. "Men, I hate to ruin the party but we have a little over an hour before nightfall. The homing device indicates the alien power source is emanating from that direction." He points out across the desolate wasteland to the low-lying hills. "This place is too open, I want us to reach the safety of the hills before the sun goes down. Prepare to move out!"

The squad wearily packs up their belongings and file out of the gully one by one as Lieutenant Sanders inspects their equipment and condition. About one kilometer into the march, Dell stumbles and falls. Hopper kneels by her side as the squad takes defensive positions around them. Her face contorts as she grabs the front of his shirt. "We've got to leave this area! Dozens of aliens are quickly converging on our location! We don't have much time. Hopper, save us!"

Hopper's headache returns with a vengeance as ten trusting faces look toward their leader. His eyes go out of focus as he returns their gaze.

We are horribly outnumbered and have no adequate cover. Don't you guys realize I'm not a miracle worker?

His mind races as he takes out his binoculars and quickly scans the area then zooms in on the shallow gully they just left. He clears his throat before speaking. "OK guys, I'm not going to bullshit you. Things don't look good. The only cover out here is the place we just left. I suggest we prepare our defense there and fire when they get within range."

He scans their sweaty, dirty faces before speaking again. "But remember this—don't give up, no matter what. It's times like this when your faith is tested. Now…move out!" They grimly rush back to the gully and prepare for battle.

Hopper swiftly walks down the line of men redistributing ammo and providing encouragement. He pats Parker on the shoulder and hands him two ammo magazines. "Remember, trust and teamwork are the keys to getting through this. I believe in you Private Parker."

Parker gives him a solemn salute. "I believe in you too, sir."

"Good. I'm proud to have you by my side." He returns the salute then moves down to the next soldier and has a similar conversation. He finally approaches Lieutenant Sanders at the far end of the gully preparing his Wasp and laying out ammo. "Are we ready?"

"Ready as we're going to be. This isn't the best place to pitch a battle but your confidence in us makes me feel like the enemy doesn't have a chance." He grins but his expression turns serious. He extends his hand. "It's been an honor serving under your command sir."

Hopper takes it and holds it tight. They look at each other knowing they may never see each other again. "Take care Lieutenant. Fight well."

Hopper turns and rushes back to Dell at the other end of the gully. Her face is expressionless; her eyes distant and unfocused as she tries to load a magazine into her rifle but fails. Hopper crouches down and loads it for her then tenderly moves a strand of hair from her face. "Hang in there Dell. I'll try to protect you as best I can."

She nods without looking up.

While the men nervously watch the horizon, their NV9s gradually display about a dozen misty distortion fields approaching from two different directions. Upon reaching firing range, the squad unleashes a barrage of antimatter weapon fire. Several enemy fields disappear causing powerful shockwaves to pulse across the desert terrain.

Before they can re-target, plasma spheres explode around them like flashing strobe lights. The situation becomes even more critical as a half dozen more fields appear and fire in their general direction as well.

Hopper's rifle quits firing and discovers it is out of ammo. He grabs his backpack causing Thumper to fall out and roll on the ground in front of him. He picks it up then makes eye contact with Dell just as a plasma blast illuminates her face.

Without saying a word, she understands what he is about to do then nods.

Hopper prays as he prepares to detonate it. *If you're listening Lord, now would be a good time for a miracle.*

Dell hugs him tightly as he is about to press the final sequence of buttons but stops as an unnatural calm sweeps across the area.

When the dust finally settles, he looks skyward to see it lit up with scores of intense laser beams shooting across the sky from all different directions followed by dozens of exploding red-and-orange flashes that twinkle in the intense glow of sunset. Soon, thousands of disks attached to long metal streamers rain down and scatter over the landscape. Hopper secures Thumper in his pack realizing he has received an answer to his prayer.

He gives Dell a big hug. "Oh yeah! I guess we're not so expendable this time!"

Dell looks anxiously at him waiting for an answer. "I don't understand, what's happening?"

He hugs her again and smiles as a flashing streamer drifts right across their position. "We're going to be OK now. Command sent missiles loaded with thousands of D-wave emitters to confuse the aliens and it's working!" He shouts to the squad still looking up in awe. "Men, we don't have much time— we're heading for the foothills now!"

Lieutenant Sanders stumbles as he approaches then salutes. He is dazed but unhurt. "Sir, Corporal Fernandez and Sergeant Mills didn't make it. I put Sergeant Blix in charge of Alpha team. As for the rest of the men, they look like they can still walk, talk, and shoot." He looks out over the pitted landscape then back at Hopper. "I really thought we were goners. Who would have thought Command would come to our rescue?" The Lieutenant staggers off as the men fall in behind him.

Hopper nods as he watches him go. *I couldn't agree with you more.*

GENERAL WAVE

8/4/2036

General Pierce and Colonel Barland stand in front of the central fountain in the underground garden district of Fort Bliss. While the two men talk, High Guards block the entrances to keep onlookers away. Pierce's hand trembles slightly as he lights a cigar and takes a puff. He stares at the water, frustrated by having to watch the Hail Mary 2 Mission through remote satellite feeds and photos.

He wishes he could take a more active role, especially after witnessing several explosions earlier in the day at the squad's location. With a radio silence in effect, questions drive him crazy. Why are there three men missing now? What is Captain Phillips' next move? Do they still have the means to destroy the power source? The General angrily flicks his cigar into the fountain.

Barland raises his eyebrows. "Something bothering you, sir?"

Pierce turns and confronts Barland head on. "Why? Is my attitude showing again?"

Barland glances at him but remains quiet.

"I've known you for over fifteen years, and you are one of the few people I completely trust. So let me tell you a secret. It's days like these when I'm not in control that I'm reminded of being bullied as a kid. Hard to believe, huh? You see, our family was rich. Some older kids at school found out and wanted me to pay them money to leave me alone. Sometimes I paid other times I didn't. Then one day while getting my ass kicked, I realized three important things that changed my life.

"Wealth is power…fear is control…and using force can bring peace. The next day I used my money and hired the meanest thug I could find and had those guys beaten to within an inch of their lives. Do you know what? They never bothered me again. Fighting violence with violence brought peace and harmony to my life. So the point is my friend, that when I'm in charge…I feel great." Pierce laughs then continues in a subdued voice. "Which reminds me, how are our plans progressing towards Peace?"

"Perfectly sir. The High Guard Army is nearing a thousand strong and growing. I've dispersed this month's new recruits and are already waiting in standby mode. The Peace Around the World Society (PAWS) has even identified safe zones within the designated *detonation* areas. The only thing holding us up now is the time it takes to manufacture more phasing bands.

"Also, McCloud told me he analyzed the BRAVE device you gave him and said he is now trying to acquire the patents but some upstart law firm is trying to do the same. Knowing McCloud though, he'll do whatever it takes to get them. He said the devices have an incredible ability to manipulate thoughts, behaviors, and if necessary, erase memories in case we're caught."

Pierce lets out a grunting laugh. "Well done Colonel. You and McCloud will be greatly rewarded in the years ahead." Pierce smiles, "You know this talk is just what I needed. I feel better already. Now let's get back to Command before they miss us."

Both Pierce and Barland laugh knowing they are both despised and feared.

As they reenter the Command Center, officers surround a display terminal showing a live feed from Eagle Eye 7. Pierce pushes them aside to see the squad bombarded by a barrage of intense energy explosions. He swears under his breath. "What the hell are you guys standing around for? Get to your stations!" As they scurry off, he quickly sits in the command chair and dons a headset. "McCloud, you there?"

"Right here sir."

"Activate the orbital missile batteries now! Program the D-wave missiles to detonate over the squad's location as soon as possible!"

"I'm already on it sir, I've reprogrammed the missiles to shut down as soon as they attain the correct speed and trajectory. If the simulations are correct, they should safely reach the target area. At that point, ground-based lasers should be able to detonate them. Looks like the missile batteries are now fully active. Firing in three…two…one."

Pierce watches two dozen missiles fire in quick succession through a nearby Eagle Eye satellite feed. Almost instantly, a plasma beam originating from the Zone blazes skyward and engulfs the launch satellite in a ball of energy causing it to explode. He switches to another display showing trajectory readings on about a dozen missiles still heading toward earth. Tense minutes go by as they enter the upper atmosphere. Suddenly, the sky lights up for hundreds of miles as scores of ground-based lasers chase supersonic projectiles. One by one, brilliant red-and-orange blooms of light blossom and shimmer in the evening sky as thousands of D-wave emitters spread out across the Zone. Everyone in the Command Center scrutinize grainy satellite images searching for survivors. They finally see nine soldiers slowly marching on a northwest trajectory through a heavily cratered landscape.

General Pierce sits back in his chair and relaxes for the first time in days. *And you call yourselves soldiers? Ha! You're a bunch of troublemakers. That's what you are. If it wasn't for me, you would all be dead right now. Captain Phillips, you owe me big-time.*

He grins as he imagines crowds of people honoring him for saving the mission.

STORM

8/4/2036

With D-wave emitters scattered throughout the region, the squad safely passes through enemy forces toward the foothills in the distance. It is near 2100 hours when they finally set up camp at the base of a hill strewn with boulders.

Sergeant Blix establishes a one-hour guard duty rotation as the rest settle down for the night. Hopper watches the eight of them scattered among the rocks with pride. *You have all performed admirably, even in the heat of battle. You have bonded well and trust is no longer an issue.*

Hopper approaches Dell and sits near her as she unrolls a thermal blanket. "It's been a rough few days for everyone. Hope you can get some sleep. We should reach the power source tomorrow. It's less than twelve kilometers away."

She looks up, her face covered in dust and sweat. "No worries there. I could sleep for a week." She gives him a tired smile. "You should try to rest as well. We need you to be alert to handle anything the aliens throw our way and bring us home safely."

Hopper nods as he unpacks his thermal blanket and wraps it around his body. "You're right. I'll try to get some sleep too. Sweet dreams."

Comforted by Hopper's presence, Dell smiles again then turns over and closes her eyes. "Good night."

He watches her for a while then dozes off himself. The night passes uneventfully. At daybreak, the sky brightens as the sun crests the horizon.

8/5/2036

A couple of hours later, Hopper wakes sensing danger as a cold breeze blows through camp. In the clear-blue sky above, raging clouds appear and form into a growing ring of turbulence. Before he can even get to his feet, dust devils begin to dot the landscape. "Everyone wake up!"

The squad barely has time to respond as a red, dusty haze engulfs the camp.

Moments later Lieutenant Sanders approaches and yells over the growing sound of the wind. "I hope you don't mind. I just sent Corporal Bennet to search for a cave he found on guard duty."

Hopper acknowledges his approval with a pat on the back. "Good idea. Seems like conditions are getting worse by the second. Group the men together until he gets back!"

The men find themselves battling fierce winds as the Corporal emerges from the dust holding onto a cord that whips in the wind, clearly tied to something obscured in the distance. Weary and out of breath, he approaches Hopper and Sanders. "Sir, I've located…the cave!" He points in the direction from which he came. "It's near some rocks about twenty meters from here!"

Hopper breathes a sigh of relief then yells. "Do you need a few minutes to rest?"

The Corporal shakes his head. "We should go before the wind gets worse!"

Hopper nods then signals the men to follow Corporal Bennet. Using the cord as a guide, he leads them to the hillside and disappears between two boulders. One by one, the men follow him inside. Hopper is the last to enter and crawls through a hole no wider than his shoulders. He emerges into a large rocky cave with white stalactites illuminated by the squad's flashlights. Dell helps him get to his feet as Lieutenant Sander approaches. "Sir, the cave only extends about thirty meters or so then dead-ends."

"Thanks Lieutenant, have the men setup camp here. Dell, come with me." Dell and Hopper walk the length of the cave then return to the entrance where Sergeant Blix is sitting. His squad radio is out of its case with the battery compartment open. The look on his face confirms the worst. "Report Sergeant."

He looks up at Hopper. "Sir, we have a possible situation here. The squad's backup radios have been off line since this storm started."

Hopper looks at his phasing band to verify his words then pulls out the homing device to see it blinking red indicating it is unable to lock onto the alien power source. His face turns grim as he rubs his temple subconsciously. He looks at Dell then turns his flashlight on himself.

"Listen up men. Gather 'round." He waits for everyone then continues. "This is for those who haven't figured it out yet. It appears the clearing has ended earlier than expected." Most express groans or curse.

Private Parker peeks outside the cave. "Sir, does that mean we are going to die? What about the mission?"

Hopper keeps his voice neutral as he looks at their faces. "I agree—it looks bleak. However, that doesn't mean we just give up. If we're going to die, it's going to be for *something*. In the meantime Parker, I suggest you take inventory of our supplies and start rationing the food. Looks like we are going to have to wait here until the storm clears or for some other opportunity to present itself. Sergeant Holloway, pick one man to secure the entrance. As for the rest of you,

I want you to put your heads together to come up with some alternative plans to continue our mission. Dell, Lieutenant Sanders—come with me."

Hopper's expression of confidence turns to worry as he walks to the back of the cave and sits against the wall. He looks at Dell and Sanders as they settle down. "Dell, what's the mental state of the men?"

Dell closes her eyes to find out. "They're fine under the circumstances. They knew what they were getting into when they volunteered." She feels Hopper's despair. "I'm more concerned for you at the moment."

Surprised by her comment, he decides to share his feelings. He puts his head down and whispers. "I am deeply disheartened that five good men, who put their complete trust in me, have already died. On top of that, our own survival is now in doubt. With the storm's arrival, even General Hamrick didn't think we could survive. All of our radios are out of commission as well as the homing device. It's possible we could briefly survive the elements but we don't have the means to locate the power source. I suppose we could stretch out our food supply but it could be a week or even months before the next clearing period arrives."

Hopper stops talking leaving Dell and Sanders in shock. The Lieutenant's mouth moves but no sound comes out. A shiver runs down Dell's back as she realizes this place could very well be their grave. She takes Hopper's hand and tries to comfort him telepathically.

Don't worry. We're all in this together.

Unaware of Dell's secret message, the Lieutenant lays his hands on top of theirs. "You said teamwork could achieve the impossible, right?"

Hopper looks up embarrassed but grateful for their support. "You're right! Thank you both, I needed to hear that. Let's get back to the men to see what kind of ideas they came up with." He stands and helps Dell and Sanders to their feet. They all return to the front of the cave to find them in a heated discussion. Private Parker asks Hopper a question as soon as he arrives. "Sir, why don't we use your phasing band to get us out of here?"

Hopper looks at the men's faces and decides to give them straight answers. "Good question Parker. The device is wired to run on the alien power source which we cannot use or locate right now."

Sergeant Holloway raises his voice. "Then let's use Thumper and get it over with. At least we can go out in a blaze of glory."

Hopper tries to laugh but realizes how close he came to doing that earlier. "I don't know about you, but I'm not ready to give up and meet my maker just yet."

After discussing and rejecting even the most absurd possibilities, the meeting ends in silence. With winds gusting well over one hundred twenty kilometers per hour just outside the cave, hopelessness lies heavy in everyone's hearts as they contemplate their dismal predicament.

Over the next four days, the squad continues to discuss ways to reach the power source but all ideas seem futile. As time goes on, the odds of surviving fade even further as they consume the last of their food rations. Out of necessity, they start supplementing their diet with worms, insects, snakes and bats.

Hopper's Despair
8/11/2036

The confines of the cave have become too much for Hopper to bear. He stands alone at the entrance of their tomb welcoming the fierce beating by the weather. The deafening roar of the wind enforces the harsh reality of his dire situation and pushes him nearer to the edge of insanity.

Rain hides tears running down his face as lightning exposes the desolate no-man's-land in front of him. He puts his hand over Eileen's letter in his pocket and takes a step forward into chaos.

Eileen, it's been a long time since I last saw you standing so pure in your white summer dress. I need your love now more than ever. I don't know what else to do. It seems like everyone I get close to ends up dying. I don't have the strength to watch them perish one by one, especially Dell. I hope you can forgive me for having feelings for her. I've tried hard to keep my distance, but the stress inside of me is overflowing. Eileen, we've been apart too long. Maybe now is the time we should be together...Yes, I think it's time. Hope you're out there waiting for me.

His eyes scan the dark horizon then he takes another step forward and then another.

Out of the swirling dust and stinging rain, a hand reaches out and grabs his shirt preventing him from going any farther. He turns to see Dell's frail body standing behind him. Her hair and clothes are dripping wet as if she's been standing there awhile. Her deep-blue eyes are wide and desperate but her voice is soft and clear in his mind.

Please don't lose hope, my love. As long as there's a single breath left in my body, you don't have to carry all your burdens alone. Come back from the edge. Gain strength through me and live again.

Without waiting for a response, she holds her medallion tightly to her chest then falls to one knee as her spirit energy flows from her body and into his.

In Hopper's mind, the raging storm fades away until he finds himself standing in a field of wild flowers and windblown grass with blue sky and a bright sun shining all around. Dell is still on her knee holding onto his shirt as her energy continues to flow out of her. He is exhilarated to witness such a perfect day as he takes a deep breath and smiles.

For the first time in almost a week, he can see things clearly and realizes the squad needs him now more than ever. He looks down at Dell who is smiling back, but her deep-blue eyes brim with tears. Her mouth moves in sync with the voice in his mind.

It's beautiful isn't it? My dream is to be with you on a day like this. Remember this precious moment when you're down. Someday when we're older, this could become a reality. I love you more than you'll ever know so please come back inside. I need you. We all need you. Even if things seem hopeless right now, have faith we will survive.

Dell loses her grasp on his shirt as her head sinks down to her chest. A strong gust blows through the field as dark clouds form on the horizon. Seconds later, a fierce gale obscures his vision causing the blue sky to fade from sight.

Suddenly, Hopper finds himself back in the Zone pounded by a wall of rain, wind, and dirt. He sees Dell lying face down in the mud but conscious. He gently picks her up as she guides them back to the cave entrance. The men are arguing with each other but cease when Dell crawls in and collapses on the floor.

Hopper quickly enters after her then motions Lt. Sanders to give him a hand. Together they carry her to the rear of the cave and lay her down. Hopper quickly covers her with his thermal blanket then whispers in her ear. "Thank you for opening my eyes, I now have faith we will succeed. Please don't worry about me anymore and save your strength." Dell wearily nods then closes her eyes to rest.

Later that evening Private Parker approaches then salutes Hopper, Dell, and Sanders. "The squad wanted to show all of you our gratitude for keeping us alive this long. We pitched in to give you this." He nervously holds out a used food wrapper with pieces of crackers, worms and bugs inside.

Dell looks at Hopper and Sanders, then gratefully reaches out and accepts it. "Thank you Parker. I speak for all of us. Tell everyone we are proud to be on the same team and we'll try to come up with something soon."

She looks into his eyes and smiles as she sends him a secret message of hope. Parker's expression of concern changes to a grin as he turns and leaves.

8/12/2036

After collecting radios from other squad members, a scruffy Sergeant Blix attempts to use their parts to amplify the homing device's receiver. He finishes re-assembling it then turns it on but nothing happens. In frustration, he hits it with his fist causing it to beep. Surprised, he quickly scans the data on the circular display then rushes to the back of the cave.

His voice trembles with hope as he hands it to Hopper. "Sir, I've modified the homing device and it now appears to be picking up a weak alien power source near our vicinity. It's moving slowly so it could be a damaged vehicle or somehow affected by the storm."

Hopper scans the device to verify the power source location, speed and direction then rubs his temple to think. A grin forms on his face as he turns to Dell. "Can you detect any alien activity in the area?"

Dell closes her eyes then slowly nods. "Maybe, I feel some sort of presence but I'm not sure what it is."

Hopper quickly formulates a desperate plan as he taps on the device. "Do you think you have the strength to guide us through the storm to *this* presence?"

Dell feels his excitement growing then realizes the possibilities. "Yes, I believe I do!"

Lieutenant Sanders looks at them confused. "Care to let me in on the plan?"

Hopper nods as he holds up his index finger then yells at the squad. "Men, quickly don your equipment, and prepare for combat. I'll explain while everyone's getting ready. Sergeant Blix just informed me the homing device located a nearby alien power source. It's currently slowly moving west but will soon be out of range if we don't hurry. Dell assured me she's able to guide us to its vicinity. The plan is to follow this object; I hope that it's heading towards their main complex located inside the Carlsbad Caverns—if not, then maybe to the outer perimeter. In any case, this is our only chance to survive. Assemble outside as soon as you're ready. What are you waiting for, an invitation? I said move it!"

Enthusiasm builds as the men quickly file outside. Lieutenant Sanders unrolls a long cord for them to hold to keep them from separating in the harsh environment. As soon as everyone has a grip on it, Dell guides them on a nightmarish journey through violent hurricane winds, sheets of rain, stinging hail, and thunderous lightning.

Forty-five minutes later, she stops and points at a moving outline of a strange-looking vehicle exposed by the spray of mud, rain, and hail driven by the fierce wind. Dell opens her mind to Hopper and points.

Do you see it? Good! The PSI bands are working perfectly. The alien inside hasn't sensed us yet.

As the vehicle begins to move out of sight, Hopper makes a snap decision and motions his intentions to Dell who relays it to the squad.

Approach the vehicle with caution and carefully mount it as the Captain did earlier. Follow my example.

Dell catches up to the vehicle and feels for the gaps in the plating then carefully crawls on top. One by one, the men approach and do the same. As if riding some magic carpet, they appear to float through the raging storm at about four kilometers an hour.

With difficulty, Hopper takes out the homing device and slowly moves it back and forth. A few minutes pass before it locks on to a strong signal. He smiles with renewed hope as he realizes the vehicle is traveling towards their main objective.

CARLSBAD CAVERNS

8/12/2036

Hours later, the squad emerges from the raging storm and enter the mouth of a dark limestone cavern. As the rain and lightning flashes recede in the distance, an amber light surrounds them causing the vehicle to become visible. They discover themselves sitting on top of a beautifully crafted machine, cross between a recreational vehicle with smooth rounded corners and a racing yacht.

Several alarms begin to blare as a spotlight focuses on them from above. The squad scrambles off and takes defensive positions behind large, broken pieces of stalagmites and stalactites littering the cave floor. Working together, they slowly advance to a large open area with many connecting passageways. The Lieutenant and the three remaining members of Beta team suddenly find themselves pinned down out on the rocky floor as a barrage of blasts force Alpha team into a side passageway.

Dell sends Hopper an urgent message. *We should try another route! There are too many enemies that way!*

Hopper fires his Wasp several times before shouting back, "We don't have much of a choice! Tell Alpha team to provide suppression fire for Beta!"

She obeys but is extremely frustrated that Hopper isn't listening to her. The gunfire pinning Beta down lets up immediately. Dell's fingernails bite into Hopper's arm as he prepares to move out. She pleads with him one more time. *Please let me tell Beta team to fall back to our position!*

Dell's expression changes to horror as an energy blast disintegrates the ceiling above Beta squad causing large boulders to rain down on them. Their last agonizing thoughts flood Dell's mind. She starts to walk towards them as tears form in her eyes.

Hopper grabs her hand then leads the remaining members of his squad down the side passageway. They emerge into a brightly lit cavern full of bulky mechanical contraptions and take cover behind them. Hopper has difficulty containing his emotions as Dell, Private Parker, Sergeant Blix, and Corporal Bennet wait for orders. His expression changes to anguish as he searches for words, finally he addresses them in a grave voice.

"I know we just lost a lot of good men back there but we need to accomplish this mission at *all* cost. Blix, Bennet—cover the rear. Dell, Parker—shoot anything that moves. I need to get a bearing on the power source."

Somber thoughts race through his mind as he takes out the homing device and turns it on. *So…we are now down to five. How many more deaths must I bear? I will never forget their sacrifice.*

He glances at Dell who is watching him intently; suddenly his thoughts clarify. He looks at the device in his hands to see a green arrow pointing towards the power source. He turns and motions everyone to gather.

"Alright, here's the plan. The power source is located deeper underground and roughly six hundred meters from here. Disperse your D-wave emitters whenever possible and use your Wasps from here on out." He looks at their torn clothes and scruffy faces then holds out his hand with pride. Looks of determination and hope spread across their faces as they put their hands on top.

"Today, I believe we will achieve the impossible. After I activate Thumper's countdown, I'll initialize a portal and we can leave this god-forsaken place. Alright, let's go!"

They head out and enter a narrow twisting tunnel that descends rapidly. It finally opens up into a cavern with many exits. Humanoid figures in bulky, black bodysuits temporarily pin them down with some type of electrical discharging ammo. Soon the air fills with weapon fire, explosions and smoke.

Dell screams as an energy beam nicks her thigh and crumples to the floor in pain. Blix and Bennet immediately unload another burst of weapon fire to provide cover as Hopper and Parker drag her into the farthest tunnel. Trained for such an incident, Parker takes out a hypodermic syringe from his belt and injects it into her buttocks then quickly applies a compression bandage around her thigh.

Dell's eyes become glossy as morphine courses through her system. She struggles to talk to Hopper. "I sense…aliens massing in the tunnels behind us. Must move forward…or we'll be trapped here!"

Hopper looks at her with concern then to Parker who nods with assurance. They help her to her feet and all five slowly advance down the tunnel but Dell's strength finally gives out and slumps to her knees. Panting with effort, she makes one final plea. "Leave me here! No one ahead—go now!"

Hopper crouches and caresses her forehead as he looks at Parker, Blix, and Bennet. "Stay and protect her. I'll be back as soon as I can." They nod and solemnly salute him as he struggles with his feelings. *Someday Dell, I promise to tell you how I feel.*

Hopper turns and runs down a long dark tunnel, which opens up to an immense brightly lit cavern. However, three-meter-high storage containers block his view. He climbs up one and glances inside to discover it full of black-plated material the aliens are wearing. From his elevated vantage point, he gazes around the immense cavern but his attention draws to its center.

Less than one hundred meters away an immense, golden triangular structure rises from the floor all the way to the ceiling of the cavern. Inside the structure are two tiered, circular platforms slowly rotating on top of the other. Hopper quickly checks the homing device to see it blinking green circles around the red center button.

Hopper quickly takes Thumper from his backpack and sets it on five-minute delay then carefully puts the active bomb inside the container. As he prepares to leave, he looks once more at the strange power source. This time he notices a humanoid figure at the base of the lower platform.

He watches as a clear, cylindrical tube ejects horizontally from the wall and exposes a nude, pregnant woman attached to a multitude of wires. The odd scene confuses Hopper. Are the aliens breeding with humans? Will the child within be removed and experimented on? He has little time to ponder these thoughts as Dell sends him an urgent message.

Hurry back! We can't hold out much longer!

Dell faints from the effort of sending Hopper the message and smacks her head on the hard ground causing the PSI band to dislodge. Blood immediately oozes from her scalp and spreads out across the uneven floor.

A few moments later, she wakes to see a shadowy black-suited figure crouching over her. Unfocused and dazed, she opens her mind and is overwhelmed by a stream of visual images and intense feelings. In horror, she realizes the aliens are not the enemy they thought they were. She tries to warn the ominous figure of the danger Hopper just unleashed but it disappears into the shadows before she can finish.

She lays her head back on the ground and closes her eyes as a wave of dizziness overcomes her.

Out of breath, Hopper returns to find Dell lying in a pool of blood with her PSI band next to her. In the distance, he can hear echoes of Wasps firing near the entrance to the tunnel. His heart pounds loudly in his chest as he quickly reattaches the PSI band to her temples then gently shakes her.

"You OK Dell? Talk to me! Please wake up!" He looks around for help then whispers in her ear, "Everything's going to be OK. Don't forget about being with me on our perfect day."

Hopper starts to tremble as he gently runs his fingers through her bloodstained hair.

Dell slowly open her eyes and tears immediately stream down her face. She struggles to sit up but fails. "Hopper, we've made a gigantic mistake! I don't have time to explain. Is there a way to deactivate Thumper?"

Hopper's concern grows as he realizes the blow to her head; the morphine shot, hunger, and exhaustion have impaired her thinking. "I can't do that even if I wanted to…the chain reaction has already begun." Hopper doesn't wait for an answer as he prepares the phasing band for activation. "Recall the men to our position immediately. Tell them the mission is complete."

Dell continues as if she didn't hear. "I was in contact with one of *them*."

He looks at her quizzically as the portal materializes in the tunnel in front of them. "We don't have time to talk and you need serious medical attention. Recall the men *now*!"

Dell continues undeterred. "The aliens are human—just like us. They're here trying to save us. If we blow up this place, we'll destroy any chance for life on earth. What we thought were acts of war were defensive measures for their survival…and ours. They've been trying to protect their technology from us while searching for a way to save mankind—now, and in the future. Hopper, I'm not going crazy! You *have* to believe me!"

Hopper's phasing device emits a tone followed by a computer-generated voice. "Thirty seconds to antimatter detonation."

Hopper begins to perspire as he tries to get Dell to her feet. "Dell, we don't have time to for this. We need to get the hell out of here. Like right now!"

Another tone emits from the device. "Twenty seconds to antimatter detonation."

"Dell, do you want to die here? Let's go!"

Her eyes go out of focus as she slides back down the wall. "Can you reactivate the portal on Thumper's location to phase it to our rendezvous point?"

Hopper looks at her in horror. "Even if that was possibly, for all I know, our rendezvous point could be at the Command Center!"

A solid buzzing tone emits from the device followed by, "Ten, nine, eight, seven…"

Dell's eyes flutter close then lets out a deep breath. Hopper hastily discards his rifles then reaches out with both hands to drag her the remaining few meters but never makes it to the portal.

Standing in the shadows, Reckston struggles to decide the fate of this unusually talented woman and her companion. *You both have doomed the world to die. Why should I save you now?* He shakes his head, torn between vengeance and compassion.

With only seconds remaining, his conscience decides for him. He steps from the shadows and stuns the man with a sharp blow to the chin. As the traitor falls to the floor, Reckston initiates a phase as the BTC disintegrates around them.

~MEETING OF THE MINDS~
FOUR MONTHS, TWO DAYS AGO...

4/09/2036

With Bunker 24 now thousands of kilometers away, O'Connell arrives on a two-meter wide circular platform at the Ryedale Research Center in Houston Texas amid a shower of sparks and emergency lights. Instantly she realizes something must have gone terribly wrong with the phasing cycle. She takes a cautious step forward and stumbles over a bulky black suit. Curious, she peers inside a semi-transparent visor to see the face of a middle-aged man. With all her strength, she drags him from sparking electrical equipment to the center of the room. The man in the strange outfit slowly comes to as she catches her breath.

He sits up and removes a three-centimeter cylinder from a compartment on his side then squishes it into a small pancake causing the outer edge to glow. With effort, he detaches his helmet exposing a hairless, unnaturally white head and blue-flecked eyes. Sweat runs down his face as he stands and puts the helmet and device on a workbench then motions for her to sit in a nearby chair.

Intrigued, she complies then nervously introduces herself. "Hi... My name is Kathleen O'Connell. Whom may I ask are you?"

The man moves his hand back and forth across his mouth, points to his eyes then taps his head. Immediately her vision blurs as her mind fills with a cold probing sensation. Surprised, she realizes he is trying to communicate with her telepathically. Determined to know more, O'Connell looks deep into his eyes then nods for him to try once more.

A few seconds later, she hears a distant voice whisper in her mind until it grows loud and clear.

My name is Reckston...I am the one you captured at Bunker 24.

He stops to make sure she understood then continues.

I'm sorry to inform you that the location you came from was destroyed in an effort to prevent further study of my vehicle and its technology. It also served to cover my escape from your people and my own.

O'Connell's eyes grow wide with questions as he lowers his head in shame.

Breeding Tube Command, or what we call the BTC, would never allow me to live or work with your people if they knew I was alive. At the same time, I cannot allow your military to gain any more information about us.

O'Connell is stunned to hear about the destruction of Bunker 24 but puts her anguish aside and continues to listen.

I will try to explain in detail why I did it. You see, we arrived here from the year 2209. Watch what this world will soon become.

Images bloom in her vision as she witnesses an earth darkened by thick floating dust; pummeling torrential rains, never-ending hurricanes, severe flooding, and earthquakes all dominated by intense heat. The vision passes but it shakes her to her core and is desperate to know how such a catastrophe could happen.

Reckston glances around the room as he senses increased activity outside the building. *We don't have much time so it's crucial you understand who we are and why we're here. My people are the second of three remnant groups alive in the future.*

He stops to read her thoughts to reaffirm himself then continues. *We only knew the year 2033 coincided with drastic weather changes and its general starting point in an area called The Zone. Information from military and civilian sources gave very little clue as to its cause so we investigated ways to travel back in time to somehow prevent the event from taking place. After years of intense research, our scientists finally understood the physics of such a task. The key was through a scientific reaction called quark-step acceleration. This process allows chain-step phasing in four-year intervals. We didn't know if our antimatter generators could provide the energy necessary for forty-four consecutive jumps, but they did. It appears it takes less energy to travel in the wake of the past than to forge forward into the future.*

While in transit to this time period, a huge subspace distortion wave preceded us. On reentry, the wave exploded and contaminated earth's subspace with distortion bubbles. These bubbles are now interacting with a newly discovered ninth dimension. The interaction between the two is what we call the Radiantnine Effect. Because of it, the vision you saw will eventually come to pass. The earth you love and all its creatures will cease to exist.

He pauses to collect his thoughts as O'Connell sits in a state of shock trying to cope with the images she just witnessed. Reckston doesn't have any choice but to continue, hoping her mind can quickly accept it.

What were once the countries of Russia, China, and United States, immediately began building the huge pyramidal structures necessary to transport the BTC, equipment, and personnel back in time. We eventually lost contact with the Russian group but now believe an explosion over Tunguska, Siberia in 1908 was the result of an unsuccessful attempt of their transport center to reenter the timeline and possibly their demise. We continued working with China until they fell behind looking for certain precious metals. With our transport center finally complete deep inside the Carlsbad Caverns, it was our turn to travel back in time. With great trepidation, we left our homes and in my case...loved ones.

He pauses briefly as a surge of sadness flows into O'Connell's mind.

After witnessing the destruction created upon our arrival, we realized our method of time travel produced the destiny we were all trying to prevent. Even worse, we have no way to warn or avert the third group from arriving, which is going to cause even more catastrophic disruptions.

Reckston stops sending perceptual images and picks up the flat, circular device off the table to make some sort of adjustment.

O'Connell is overwhelmed but decides to ask a few questions of her own. "There is so much to ask...like what's that device in your hands?"

Reckston lifts it up to show her. *We call this a Nullifier and it's currently scrambling all electronic signals in this room by shifting time on a minute scale.*

O'Connell shakes her head in disbelief then asks another question. "This Radiantnine Effect you talked about...can you please explain more about it?"

Her mind is flooded once more by a swirling sea of images as Reckston tries to enlighten her. *The ninth dimension is currently colliding with local subspace distortion bubbles causing friction that is having a devastating impact on local space and time. You have already seen some of the effects with the strange weather in and around the Zone. Your newly developed quark technology and our own advanced phasing methods generate even more of these distortion bubbles, which is adding to the problem. We believe the arrival of the third group will be the tipping point for the Radiantnine Effect to encompass the whole world. Weather patterns will drastically change causing the sky to fill with choking streams of dust that will block all sunlight and kill most plant and animal life. Ultimately, sterility will spread throughout humanity and animals alike.*

However, not all will be lost. At least not in our version of history. You see, over time our scientists will use tubes lined with transmuted lead—vastly harder and denser than any known metals of the twenty-first century—to provide protection for a selected few from this dimensional phenomenon. In the beginning, only pregnant women will use these tubes to protect their unborn children or prevent sterility of the young until they come of age.

In about a hundred years from now, the surface of the earth will become unlivable and all forms of electronic communication will fail due to this Radiantnine Effect. With humanity forced underground and faced with no way to communicate, the world council decides to enlist females with empathic abilities. These psychogenetic traits are more matriarchal in nature; therefore, thousands of women from around the world volunteer or are forced to take drugs at military complexes to enhance their abilities. Those who show promise are immobilized and neural-linked together in large, circular, underground silos that will eventually lead to communication centers.

Within a decade, scientists create a working telepathic network but it will have major limitations. In an effort to increase telepathic efficiency, they impregnate most of the volunteers with genetically altered embryos. The experiment exceeds expectations and eventually the children born in the silos become part of a new, more powerful communication network called Breeding Tube Command, or BTC.

Finally, by sheer chance, our scientists will find an effective means to protect us from the Radiantnine Effect. It happens when they create a dual, synchronized phasing process that allows objects to oscillate simultaneously in the minute past and future, allowing it to retain physical properties in the present but is optically and electronically invisible. We call this condition, null state.

In the beginning, there were many problems with this technology. Test objects for instance, would destabilize and wink out of existence for unknown reasons. To understand why, a human volunteer phased into null state. Initially, all communication was lost but quickly reestablished through the BTC's neural network. The volunteer told them the surrounding energy fields fluctuated too erratically which prevented him from seeing beyond it. It was then determined that conventional energy sources were too unreliable. What they needed was a constant stream of pure energy. Unfortunately, the scientists weren't able to bring the volunteer back and he ceased to exist. Nevertheless, armed with that knowledge, they created Dynalink Converters—an upgrade to your quark-phasing platforms—to use a new powerful form of energy called pulse waves. These waves emanate from subspace itself. Our massive transport center currently taps into this vast energy source and can transmit those waves over great distances to receivers in the field. Finally, we had a pure, stable energy source that allowed us to phase in and out of null state and protect us from Radiantnine at the same time.

O'Connell presses her lips together and nods as she looks at Reckston. "OK, I'm now getting the big picture. To compensate for all the issues caused by Radiantnine, you created telepathic communications and null-state technology that keeps us from detecting your vehicles in the Zone. I'm still confused though, how are you able to locate us so easily if you are blinded by your surroundings?"

Reckston gives her an understanding nod, happy to know she is past her shock and fully able to comprehend what he is sharing. *The BTC's Neural Net creates a telepathic visual loop with people outside the null state field then sends that data to us, allowing personnel operating vehicles called Crawlers to see, so to speak. This method has been very effective locating people who enter the Zone but it makes us almost completely reliant on the BTC for information.*

O'Connell's mind races with even more questions. "So why didn't you guys stay in the future when you finally found a means to protect yourselves?"

It's simple. The planet was already dead. There is absolutely no place to go truly free of Radiantnine except in high-earth orbit at a space station called Arcadia.

His answer surprises her. She looks deep into Reckston's eyes. "Ok, you seem very open and sincere about saving mankind, so why are you killing everyone who enters the Zone?"

Reckston glances away embarrassed. *Yes, well…that does need some explaining. On our arrival, the Neural Net went down due to the massive Radiantnine storm raging around us. Luckily, our transport center and crawlers were in null state keeping us both invisible and protected from it. When it finally came back online, we discovered many of your people believed the initial blast was an alien attack. The BTC Collective liked the idea and thought it would be wise to play the part to protect our identities and harmful phasing technology from you. At the same time, trying to reverse the damage we caused and prevent more of it from occurring in the future. The boundary where most of the effects of Radiantnine end was the dividing line for us to go no further, and an area to prevent your people from entering. It was not my decision and I had no choice in the matter but I never killed any of the humans who came into my sector. In fact, I was trying to make contact with a two-man team but unfortunately, the BTC read my mind and activated my weapons remotely. The only thing I could do then was follow them through their portal hoping to break contact from the BTC. However, before I could catch up and bring the two inside my Crawler, your military captured me. As for trying to keep phasing technology from you, I see we are already too late for that.*

Reckston stands as he senses people entering the building and slowly approach their location. He looks at O'Connell who is unaware of what is happening outside the walls of the lab. *We really are not the cold-blooded murderers as you think. We are here only to survive and somehow correct the past! Our technology is more advanced but we definitely don't have all the answers. We need your help to neutralize this Radiantnine Effect and to prevent the third transport center from arriving. I believe your society may hold the key to knowledge we lost over time. It's quite possible the solution lies in a combined effort between our people. So my question to you is…are you willing to work with me, independently from your government and mine? I will share our advanced technologies, resources, and expertise if you are willing to do the same. Help me, save our world!*

His commitment to take on such a daunting project touches O'Connell deeply. How could she refuse? She smiles and nods. "I'm up for the challenge. Yes, let's save our world!" She leans forward. "Looks like I've just made your job fifty percent easier." She holds out her hand as Reckston removes his right glove and shakes it.

O'Connell looks around at the destroyed lab. "Well, if we're going to save the world our first concern is to find a secure place." She points to the device on Reckston's arm. "Can you phase us from this location?" He looks down at the device then nods. "Good, I have just the place in mind."

Reckston does a summation of O'Connell's thoughts then inputs coordinates into his Dynalink phasing band as O'Connell quickly gathers supplies and erases traces of them being there. Just as the doors open to the lab, they phase to an underground cavern dimly lit by a string of emergency lights.

O'Connell turns on her penlight and points it back and forth between two tunnels leading from the main chamber. "This cavern was initially going to be used to construct a Command Center but several potential fault hazards were discovered and it was abandoned for more stable bedrock to the east. The tunnel sloping upward leads to the surface, the other to several more passageways. One actually links to the current Command Center at Fort Bliss as an emergency escape route—or, in our case, a way to access their facility. Let me try to illuminate this area a little bit better." O'Connell walks to an old breaker panel used during construction. With a few flicks of some switches, she activates the area's lighting.

Reckston looks around then nods in approval. *I see you have chosen well.*

As they continue to examine their surroundings, they discuss what the next step should be and come up with four areas to resolve. Create a lab, get personnel, prevent the third transport center from arriving and somehow neutralize the Radiantnine effect.

4/11/2036

Over the next two days, Reckston and O'Connell use the Dynalink phasing band to travel in and out of several large storage facilities around the world to pilfer equipment and supplies. As a makeshift lab takes form, O'Connell christens the area as Shadow Base.

Needing some advice on power amplification, Reckston removes the Cry-Comm unit from his pack and brings Ritan out of cryostasis. Intrigued, O'Connell stops her inspection of a junction box to look at the octagon cylinder with what appears to be a dark oval shape inside.

After a sequence of blinking lights on the end caps, Ritan's icy presence fills the air as she reads their minds. Reckston relaxes when he hears her voice inside his head. *I sense you're troubled my friend. No need to worry, we'll figure it out. You two have already accomplished much in the last two days.*

Reckston subconsciously holds the cylinder to his chest. *Yes, once more you've come to my rescue. My dream of working with these people to save humanity is coming true, but I don't believe we can succeed without you.*

Ritan shushes him with her mind. *I'm glad to help; our future is at stake. Anyway, we can't go back to the BTC, we broke all the rules by making contact.* Ritan focuses on O'Connell. *This woman is more valuable than you think. Her knowledge of quark theories is unparalleled in this age. You couldn't have picked a better person to work with.*

Reckston looks over at O'Connell and nods. *Her drive to make a difference is similar to mine. I hope together, we can surpass our wildest dreams.*

O'Connell's curiosity continues to grow as she watches Reckston look at the cylinder and then to her several times. She clears her throat to get his attention. "I hate to interrupt but my ears are burning. Care to tell me who you're talking to?"

Reckston gives her a big smile then holds the cylinder out in front of him. *You're quite right. Let me introduce you to Ritan, she was once part of the BTC neural network. Ritan, this is Kathleen O'Connell; she was a scientist at a place called Bunker 24 and now here at Shadow Base.*

O'Connell winces at the words *Bunker 24* then hesitantly greets the device. "Hello Ritan, it's an honor to meet you."

A pleasant female voice enters her mind. *Thank you Kathleen, I feel the same about you as well. I look forward to working with you and Reckston. I can see we have a lot to do.*

O'Connell looks down at the power cables running out of the junction box. "Indeed. At the moment I'm trying to figure out a way to boost our energy output without being detected."

Lights on both ends of Ritan's container flicker then a beam of light emits from one end as she scans Reckston. *Reckston, your biosuit's power module is capable of receiving and converting pulse waves for energy. It's possible we can use it to supplement the power here to run several labs. I also believe you can link your suit's onboard computer to one of Command's data cables. By doing so, I should be able to gain access to their mainframe computer for information and to prevent our detection now and in the future.*

Amused, O'Connell looks at Reckston and points to his helmet. "Wow! I guess if I'm hungry, you have food in there too?" Laughter echoes in the cavern and in O'Connell's head as she addresses the device. "Glad to have you on board Ritan, now let's get started with those modifications you mentioned. You know the world won't save itself."

Under Ritan's diligent guidance, Reckston and O'Connell succeed in making the necessary modifications and soon have an abundance of untapped energy and unrestricted access to the Fort Bliss' mainframe computer.

As Shadow Base takes form, Ritan shares with O'Connell the theories of multi chain-step phasing and other technologies developed in the future. It is clear the time has come to recruit a specialized group of geniuses. After careful consideration, they devise a safe method to get the additional staff they need.

Using Reckston's phasing band, they covertly contact O'Connell's friends and colleagues and share advanced technologies while telling them about the world's bleak future if time runs its course unimpeded. Most agree to help but for those unwilling, Ritan uses her abilities to fade the memory of the meeting from their minds.

Soon, Shadow Base is buzzing with activity as more personnel and equipment arrives each day. With everyone helping out, they quickly build a makeshift lab, mess hall, first aid center, community quarters and a bathing area.

5/9/2036

Within a month, O'Connell's team nears thirty members. With some of the best minds in the world focused on resolving issues, they quickly discover the physics behind the mystery of the clearing periods. They occur when local subspace distortion waves emanating from the Zone intermix with incoming distortion waves from the third transport center, temporarily neutralizing each other.

However, there is no celebration for their discovery. In fact, the Shadow Team sits in silence around a table of crates inside the community quarters contemplating Ritan's proposal. Her idea is for them to recreate the chain-step method of time travel like the BTC's in hopes of sending a message to the incoming transport center to self-destruct before reentry or a mass extinction event will occur. Most realize the plan is too drastic and well beyond their 21st century technology to build.

O'Connell stares at her hands, frustrated by their continued silence. "Does anyone else have an idea how to prevent the third transport center from arriving or to neutralize the Radiantnine effect?" She looks up and points to one of the engineers, "Ethan?" He presses his lips together then shakes his head no. She gazes at their faces then turns to address her new lab assistant. "How about you Camille? You always have something to say."

The dark haired women puts a finger to her mouth then rolls her eyes and looks away as if she didn't hear.

O'Connell stands up and slams both fists down on the table. "Come on you guys! We're wasting time. Nobody's leaving until we figure out a solution, so get creative people!"

Reckston feels their disappointment then decides to offer up his own suggestion. He makes eye contact with O'Connell who nods in his direction. He stands and walks around before speaking to them telepathically. *My idea may not be as grand as Ritan's, and in reality, is the poor man's way of doing things.* Reckston can feel everyone's attention starting to focus on him. *Ritan is on the right track but I think an easier solution would be to infiltrate the BTC and pilfer a device called a SOL, or a Small Object Launcher. Its purpose is to transport small inanimate objects short distances in time. They came in handy when developing time travel technology. I've seen them myself in their main storage facility. If we can get our hands on one, I feel confident our team can reverse engineer it and gain valuable technology, or possibly even integrate it directly into one of our designs.*

Now, I don't like the idea of requesting our time travelling friends to sacrifice themselves. Instead, we can prevent their reentry and spare their lives at the same time by deflecting them to the extreme past. However, it will require us to create a small craft based on Crawler technology so we can duplicate a null state environment. We should then be able to destabilize its phase fields in a controlled manner and send it on an intercept course to bump the incoming Transport Center into a new trajectory. If outfitted properly, we can even have the craft generate a deionizing wave. The impact should disperse it enough to neutralize earth's subspace distortion bubbles and allow Radiantnine to pass freely once more.

The room is silent as Reckston pauses to think, but before he can say another word, all chaos break loose. Everyone is on their feet clapping, hugging, yelling, or jumping up and down, excited about the possibilities of his ideas.

With everyone now bubbling with energy, the meeting progresses at a furious pace. They name the transport craft an antichamber and are soon discussing its size and shape. However, they quickly realize an unmanned version isn't feasible due to the need to correct minute variances in real time. They speculate that if the trajectory angles where plotted correctly, a person could actually survive the deflection process and reenter the timeline some point in the future.

Reckston immediately volunteers to operate it in hopes of returning to his family in the year 2210. However, most of their plans are contingent on retrieving the SOL device, much needed technical data and valuable support equipment from the BTC located deep inside the perimeter of the Zone.

8/3/2036

As the Hail Mary 2 mission commences, the Shadow Team prepares for the dangerous scavenger raid. While the BTC's attention focuses on trying to find and eliminate Captain Phillips' squad, Reckston plans to use his access code to phase safely through their defense grid to retrieve critical equipment from one of their storage facility. To ease Reckston's mind, O'Connell supplies him with a device to locate the squad and if necessary, physically prevent them from setting off Thumper.

In an improvised control center, most of the Shadow Team watch Command's satellite and video feeds to follow the squad's progress across the Zone hoping to receive word that they reached the Carlsbad Caverns.

However, when the clearing ends a day and a half earlier than expected it puts their raid on hold. After nine frustrating days of waiting and trying to come up with alternative solutions to infiltrate the BTC undetected, the team takes a well-deserved rest.

Exhausted, O'Connell lies down on her cot and quickly falls asleep. In the middle of the night she is awaken by Ritan's urgent voice in her mind. O'Connell rubs her eyes as she tries to understand what she is saying. "Ritan, can you please repeat that?"

Sorry to wake you but about five minutes ago, seismographs at the Command Center began registering what they think are explosions within the Carlsbad Caverns area. I'm also sensing desperation emanating from BTC's Neural Net. There must be something seriously chaotic happening there if I can sense them from here.

O'Connell sits up quickly and swings her legs off the cot. "Definitely sounds like they're under attack. How Captain Phillips and his squad reached the caverns with the raging storm out there is beyond me. I guess we don't have much time to prepare. Have Reckston and my lead lab assistant Camille report to the lab immediately then notify the rest of the team that the scavenging raid is on and will commence as soon as possible."

Reckston enters the lab fifteen minutes later, bleary eyed but ready. He walks over and stands on the lab's new Dynalink Converter run by pulse waves. O'Connell approaches and puts a modified PSI band on his head while he dons his bulky black suit. "This should hide your thoughts from the BTC." He looks at O'Connell apprehensively as Camille hastily enters wearing only pink pajamas and slippers. The slim, dark haired woman's face is flush with embarrassment then shrugs. O'Connell smirks and points her to a bank of portable computer terminals. Camille nods and immediately walks over and turns them on. After verifying functionality and synchronicity, she enters phasing coordinates deep inside the Zone's boundary.

Tinged with anger, Reckston's voice enters their minds. *You know, whatever happens out there please understand I cannot allow anyone to harm my people, not with the human race at stake.*

O'Connell looks away then nods but says nothing.

Camille looks at O'Connell then back to Reckston. Her voice is light and cheerful as she addresses him. "I know the squad is a threat, but maybe you can explain to them who you are and why you're here. I'm sure you can make them understand."

Reckston glances at her then lowers his eyes.

O'Connell approaches Camille at the computer terminals and puts a hand on her back as she verifies the settings. "It's time." She looks over at Reckston, "Please be safe my friend. May you find all the things we need to give us a fighting chance to save humanity and our planet." Her forehead creases with worry then flips a switch on the computer terminal. As the platform energizes, he waves before disappearing in a flash of light.

Reckston finds himself standing in a large, dimly lit cavern with hundreds of shelves lined with electronic equipment and only an occasional workbench here and there. He scans the area for life and is relieved to find no one in the vicinity. The plan to use the squad as a decoy was working well. All available personnel must be either pursuing or fleeing Captain Phillips' squad right now.

With no time to spare, he quickly finds a flat-panel optic reader along with several red holographic disks loaded with much-needed data. On the floor near the back, he locates a small, but heavy spatial generator shaped like a flattened beehive with a scorpion's tail needed to help power the antichamber and a newly proposed subspace radar console to plot trajectory angles. He puts the items in his hands on top of it then looks around anxiously.

He searches dozens of long shelves before finding the most critical item of the raid, a Small Object Launcher. It's a circular device twenty-centimeters wide, two-centimeters thick with an eight-centimeter solid gold center. Covering the remaining surface is a layer of dark, polarized refracting crystals that shine even in the dim light.

The last time he actually saw one functioning was almost a decade ago while working on the Transport Center. He lays a hand on the surface then opens his mind to create a link. Immediately a faint blue haze of an immersion display appears above the device. He slowly lifts his hand and is able to interact with three-dimensional objects within. He touches one causing the outer surface of the SOL to activate and glow in deep rich colors waiting for an object to be place at its center. He wishes he had more time to investigate then touches the same object causing the SOL to deactivate. He lowers his hand to the surface ending the link, immediately the blue haze disappears.

He carefully picks up the device and places it on top of his growing pile of equipment. With precious time slipping away, he searches a workbench for one last item—another Dynalink phasing band similar to his own. He picks one up and turns it on then enters Shadow Base's coordinates. He sets it on the scavenged equipment, moments later the pile disappears. As he prepares to head out to look for the squad, the ground shakes beneath his feet knocking several items to the floor. Seconds later, he hears a loud explosion followed by echoes of gunfire.

Reckston pulls out the modified homing device and quickly locks onto the squad's PSI band frequency. He cautiously heads toward the pyramidal transport center through several cross-connecting tunnels then goes down an empty passageway. He slows as a pitched battle intensifies up ahead.

He rounds a corner in the tunnel to see an unconscious woman lying in a pool of blood. Her eyes flutter open as he kneels down and inspects her head. His body turns numb as he scans the woman's mind to discover it's too late to prevent Thumper from detonating. Anger courses through his veins as he tells her where they're from and what they are trying to achieve but is interrupted by the sound of running footsteps.

He scans her mind to discover the one approaching is the person responsible for setting off the antimatter bomb. Unsure of what to do next, Reckston stands then fades into the shadows to contemplate the fate of these two traitors.

TAINTED VICTORY

8/12/2036

    A brilliant sphere of light temporarily pierces the chaotic storm inside the Zone bathing the entire region in an intense eerie white glow. Colossal boulders rain down from the sky as a massive shockwave expands outwards. As it reaches the outer edge of the perimeter, countless smaller explosions erupt throughout the entire quarantined area as if powerful sticks of dynamite were going off.

    The fierce storm inside the Zone temporarily subsides but continues to affect communications and block optical and electronic topographical scans. In the following aftermath, watchtower guards are finally able to report the sudden disappearance of all alien distortion fields in their vicinity. However, the military has to wait for the next clearing period to investigate what happened this day.

    Several months pass by before the storm finally dissipates. With the Zone once more basking under a clear blue sky, General Pierce immediately launches a multi-prong attack force of mechanized infantry, escorted by hundreds of hover jets; all armed with Kaon particle weapons. When they cross into the Zone, they encounter a landscape littered with millions of jagged boulders but meet no resistance as they advance towards ground zero. At its center they discover a massive, cone shaped crater almost two kilometers across located where the Carlsbad Caverns used to be.

    After scouring the entire area for over a week, they are unable to locate any alien distortion fields or discover any physical evidence of them being there. With the elimination of the enemy, Command deems the Hail Mary 2 Mission a complete success. However, several disturbing questions remain unanswered. Who were the aliens? Where did they come from? Why are there no bodies or physical evidence? It's as if they never existed. Moreover, why are the disruptive storms still occurring inside the Zone now that the enemy is gone?

Heroes
8/20/2036

To shift the world's attention to happier times, President Wellington stands in front of a podium inside the Oval Office and looks out at a dozen or so reporters waiting to telecast the courageous deeds of the men and woman of the Hail Mary 2 mission. He taps one of the microphones and grins. "Is this on?"

Several reporters chuckle as he continues. "Let me begin by saying it's an honor to be here today to remember and celebrate the squad who gave their lives to protect not only our country but the world. When the Zone first appeared three and a quarter years ago, we didn't know if it was from terrorists, natural phenomenon or from something even more mysterious. However, we soon learned it was an attack by an unknown enemy force whose technology is vastly superior to our own. I am proud to stand here today and say we faced this challenge as a united world, and in the end, we were victorious.

"We may not know everything about them but I assure you, we will be prepared if they return! With me now is my chief adviser, General Shadley Pierce and Major General Dave Hamrick. They commanded the missions and oversaw all aspects of the operation. Without their careful planning and attention to detail, this mission may not have succeeded. Both will receive the Medal of Honor here today. But first, would either of you like to say a few words to honor the fallen?"

Unwilling to praise Captain Phillips, General Pierce clears his throat as he glances at General Hamrick. As they lock eyes, Pierce's head moves almost imperceptibly back and forth. Hamrick frowns then stands up and smiles as he approaches the podium.

"Thank you Mr. President. It would be my honor." Hamrick shakes the President's hand then turns to the cameras. "Since the beginning of this crisis there have been over thirty-one thousand military and civilian casualties. Each life is precious which makes it difficult to pick out certain individuals. However, I want to share with you the courage of an extraordinary group of soldiers who went into battle and defeated an enemy who many thought were untouchable."

"Captain Lucas Phillips was their leader, a man who understood the challenges but never wavered from his conviction to succeed... Who outwitted an enemy he could not even identify... His belief and trust in his squad inspired them to accomplish what a whole army could not do—to destroy the enemy residing within the Zone. The squad gallantly gave their lives to rid the world of this fear and oppression. I'm proud to have known Captain Phillips and his squad personally."

He looks solemn as he sighs at the cameras and reporters. "I will greatly miss each and every one of them. It is with a heavy heart that I read their fourteen names, so America and the world, will not forget the brave soldiers who lost their lives to save ours. May God bless them and the thirty-one thousand other precious souls."

General Hamrick removes a piece of paper from his uniform and clears his throat. He speaks proudly as he begins reading their names aloud. "Captain Lucas Phillips...First Lieutenant Brian Sanders... Second Lieutenant Annadell Thompson...Sergeant Johnathan Blix..."

In the background, Pierce glares at Hamrick and the President as they glorify the memory of the squad. He struggles to maintain a calm composure as he whispers to himself. "Why are you honoring those men? They were only pawns in *my* plan. Without me, the Captain and his squad would never have accomplished their mission. I'm so tired of kissing up to this sorry excuse of a President. I can do a much better job…and if you want to rid the world of fear and oppression, I'll be all too happy to show you how to get the job done right, because I'm a man of action…not empty words."

SHADOW BASE

8/12/2036

Hopper wakes with a sore jaw then looks around to discover he is lying on a large circular platform with a bald, oddly white-skinned man towering over him. The man clenches his teeth as a voice full of hatred enters his mind.

I should have let you die.

Hopper immediately reaches for his rifles but realizes he left them on the cave floor inside the Zone. He starts to unsheathe his knife as a woman with white hair comes into his field of vision. "Hold on there, no need for that Captain Phillips. My name is Kathleen O'Connell and I welcome you to Shadow Base." She smiles then reaches down and helps him to his feet as Reckston hesitantly steps back.

Confused, Hopper quickly glances around to locate Dell but sees only blood splattered about. Off to his left, several men and women wearing lab coats are busy analyzing a strange pile of electronic equipment. Looking at how sophisticated it is he surmises he must be in some sort of advanced military laboratory. Hopper wearily keeps his eyes on the strange-looking man while addressing O'Connell. "Where is the woman who was with me?"

O'Connell frowns then shakes her head. "She is seriously injured and is being taken care of as we speak. Try not to worry though our doctor will take good care of her." O'Connell shifts the topic of conversation to the angry man standing next to her. "For now, let me introduce you to Reckston. He is one of the so-called aliens."

Hopper's adrenaline rises as their eyes lock and more words enter his mind. *It is rare to meet someone who is a hero and a traitor to the human race. However, the question I should ask you, are you its annihilator?* Reckston abruptly walks off the platform and disappears into a dark passageway.

Confused by the comment, Hopper looks to O'Connell. "Who are you people? How did I get here? And how in the blazes did you team up with an alien?"

O'Connell's gaze drifts over to the equipment her fellow scientists are inspecting. "Your questions will be answered in due time Captain Phillips. However, you might not like the answers you receive."

Not satisfied with her response Hopper asks another question. "And how do you know my name?"

O'Connell's patience finally gives out as she gestures a woman wearing pink pajamas and slippers to come over. "As you can see, we've just concluded a dangerous recovery mission and now need to take inventory of the acquired items. So let me introduce you to Camille, she's my lead lab assistant here at Shadow Base. I'm sure she'll be happy to answer your questions and show you around."

The woman smiles as she approaches then extends a hand. "Pleased to meet you. May I call you Hopper? I've heard so much about you and your team."

He glances at her cloths then rolls his eyes as he fights his growing confusion and frustration. With effort, he shakes her hand.

O'Connell ushers them off the platform. "Camille, please take Captain Phillips to the med center so he can see how Lieutenant Thompson is doing and then to the community quarters. Feel free to answer *any* questions he may have." O'Connell turns to Hopper. "Captain Phillips, you are not our prisoner and are free to go wherever you wish but I beg of you, don't touch anything that looks important."

She looks at the knife on his utility belt with distaste. "I assure you, you won't need that any time soon, so please be careful with it."

In the background, the scientists become excited over a small circular device with a golden center. O'Connell glances at it then impatiently escorts Camille and Hopper from the lab. She waves goodbye before closing a makeshift wooden door behind them.

The apparent crudeness of the facility surprises Hopper as Camille leads him through a narrow underground passageway carved from solid rock, lit only by a single string of construction lights hanging from the ceiling. Her voice startles him as she tries to break the ice.

"Are you wondering why you haven't heard of Shadow Base before?" Intrigued, Hopper nods as she continues. "It's because it doesn't exist...well, at least not in the world's eyes." They stop to let two men in lab coats hurry by then resume walking. "O'Connell and Reckston created our secret group out of a need to save the human race and the world from total annihilation in the future."

Hopper clears his throat as a feeling of dread overcomes him. "This Reckston person...who is he?"

"Let me start by saying he's the *alien* who chased your team through several phasing portals during the Hail Mary One mission, but eventually trapped inside the Bunker 24 containment area. From there, he escaped by piggybacking on O'Connell's quark phasing signal when she left for the Ryedale Research Center in Houston. I must say, it was an incredibly risky maneuver. Somehow, the two started talking and decided to work together to prevent another large-scale explosion similar to what happened in the Zone and the spread of an effect called Radiantnine." Camille stops walking and faces Hopper. Her voice turns serious as she tenses. "Now, I didn't want to be the one to tell you this but the aliens are...*were*...from our future. I'm sure Reckston's anger at you is off the charts for killing everyone at a place he calls the BTC. I highly suggest you stay clear of him till he cools down."

Hopper's horror builds inside as he realizes the man had every right to be furious at him. He single-handedly destroyed countless lives trying to do General Pierce's bidding.

Camille touches his arm to comfort him. "You mustn't blame yourself though; we took a calculated risk to let your mission continue. Besides, there's still hope the Shadow Team can continue their efforts. It's quite possible Reckston retrieved all the essential equipment and data disks we needed before the BTC was destroyed."

They continue in silence and approach a poorly constructed door labeled FIRST AID with a hand painted white cross underneath. They pass through to see Dell lying motionlessly on two padded wooden crates hastily pushed together. Her head and thigh are wrapped in white dressings already seeping blood. Several intravenous tubes are attached to her arm. A woman in a white coat finishes administering an injection before looking up. Her worried expression tells Hopper how desperate Dell's condition is.

Her latex gloves drip with blood as she addresses him. "You must be the Captain everyone is talking about. My name is Faith, I'm just a part-time medic here but everyone calls me a doctor. She looks at her patient. "I'm sorry, but your friend here is in a coma. I hope you understand, but I really don't have time to talk right now.

She quickly moves to Dell's feet and removes her combat boots then carefully elevates her legs. She turns to Camille, "Can you bring the Captain back later? She needs all my attention and our prayers." She motions for them to leave as Hopper starts to tremble.

Camille puts her arm around Hopper and leads him out the door. "Don't get too worked up, she's good at helping people. We'll come back later, OK? Let me take you to the community quarters now."

Camille guides him down several more dimly lit tunnels. At one point they squeeze around a dozen or so empty wooden storage containers. On the other side is an opening to a cavern in the shape of a perfect circle.

Camille tries to focus Hopper's attention on it. "Are you wondering how this was done? Reckston used his Dynalink phasing band, which is similar to your own band."

Hopper looks at the device to see the display broken and powered off.

"You see most of the rooms and halls down here were created by inducing a phase field through solid rock which was then transported to another location. This one just happened to open up to a cave like the one in community quarters."

Hopper walks through to find himself in a large cavern lit by several floodlights that illuminate delicate stalactites with a shallow stream running through its center. Camille follows him inside.

"When we get the time, we'll eventually use these containers to make a bridge over the water to create a sanctuary on the other side." She guides him back into the hall as several more technicians pass by. They stop to look at his scruffy face and ragged battle fatigues then nervously continue on their way. He stares back as Camille motions him to follow her down the narrow hall to a connecting tunnel.

They finally encounter an opening with two large sheets of plywood as doors. She pushes them open and enters a chamber filled with an assortment of crates used as furniture. At the far end are several cots that line the wall near a natural cave entrance. Camille points to it as steam drifts out. "There's a natural hot spring in there. You can clean yourself up, even shave if you like. I think you'll find it quite refreshing. As for your bed, take your pick.

She points to the cots. "I'm going to go back to the lab now for a few more hours. In the meantime, you can try to get some rest or if you're hungry, just follow your nose." She turns to leave then stops and touches a black wall plate near the door. "Oh, if you want to contact someone here, just press your hand against this. Say your name and then the person you want to communicate with. Ritan should be able to relay any messages you may have." She smiles at him, "OK, that's the end of the tour so please make yourself at home." She waves, "Bye-bye for now."

Overwhelmed by so many unfamiliar experiences, Hopper doesn't ask who Ritan is. Instead, he waves back as she departs then realizes he forgot to ask her about clothes.

Hopper looks around to see he is alone then decides his first priority should be to clean himself up. He enters the steaming cave and undresses near a hot pool of water. He slowly submerges himself and tries to relax by watching a drop of water slowly form at the end of a stalactite. It finally falls into the pool causing ripples to spread out across its surface. He takes a deep breath then dunks his head as thoughts of regret race through his mind.

Well, you did it again. Another squad decimated, Dell's in a coma, and quite possibly, wiped out the future of the human race. I had to accomplish the damn mission! How was I to know the consequences of setting off Thumper? If only Dell could have told me sooner about this BTC...

Hopper lifts his head then emerges from the water to retrieve a towel from a nearby stack and dries himself off. He peers at his reflection in a mirror hanging over a primitive water channel as he wraps it around his waist. His haggard unshaven face stuns him. The stress over the last few weeks has been hard on him. Crow's-feet have developed around his eyes as well as a streak of white hair growing from his frontal hairline. Sadness overcomes him as he puts a hand to his face as if to verify it's his own. He finally looks away and finds some toiletries nearby.

With each stroke of the razor, he removes years off his face and finally starts to feel better again. He picks up his belongings then reenters community quarter and places them under a cot away from the others. Wanting new clothes, he searches some open crates and discovers one full of mixed clothing. To his relief he finds a pair of brown maintenance overalls, a tan long sleeve shirt and some under garments then immediately puts them on. Before tossing his dirty clothes in a container marked waste, he searches and retrieves an old, ink-stained envelope sealed in plastic.

He carefully holds it to his chest and whispers. "Well Eileen, look at me now. I'm still trying to hold my feelings in, the very thing you wanted to prevent. I feel like I'm slowly losing it without you. How can I go on now knowing that in trying to get revenge for your death, I've possibly doomed the world instead."

His hands tremble as he caresses the seal on the back of the letter. "I promised myself I would never open this because it gives me strength and comfort knowing we can still share one last intimate moment together. I wonder what will happen to me after I read it."

He wearily shakes his head and takes a deep breath. "Today is not the day to find out. My heart is just too burdened to take anymore." He wipes tears forming in his eyes then carefully puts the envelope into the pocket of his overalls. Heavy with fatigue, he returns to his cot and lies down. Within in minutes, he falls into a deep slumber.

The walls of mist surrounding Hopper slowly dissipate only to find himself struggling behind the tiller of a small sailboat surrounded by monstrous, jagged waves in every direction. His tired eyes look out over a vast, angry sea and realizes he is alone with no one to save him. The roar of the water is deafening as he tries to keep the boat on course but the effort is futile. Wind and waves have long shredded the sails.

Exhausted, his hope of rescue fades. A huge dark wave crashes into the boat causing him to lose his grip on the tiller and forces him against the rail. Shivering from the cold, he lowers his eyes to see angry distorted faces in the frothy seawater.

Dread fills his heart as Eileen's face emerges among them. He reaches out to her in anguish then cries out, "Eileen, not you too!" Haunting laughter echoes around him as other dying friends and loved ones float in and out of his vision. He quickly realizes they have come to take him into the watery depths below. He fights to regain his grip on the tiller but it is to no avail. Another huge wave crashes into the boat throwing his battered body overboard. He desperately struggles to keep his head above water as the little boat drifts out of sight.

Cold water fills his lungs as he tries to catch his breath. Ready to succumb to his demise, Dell's loving face appears before him and waves her hand in front of her, urging him to wait. Her apparition slowly disappears but an awful laughter grows louder and closer until it consumes all his thought.

The doors to the community quarters slams open and a group of celebrating engineers wearing various-colored lab coats enter. Hopper wakes gulping for air then instinctively rolls off the cot and draws his knife from its sheath. As his mind clears, he looks at the men with relief.

They immediately stop talking when they see the knife pointed in their direction. Embarrassed, Hopper promptly sheathes it then lies down pretending to go back to sleep. He hears them whispering to each other as they gather some belongings and quietly leave.

Hopper sits up as their voices recede in the distance. Worried about Dell's condition, he latches his utility belt to his waist then walks over to the door and inspects the plate Camille pointed to earlier. To him it looked like the standard ID scanners used on post to allow access to restricted areas. Curious as to how it functions as a communication device he puts a hand on it and speaks in a loud clear voice. "Captain Phillips to Annadell Thompson."

Seconds go by then a cold sensation fills in his mind, the same sensation he felt many times inside the Zone and just recently with Reckston. Moments later a response enters his mind. *Unable to fulfill your request. Annadell Thompson is currently under medical attention. I will notify you when her condition improves. Ritan out.*

The message shakes Hopper to the bone, getting use to mind-reading humans from the future will take some time. Only a few hours ago he called them his enemy and thought they were aliens. Now, through some sort of twisted fate, he's probably going to work with them to save the world. He shakes his head then decides to explore his surroundings. He pushes open the swinging doors of the community quarters and enters into a gloomy passageway beyond.

The smell of food is thick in the air as Hopper passes numerous openings as he tries to locate its source. He finally enters a well-lit cavern where several tables surround a steaming food cart as soft music plays in the background. He waves to the group of men scared off earlier but they ignore him and continue to talk amongst themselves. *So much for making friends.*

He shrugs then walks over to the cart and dishes himself a plate of meat, potatoes and some vegetables. To minimize disturbing them, he sits near the entrance to eat. Halfway through his meal Reckston emerges from an adjacent tunnel then abruptly leaves.

Realizing the negative feelings between them could get worse; Hopper decides not to heed Camille's warning. He stands and approaches the three men and gets directions from one of them named Ethan. Moments later, he is traveling down unfamiliar tunnels to the makeshift door of Reckston's room.

Knocking produces no response. Hopper turns to leave when the door slowly creaks open, he peeks inside expecting to see Reckston.

Suddenly, Hopper is slammed face first against the hard rock wall of the cave, his right arm pinned painfully behind his back. He struggles to break free but stops as Reckston's bitter voice enters his mind.

Find anything interesting in there traitor? You've come here to make amends and this is how you show it? You are an ignorant fool! Nothing you can say that will make a difference to me. If it wasn't for the injured woman's love for you, I would've let you die with the rest of your squad!

Hopper realizes the man's anger is beyond reasoning as he tries to turn his head. Reckston pushes him even harder against the wall and continues venomously.

You want to see beyond reasoning? I can read your mind as easily as if it were my own. You're thinking now I should try to see it from your point of view. Reckston grits his teeth. *You've come to the wrong place, looking for forgiveness. You destroyed my people and all they have tried to achieve. Only time will tell if I retrieved all the equipment necessary to continue their work. If not, the blood of the human race is on your hands.*

Reckston releases Hopper's arm then spins him around then stares at him with intense, blue-flecked eyes.

You and I come from two different worlds. I suggest you keep it that way. Now leave before I change my mind about saving your miserable life! Reckston releases him then enters his room, slamming the door shut behind him.

Shaken, Hopper massages his shoulder, contemplating what the man just said. He carefully forms words in his mind.

Yes Reckston, you have every right to hate me. Have no doubt I'll stay out of your way, but I'm not going to take full responsibility for the extinction of the human race. You forget that your people created this situation in the first place. If you want to place blame for what happened in the Zone, I think we're both guilty.

Hopper slowly turns around and walks back to community quarters trying to shield his thoughts from the man from the future.

RITAN

8/14/2036

Located in the first aid center of Shadow Base, an octagonal tube displaying a dark oval shape inside, rests on an empty wooden crate standing on end. Lights on both sides flash before it emits a beam of light and scans an injured woman lying on a makeshift bed.

Ritan is relieved to see the young woman's condition stabilizing. Being able to scan for vitals still amazes her. Her second life as a Cry-Comm has given her even more abilities than when she had a complete physical body. Along with retaining her extraordinary telepathic abilities, she now can access computers, networks, scan items and compute large amounts of data. Under the right conditions, she could even live in her extruded crystal housing for over a century. However, memories of running and playing freely with classmates in the holy garden made her wish she could return deep underground to those carefree days.

Ritan's thoughts turn negative when that all ended once the elders arrived on her thirteenth birthday. After a sacred ceremony, they took away her ability to move after integrating her body into the silos to become part of the BTC worldwide network. Even worse, when she turned eighteen they artificially inseminated her and forced her to conceive a child.

Ritan's emotions flare remembering that painful moment when labor began…the day they removed her mind from her body. Soon after regaining consciousness, they told her she had suffered a massive heart attack. To preserve her valuable mind, the elders transformed her into a Cryostasis Communicator, in other words, a Cry-Comm so she could participate in the upcoming jump to the past. Although she resented them at the time, she is now grateful. She may never have met Reckston otherwise. However, his anger over the destruction of the BTC made it difficult for her to communicate with him. It took several requests just to persuade him to allow her to stay with this woman during her recovery. It excited her to know she will meet someone from this age who has a telepathic gift.

While relaying messages for the Shadow Team and offering advice to O'Connell on how to access the holographic disks in the lab, Ritan decides to probe the woman's mind only to discover a weak but sophisticated psychogenetic pulse emanating from a silver medallion around her neck. *What is this?* Curious, she focuses her attention on the medallion's center. Slowly it grows within her mind until she finds her own naked spirit body standing on a deep-blue platform surrounded by four large floating spheres.

Ritan's slender, elegant spirit body glistens as the spheres change color and float about. *How incredibly beautiful! Even our own scientists were a few years away from perfecting something like this. I bet its monitoring your mind waiting for you to attain certain levels of telepathic awareness. Maybe even release messages or skills of some sort. Who are you?* Unable to quench her desire to know more, she fully opens her mind but the spheres colors immediately fade. She realizes there must be some kind of psychic lock to keep intruders from accessing it. Disappointed, she touches one of the spheres and Reckston's weeping face appear inside.

Overwhelmed by the implications, her spirit body stumbles back. *How is this possible? What does this mean?*

Driven to know the truth, Ritan wills herself forward. Her spirit arm trembles as she reaches out and touches the sphere to see Reckston's face once more. In a leap of intuition, Ritan realizes Dell's true identity. *Heaven above, have mercy on this woman's lost soul! How could she be a stranger to her own father? Something must have gone terribly wrong in the future.*

Ritan focuses her mind on Reckston's face and is able to arrange the other spheres into different combinations but is still not able to gain access to the device. The effort to keep the medallion energized causes her spirit body to react as if it was real. Her breathing intensifies and sweat forms on her skin. With her frustration continuing to grow, the spheres lose color and float about randomly. She contemplates a moment then smiles realizing Reckston's face is the key. Remembering her studies in cryptography when she was younger, she realizes the lock could be part of a three-dimensional puzzle. *Of course! Like a pyramid...one to center, three to complete.*

Her arms move gracefully as she wills three of the four spheres into a triangle around her and then positions the one with Reckston's face directly overhead. As she completes the task, the spheres pulsate as one. *Yes. Yes! Next will be to discover the most traumatic events in this woman's life to unlock the medallion.* Excitement energizes her mind as she begins to move rhythmically to the pulsating light. Her mystic dance becomes one constant beautiful motion as images of Dell's early life flash around her.

An intense feeling of abandonment overwhelms her senses as she sees a bald little girl bravely looking out a window at a multi-ringed space station floating over a rusty brown, cloud-covered planet with a moon rising on the horizon. Ritan controls her feelings as she passes her spirit hand over one of the spheres. It ceases to pulsate as the image of the space station freezes inside.

She continues to view Dell's life in fast-forward one scene after another. Suddenly, the images slow to show a terrified little girl wandering aimlessly in a bizarre city, frantically calling out for her mother. The next scene is of a kind-hearted man with open arms and a little girl with short brown hair running to meet him. The images speed up again and span several years into the future. They finally slow again to show her as a sobbing teenager lying facedown on a barren plain. Ritan struggles to retain the link as Dell's young spirit floats from her body to search for her father with a broken leg. Ritan's hand trembles as she passes it over one of the remaining two spheres. Another ceases to pulsate leaving the image of Dell's agonized spirit body frozen inside.

Ritan has little time to recover and isn't prepared for what comes next. Out of the swirling chaotic images, Dell's adult spirit body materializes over a severely injured man in a blasted desert environment to touch his forehead. Dell's spirit reacts as if struck by lightning as their auras merge. Ritan immediately recognizes him as the man Reckston just rescued in the Zone. As the scene continues to unfold, an intense feeling of love blossoms within her and grow until it saturates her mind, body and soul. She realizes everything in Dell's life just paled in comparison. Without his love, her will to live will cease to exist. Ritan weeps as she puts both hands over the last remaining sphere, freezing the image of Hopper's battered body inside.

Ritan's spirit body slowly rises off the medallion until her head immerses in the sphere above and comes face-to-face with Reckston kneeling next to her with tears in his eyes. She looks around to discover herself inside the Arcadian Space Station. In the background, floating bioluminescent spheres of light illuminate the main navigation room. It is mostly quiet except for the low-level hum of the ship's massive gyroscopic outer rings.

Near a huge transparent window, a beautiful but distraught bald headed woman wearing a blue jumpsuit looks out into deep space. Her body trembles as she looks over to her then holds a silver medallion with a blue center tightly to her chest. Ritan focuses her attention back on Reckston as he begins to speak.

Eva, my precious child...or should I call you Dell? I don't know where to begin, but you know me as Reckston. I am your biological father. He gestures toward the woman behind him. *This is your mother Anna who has abilities even greater than Ritan. I see you have inherited much of her skills already. If you ever get this message, you will have finally reached your full telepathic potential.*

I'm sorry I didn't realize you were my daughter until I returned to the future. I don't have much time to explain all the things you would like to know but I'll try my best. The antichamber worked far better than expected, sustaining very little damage. However, I arrived two years later than expected and was devastated to find the BTC facility abandoned. I was finally able to phase to a hellhole called Mech. City. It was the last place where you, your mother, and I briefly lived. I desperately searched that empty city for days. The pain of never seeing you again was almost too much to bear. If it wasn't for Ritan, I would never have discovered you both living with others on a space station called Arcadia. They now just call it "The Ark," and it's heading toward Mars. This ship carries with it the last remnants of life on earth in hopes of creating a new living environment in a cave deep underground.

After fixing a defective Dynalink Converter, I was then able to phase directly to the station. It was a joyous moment for all of us to be together again but it was short lived. Even before I arrived, the fabric of time was already starting to unravel. When the antichamber deflected the third transport center, I skipped like a stone on water ahead of the changes.

In order to survive the new approaching timeline, we must outfit the Arc for a shift into subspace before the time wave arrives in about fifty-two hours. If we fail...we will cease to exist as history rewrites itself. Even now, spatial shockwaves are buffeting the ship. After some discussion with the crew, we decided to use the antichamber to allow one person to escape to the past. You, my much-loved Eva, was chosen because of your size, age and for having the least exposure to the destructive effects of Radiantnine.

Modifications to the antichamber for a return trip should be minimal but it pains us greatly to see you go. Ritan will guide you on your journey and phase you out of the time stream around the year 2008. I try not to think about what will happen to her after the antichamber's fuel cells run out.

Reckston lowers his head. *We will forever be grateful to her for volunteering to save your life.* He pauses then looks up. *Something must have gone wrong with your medallion or your telepathic development. Even with your untrained mind, you should have received this message long before the Zone appeared. We hope someday you may still discover the medallion's secrets. For now though, knowing you made it back safe and grew up to become a beautiful, talented woman comforts us all. Dell, you are our last hope and dream. If we fail the transition, you will be the last remaining survivor of our time.*

Reckston gestures Anna to move closer. They embrace each other as he continues with confidence rising in his voice. *The year is 2212, and if everything goes according to plan, we will arrive in the new timeline and return to earth. I know this message is short but we must help prepare the ship for the jump. Remember this my child, your mother and I love you very, very much.*

Anna gets down on her knees and looks deep into her little girl's eyes then hugs her tightly. *Little Eva, do not fear the path you take today. Try to live your life to the fullest and believe...truly believe that one day we will all be together again in mind, body and soul.* Tears stream down Anna's face as she kisses the medallion then gently presses it to Eva's forehead causing the message to abruptly end.

Ritan disengages her mind from the medallion emotionally distraught by the scenes she witnessed and of her own possibly demise. She focuses her full attention on Dell. *Until now, we have never met but we are somehow destined to participate in events beyond our control. Please forgive me for what I must do. For now, I cannot allow you to gain access to the medallion's secrets or the critical chain of events leading to this moment may never occur. I must also keep Reckston from knowing he is your father otherwise, it may interfere with his decision to deflect the third transport center and send you back in time. However, I promise you this...I'll do everything I can to help you now and in the future.*

Ritan accesses the medallion once more and changes the trigger sequence so Dell will receive the message it contains automatically after Reckston and herself return to the future—and the next time Dell is intimate with a man. She also configures the medallion so it will temporarily shut off and appear to be nothing more than costume jewelry to Reckston if he tries to access it.

After a brief rest, Ritan delves even deeper into Dell's mind to locate the damaged neural pathways preventing her from waking and re-directs them to healthy nerve endings. In the process, she realizes the traumatic event blocking Dell's childhood memories. It's the one where a frightened little girl is wandering aimlessly in a bizarre city crying out to strangers. Ritan fades the memory from her mind allowing Dell to reach her full telepathic potential when the medallion reveals its many secrets.

Satisfied for now, Ritan leaves Dell's mind with one last parting thought. *Sleep peacefully precious one, now that the time for fulfillment will soon be upon you.*

FRIENDS

8/17/2036

Dell stretches then opens her eyes to see a fuzzy white-domed ceiling overhead. She gazes at it without thought. Finally, her pupils begin to focus and wonders where she is. Confused, she carefully sits up to find herself on padded wooden crates with a makeshift door at the entrance. On a table next to her is a clear, octagon device with a dark oval shape inside and metal end caps that blink. Intrigued, she reaches out to touch it when a woman's voice enters her mind.

Don't be afraid. What you see is a Cry-Comm, a Cryostasis Communicator. From this device comes the voice you hear.

As the woman speaks, Dell feels a familiar cold sensation, the kind she felt many times inside the Zone. Strangely, she has no fear and even relaxes a bit as she projects her thoughts. *So you can communicate telepathically with me. Whom may I ask is speaking?*

The lights on the container blink rapidly as the voice enters her mind once more. *My name is Ritan...I come from the future.*

The answer takes Dell by surprise. *OK...pleased to meet you Ritan. Now, would you mind telling me where I am and how I got here?*

Information passes quickly and silently between the two as Ritan updates her on their location, the purpose of Shadow Base, some things about the future, and even of herself. The next couple of hours pass quickly as Dell learns a great deal and receives answers to many of her questions. Out of all the information though, she is shocked most about Ritan being born for the sole purpose of becoming part of the BTC and then to be turned into a Cry-Comm. However, they have to put their conversation on hold as a woman wearing light blue scrubs enters and introduces herself.

"Wow! I am amazed to see you sitting up and responsive already. Oh I'm sorry, my name is Faith and I'm the one taking care of you." She puts a caring hand on Dell's shoulder. "I was so worried about you. How are you feeling?"

Dell puts a hand on her thigh. "My leg is starting to hurt but other than that, I'm fine. I want to thank you for everything you've done so far. Ritan told me you spent a lot of time cleaning wounds and patching me up."

Faiths nods then reaches out and touches the blinking device sitting on top of a wooden crate. "It's my pleasure, I'm glad you two had a chance to talk. I figured you would have a lot of questions, Ritan here is the perfect person to catch you up to speed." Faith removes a penlight from her coat and shines it into Dell's eyes one at a time. "Do you have a headache or feel any nausea?"

Dell shakes her head.

"Well, your pupils seem fine. My goodness, you're recuperating faster than I thought possible. I wish all my patients were like you. Let me get some pain medicine for you now. When I return, I'll also inspect your dressings OK?" She smiles then turns and leaves mystified how a person with such a serious trauma could recover so quickly.

Hopper arrives a short time later and quietly opens the door to see Dell sitting on padded crates staring at an octagon device near her head. He knocks to get her attention then enters and gently takes her hand.

Dell grins as she hugs him tightly. When she finally lets go, she points to the device. "I know this may sound strange but I want to introduce you to Ritan. She's from the future and has incredible telepathic powers and other interesting abilities."

Curious, Hopper leans down to examine the device then notices the egg shaped matter inside. "So you are Ritan. I wondered who informed me of Dell's recovery. Are you a computer or human in nature?"

The lights on her container blink rapidly as Ritan laughs in their minds. *Both, I was born human but when my heart failed, they kept parts of my brain alive and integrated it with a computer to assist in emergencies. And yes, you could say this is an emergency.*

Hopper takes a step backward.

I know you're uncomfortable with me reading your mind but have nothing to fear. I hold no resentment against you for the destruction of the BTC. In fact, I hope we can all be friends.

Hopper's guilt rises as he looks at Dell then back at Ritan's container. "Friends? Maybe if you and Reckston stop reading my mind."

Dell glances at the device then smiles at Hopper. "Ritan says that information is highly classified but told me how you can block your thoughts. Consider it a gesture of goodwill and trust between us. However, I'll share it with you later. For now, let's try to get to know Ritan first. OK? Please?"

Hopper finally nods but their conversation is short lived when Faith returns with medicine and new dressings. He realizes he needs to leave then awkwardly hugs Dell. "Take care of yourself." He stands up and addresses Ritan and Faith. "Thank you for helping her. I don't know what I'd do without her." His expression changes from gratitude to affection as he looks at Dell. "Please let me know when you need anything or want some company." He reaches out and squeezes her shoulder then leaves trying hard to shield his thoughts and emotions.

8/31/2036

Two weeks later, Faith releases Dell from the med center after her thigh has healed enough to walk. Despite her recovery, Dell has to lean on Hopper as they make their way to community quarters. During a short rest period, she explains some interesting facts she just learned.

"When I asked Ritan why our NV9s weren't able to sense some of their vehicles they call Crawlers, she explained that occasionally their power grid cannot keep all their vehicles running efficiently in a null state. I believe this null state has something to do with time shifting. Anyway, it's what makes them invisible. When they switch their Crawlers over to internal fuel cells, it reduces their field strength making it even harder for our NV9s to pick them up. It also makes them more susceptible to destabilization, especially during storms. Most of the Crawlers running in this reduced state are controlled remotely by the BTC or have an active Cry-Comm unit on board."

Hopper nods, grateful to understand. "Ah, I was wondering about that, thank you. Did she say anything about their activities where the Cavern City Airport should be?"

Dell nods, "After reading my mind to understand the question, she said their scientists discovered a dimensional vortex in that vicinity generated by Radiantnine interacting directly with a massive subspace distortion bubble. They never encountered anything like it before but were unwilling to investigate further. Only after the most talented telepath at BTC said she heard the screams of thousands of lost souls on the other side did they start pulling resources from the field. Their scientists were finally on the verge of sending in a probe to discover what was on the other side when we detonated Thumper—" Dell looks at Hopper then stops abruptly and lowers her eyes. After a long pause, she continues in a subdued voice. "Ritan figures it's some sort of psychic echo of the citizens of Carlsbad when they died. We'll probably never know…"

Hopper leans against the cave wall and takes a couple of deep breaths trying not to think about the massive amount of lives lost since the Zone first appeared. To change the subject he asks Dell another question. "Is this Radiantnine Effect harmful to us?"

"I'm afraid so. Their whole reason for going back in time was to stop the spread of it. In the future, it will kill virtually every living thing on the planet. They were only able to survive this long deep underground or in a space station in high orbit. When I asked her about the space station she seemed reluctant to say anything about it but I'm sure she had her reasons." Dell feels Hopper's unease growing then decides to cheer him up. "Hey! Do you still want to prevent certain people from reading your mind?"

Hopper looks up visibly relieved at the change of subject. "Yes! I thought you were withholding that information to punish me for some reason."

Dell laughs. "No, not at all. Ritan said that if you take certain mineral supplements in high enough doses they'll shield your thoughts from mind probes but won't prevent messages like the ones I can send." She looks up and down the passageway then whispers the secret in his ear. His eyes widen with surprise then looks at her questioningly.

"Really? I wouldn't have suspected that. I promise not to tell anyone. If it works, I'll take up Ritan's offer of friendship." Hopper immediately makes a plan to revisit the med center later that day.

As they resume their walk through the poorly lit tunnels, their conversation shifts to how they might contribute as new members of Shadow Team.

Sanctuary
11/30/2036

Dell sits on the newly finished bridge in the sanctuary. Her legs dangle over the edge with toes touching the water. Bright patches of blue luminescing moss covers the cave walls giving her the feeling of being under the stars at night. She is glad Hopper let her design the place to her liking. For the first time in her life, she finally feels at home.

With Ritan's help, she was able to recreate a chemical used in the future to accelerate plant growth and at the same time produce light. At the end of the plant's life cycle, it will emit a gas that can condense into spheres and glow for weeks. Dell smiles at the thought but it slowly turns into a frown as she contemplates the difficulties she and Hopper had to endure over the last three months. Every member of the Shadow Team has a purpose for being there. When they first arrived, they seemed to get in everyone's way. It wasn't until Ritan suggested they complete the sanctuary did they finally find their calling.

Working with Hopper however, has been challenging due to his ups and downs. His painful memories and guilty conscious constantly brings him close to the edge. Time after time, she has had to support him through those difficult periods. Only recently has he recovered enough to smile again. It pains her to know that even now he continues to fight his feelings for her because of Eileen.

Frustrated, she stands and crosses the bridge to approach a large ring of beautiful glowing flowers. A meter-wide path of white crushed limestone leads through its center to where a young sapling tree sits on a mound of topsoil. Surrounding it are large flagstones followed by another ring of flowers.

Her smile returns. It seems fitting to have their own tree of life after Reckston told her earlier they lost the ability to grow trees. Asked what tree he would like to see planted here, he immediately replied an apple tree because it is symbolic of the interconnection of all life on the planet.

Happy, she turns to go back to the community quarters when she feels Reckston's presence enter her mind. She looks up to see him approaching from the other side of the bridge.

I hope I'm not intruding but I wanted to talk to you alone in this place. Is that all right?

A wave of sadness and loneliness emanates from Reckston. She holds the medallion close to her chest and nods. He crosses the bridge to stand next to her then looks around. His gaze draws towards the young sapling tree growing on a mound of topsoil. *This place is more beautiful than I imagined and is oddly similar to one we had in the future. Cave gardens like this are holy places where people would come to give thanks and remember what the world use to be like. As far as I know, in 2209 there's not a single plant or animal living on the surface of the earth.* He sees Dell clutching the silver medallion around her neck and points to it. *This must mean a lot to you. Can I see it?*

She looks down then hesitantly takes it off and hands it to him. "I'm told I've had this since I was little. I believe my parents gave it to me but due to some sort of childhood trauma, I cannot remember. For some reason though, I really cherish it."

Reckston examines the worn medallion then runs a finger over the blue disk at its center. He pauses for a moment as he loses his train of thought. He chokes up as he hands it back. *It's very beautiful and unique. My wife Anna would have liked it very much.*

He shuffles his feet before continuing. *I wanted to share something with you ever since I first read your mind while you were lying injured on the cave floor. I felt how deep your love for Captain Phillips was, so much so, I knew you would have die if he died. To be honest, I couldn't allow that to happen. Something prevented me from doing anything to harm you even indirectly. I guess what I'm trying to say is, I understand your unconditional love, because I feel the same way towards my wife and daughter.*

The BTC wouldn't allow them to return to the past after I freed Anna from the silos. When she became pregnant, she wanted our child to live a normal life. After our daughter was born, we became outcasts and had to survive on our own for a couple of years. It was a very tough time for all of us. As the transport center neared completion, they forced me to join the team to go back due to drastic personnel shortages. However, the BTC deemed my wife, daughter and a few others undesirable and left them behind to run the spatial generators. Now that were building the antichamber, I have a second chance to be with them. Life is so precious— He stops, unable to go on.

Dell feels Reckston's pain as if it were her own. She reaches out and holds his hand tightly as they console each other. She leans back to look into his watering eyes. "Reckston, you're an honorable man. You did all you could under the circumstances. I know you miss your family. So for now, consider me part of it till you get back, OK?" She wipes a tear from his face as he nods and smiles. "Good, when you want to talk to me, let's meet here in sanctuary."

Because of Ritan's plant treatments, the vegetation grows quickly and seeds. The little sapling soon becomes a vibrant young apple tree with glowing leaves and branches. The scent of flowers and blossoms is soothing as orbs of light eventually form and drift slowly around the cavern. Dell and Reckston meet in the sanctuary often as their friendship continues to grow and deepen.

Over time, Hopper and Dell find themselves valuable members of the Shadow Team fixing all kind of things, building items, or phasing to different parts of the world to scavenge much-needed materials and items for the construction of the antichamber. For Hopper, it is a time of recovery. Each passing day he is one-step closer to becoming his old self again. For Dell, she fully recovers from her injuries and for the first time in her life feels truly happy tending the sanctuary and being with the man she loves.

GENERAL PLANNING

4/28/2037

The Shadow Team chats noisily in the community quarters around a table made out of wooden crates hastily pushed together. As O'Connell arrives, she nods in Reckston's direction. The room quiets as he uses his telepathic abilities to get everyone's attention.

Thank you all for being here today. Without your help, the completion of the antichamber would never have been possible. He smiles at O'Connell, Dell, and the team but his face flushes angrily as he squints at Hopper in the back of the room. Even now, he struggles with his feelings toward the man and has to lower his eyes to clear his mind. He continues after a brief pause. *We have gathered here this morning to brainstorm how to integrate Command's equipment with our own. With that said, the floor is open for comments.*

O'Connell goes first and addresses Reckston. "I want to thank you and Ritan for trusting in us. Only by your guidance and the knowledge gleaned from the devices and data chips recovered during the raid on the BTC, we were also able to create the subspace radar needed to resolve most of the trajectory angles and timing issues. Humanity now has a chance for a brighter future."

The room fills with applause, as it subsides she turns to address the other members of her team. "We've worked hard over the past fourteen and a half months to prepare the antichamber to intercept and deflect the incoming BTC transport center to the extreme past, possibly millions of years. However, our work may still be in vain.

The lab's phasing platform is too weak and our computers are too limited. We either need to figure out a way to take over Command or to find a way to operate their equipment remotely. So today, everyone needs to think outside the box to help us overcome this one last hurdle!"

The room becomes quiet. After a few moments, Hopper clears his throat as if to speak then hesitates as Reckston glares at him.

Unable to read the traitor's mind any longer, Reckston decides to send him a message. *As you know, we are running out of time and options here. Even though I hate what you've done, the fate of the future is still unknown. Your comments may help so let us both set aside our feelings for today. Please, speak your mind.*

Hopper nods and walks through the crowd to the front of the room. He keeps his eyes lowered then turns to address them. "I want to thank all of you for making me feel part of the team and want to help where I can. I've been thinking that the best solution is to have someone else take over Command for us. If we can get that person to activate the nuclear arsenal at Fort Bliss, I believe we should be able to gain complete access to their equipment through a little-known emergency backup system. But we'll need somebody to give the required orders to initiate the process, and I have just the person in mind."

He stops as several people begin to ask questions. Intrigued, O'Connell raises her arms to quiet them down. Hopper looks around the room then continues with confidence. "There is one man who has the power to accomplish all our goals. If we can use the right kind of persuasion, I'm sure he would be more than happy to create the security breach. But this feat will take in-depth research, prior planning, some fancy equipment, and most of all...Ritan's help."

All of them are on the edge of their seats. Finally, Camille asks the question on everyone's mind. "I can't stand the suspense. Who is this person you speak of?"

Hopper grins. "None other than…General Pierce himself!"

GENERAL PERSUASION

5/13/2037

Two High Guards snap to attention and salute Pierce as he passes them on an exposed upper balcony walkway. He normally enjoys their obedience especially after a long day of dealing with incompetent staff but tonight his mind is on other pressing matters. Standing just outside his quarters, he takes a moment to peer down into the garden district. Green light reflects off his face as he contemplates his grip on reality. *I really must be losing it. How could I've seen Captain Phillips appear and vanish earlier today? He's dead; I made sure of it this time.*

Baffled, the General shakes his head and enters his plush living quarters. "Computer! Option five. Connect to level ten, lab twenty-eight." He walks over to a display terminal as McCloud's face appears on the screen.

"McCloud here."

"Are all quark phasing bands accounted for?"

McCloud looks off screen then back at the General. "Yes sir. All are out of commission except the one you're wearing."

Pierce looks at the phasing band on his wrist. "Have any been used for testing lately?"

McCloud shakes his head. "Is there a problem I should be aware of?"

Pierce grunts. "No, not at the moment. Pierce out." The display turns off as he takes a cigar and lighter from his front pocket but his hands shake too much to light it. Frustrated, he tosses them on a coffee table then removes a shiny tin from his pocket and takes out a couple of tablets. He walks into the kitchen and pours himself a glass of vodka. Without a second thought, he pops them into his mouth and washes them down. A moment later he leans against the counter as his mind suddenly gets icy cold and his eyes go out of focus.

"Whoa! Dr. Matthews, your pills seem to be getting stronger lately."

He shakes his head as he carries the glass to the living room and puts it on a coffee table. He sits down and relaxes on the couch as he feels drowsiness come over him. In minutes, he drifts off to sleep but the sound of breaking glass startles him awake. Through blurry eyes, he looks around.

A shiver runs down his back as he sees the glass shattered in front of him. He fumbles for a pistol on his belt and pulls it out. "Who's there?" He slowly rises to keep his balance then inspects a security panel on the wall to find everything secure. Perplexed, he lowers his weapon and returns to the living room just as Hopper's voice enters his mind. *You've been a very bad boy lately Shadley Pierce. Or should I say Shady, as your old schoolmates use to call you?*

Sweat beads on Pierce's face as he frantically swings his gun around looking for a target.

Without warning, the gun flies across the room and hits the wall. *Tonight, I'm going to be your worst nightmare. I'm angry that you had my phasing band switched right before the Hail Mary 2 Mission was about to begin. You made it so we couldn't have escaped after activating Thumper. I'm glad I've kept you awake at night wondering how I got all the glory and you didn't. Do you really think you deserve respect for doing things like that?*

Pierce stutters as he tries to catch his breath. "I...d-demand... you show yourself, now!" He lunges toward the security panel but an intense electrical shock jolts him causing him to fall to the floor and twitch. Saliva drips from his mouth as he tries to sit up and fails.

His gaze darts wildly around the room then puts his hands to his ears as if trying to rid the voice from his mind. "You can't be Captain Phillips. You're dead! There's no possible way you could be alive. Now, get out of my mind!"

What would your peers think if they knew you gained rank and authority by killing thousands of innocent people by destroying and poisoning food supplies during the Famine War? Or the way you murdered government officials and imprisoned some of your own troops to keep it a secret? You're a pathetic individual. Even your mother thought you were too egotistical for your own good.

Pierce rolls over panting. "How do you know these things? What is it you want?"

The voice intensifies in his mind as he receives his answer. *What else Shadley? I'm here to help you redeem yourself for your sins.*

Pierce's anger rises as he mouths the word *redeem* to himself. "I don't know who you are or how you're doing this but I can't believe you're a ghost. It doesn't matter anyway. Your fun is over." He leers at the empty room then activates the phasing band around his wrist.

The living room vanishes around Pierce only to find himself tumbling wildly out of control through an infinite sea of darkness. Freezing wind roars past him as he screams in terror. Pierce focuses on Hopper's voice to keep from losing consciousness.

Since you're not afraid of hell Shadley, I'm going to take you there now. There's no escaping it except through me. This is the other side of reality where the future and past are one. Where a mere second can last an eternity. Have you ever wondered if there's a devil? Prepare to meet your doom. Hopper's voice pauses.

In the dark depths, two glowing red orbs appear below Pierce's feet and grow larger and brighter by the second. In sheer terror, Pierce screams and struggles to get away. When Hopper finally speaks, it's from a very great distance.

I'm leaving you here now Shadley. This place will forever be your reality from now until eternity unless…you are willing to pay a price for your sins. However, the cost for your redemption is high. Are you willing to pay its price?

Terrified of dying, Pierce savagely fights to stay conscious and struggles to form his words. "Yes. What…must I do? Save…me!"

General Reality
5/14/2037

Pierce suddenly finds himself lying on the floor of his living room staring at two red lights on the security panel. When he sits up the room flows and distorts around him as if submerged in a pool of water. Hopper's voice is distant and muffled as it enters his mind once more. *Dreams can lead to your heart's desire or to your worst nightmare. However, the path to your redemption rests in both.*

Pierce's phasing band chimes on his arm. He looks down to see Colonel Barland on the display.

Barland answers hesitantly, "Ah…Good morning, sir. How can I be of service?"

Hopper's voice fills Pierce's thoughts. *Believing in one's dreams is the path to true happiness.* Overwhelmed by pleasure, Pierce grins as his plan for world peace comes to mind. He is unable to resist his desires any longer. His voice slurs as he speaks to the Colonel. "Barland, I am ordering you to initiate Peace Around the World tonight. Have all High Guards on duty assemble in the garden district ASAP. I will meet them there shortly. You know the plan. Use protocol Alpha Alpha One as the initial cover."

Barland's eyebrows furl. "Sir, we're not prepared for that yet. Most of the phasing bands won't be ready for another year or so. Some key personnel are still not in place and—" He looks off screen then back. "We still need the two fifteen-digit keys to activate the nuclear arsenal."

The security panel on the wall begins to hum and glow brightly as if on cue. Puzzled, Pierce stands up and stumbles over to see the two fifteen digit codes flashing on the screen. Pierce gives Barland an evil grin. "Looks like that's just been taken care of. Now, I don't want to hear any more excuses! Just do as I say!"

An unnatural excitement bordering on ecstasy overwhelms his thoughts as he brings up a flashing red screen on the terminal. He transfers the numbers over into the two spaces provided then presses his thumb against the display. With his plan finally set in motion, he gives Barland an evil grin as he anticipates his dream of world peace will soon be reality.

The late night staff in the Command Center are startled when a half dozen armed High Guards burst into the room. Seconds later, General Pierce confidently walks in with a crazed look on his face.

The voice says all I have to do is follow my dream to get what I deserve. Well, I'm going to do just that. Tonight, with the power of a nuclear arsenal behind me, I'll do the world a favor and show everyone how to accomplish peace through fear, fire and force!"

Deep in the recess of his mind, Pierce sees the things he must do to make it happen and begins to instruct station operators how to manipulate their computers in ways they never thought possible. To watch them do his bidding delights him even more. He looks at his phasing band. *Even computers are following my orders. It's as if they are reading my mind.* With the room flowing and distorting, the voice in his head continues to whisper instructions as his dream of Peace Around the World unfolds around him.

HAMRICK'S SURPRISE

5/14/2037

From his elevated office, General Hamrick sips coffee as he casually watches over station operators down in the Command Center. Lately, he's been enjoying the night shift mostly in part of not having to deal with Pierce. The man's antic behavior has really been getting on his nerves.

He shakes his head. *Honestly, am I the only one to see he's out of control?*

As if on cue, General Pierce and a dozen or so High Guards enter the room below and dismiss some of the operators. Hamrick almost drops his coffee cup wondering what Pierce could be doing at this hour. He turns to find out when his computer terminal starts flashing red text. "Attention! Operation Alpha Alpha One now in progress!"

Hamrick's blood pressure quickly rises as he sits down and verifies its authenticity. "Holy smokes! You're activating Fort Bliss' entire nuclear arsenal for a preemptive strike?"

He looks around in horror then notices all is quiet. He scratches his head wondering why there are no alarms or audio alerts going off. He quickly scans some supplemental info and finds several protocol discrepancies. Perplexed, he heads for the stairs when several High Guards enter and block the exit. Fear trickles down his spine as he recognizes one of them as Pierce's number-one man...Colonel Barland.

The Colonel taps the pistol on his waist impatiently then motions Hamrick back to the center of the room. "Sir, I've been ordered to detain you here for your safety while this operation gets underway." Confused, Hamrick nods as they both walk over to the observation window to watch events unfold in Command.

In stunned silence, Hamrick watches as Pierce gives strange orders to his High Guards and station operators alike. With each passing moment, more and more computer terminals cease to respond. Suddenly, the lights flicker as a ball of green energy forms over a large phasing platform in the back of the room. It takes only seconds to intensify in size and strength then pulsates with a life of its own.

Without warning, the massive energy ball becomes translucent and disappears leaving a vacuum in its place. As air rushes in to fill the void, it causes a powerful shockwave that emanates throughout Command sending station operators sprawling to the floor. The observation window in front of Hamrick and Barland cracks but withstands the impact. Seconds later, a powerful earthquake rocks the entire underground facility plunging the whole facility into darkness. Several minutes pass before the lights come back on to expose a chaotic scene down below.

Hamrick slowly gets to his feet and shakes his head trying to stop the ringing in his ears. He is speechless as he pushes Barland aside then carefully descends the stairs to enter the destroyed Command Center. Within a minute, post security arrives as General Hamrick orders Pierce to explain himself or be arrested.

Pierce wearily stands but says nothing as he looks around in bewilderment wondering how the place got that way. The High Guards in the room immediately form a defensive circle around him, guns locked and loaded, ready for all-out carnage.

Pierce clenches his fists in rage as he finally realizes what he was experiencing was not a dream. He opens his mouth to speak then suddenly slumps to the floor unconscious. Confused about what to do next, the High Guards lower their weapons and surrender without a fight.

Hamrick has them all arrested and taken to a maximum-security cell for questioning.

ANTICHAMBER

5/14/2037

With Ritan and the antichamber successfully phased into null state, Reckston paces on the Dynalink Converter waiting for the computers to recalibrate for his size and weight. He decides to use the time to say a few last-minute good-byes to O'Connell, Camille, Dell, and fellow scientists. He concentrates his thoughts to all.

Your dedication to save our world honors me. He gestures towards O'Connell. *Thank you for outfitting the antichamber with special shielding and equipment. I know you've done everything possible to insure I reach the future safely.*

O'Connell smiles. "You should thank Ritan. She was adamant about it. Some of the circuit boards we created...Well, I'm not even sure what they do." She shrugs and waves a last farewell. "May you live a long and happy life my friend." She winks then looks over Camille's shoulder to double check some settings.

Dell locks eyes with Reckston and decides to relay one final message. *Hopper wanted me to tell you he was sorry for destroying the BTC.*

Reckston's expression softens then sends her a message in return. *Tell him I forgave him the moment he came up with the solution for us to take Command over. It made this jump possible. As for you Dell, I will never forget you. You will always be part of my family. My wife Anna believes someday we will all be together in mind, body and soul.*

For some reason I believe the same goes for you and me. A sad smile forms on his face as he puts his hand across his heart then disappears from the platform.

Fighting feelings of abandonment, Dell clutches the medallion to her chest then slowly walks from the lab trying to understand why Reckston affected her so.

O'Connell paces nervously around the lab as she waits for news on events happening in Command. She jumps as Ritan's voice enters her mind. *Sorry to startle you, but I'm happy to say General Pierce performed all his tasks better than expected. You can now proceed to phase two and use the emergency backup system. Thank you Kathleen for helping us get this far. May you continue to make a difference in people's lives and know in your heart, you've done everything possible to give the world a future to look forward too. You must hurry now... the window of opportunity is closing. Good luck my friend, Ritan out.*

O'Connell is sad to see her go but knows she must pilot the antichamber to adjust for minute variances to the trajectory angle in real time. She anxiously turns to address the Shadow Team, "We've been given the all clear. It's time to send the antichamber on its way."

The assembled men and women in the room begin activating programs to auto engage computer terminals at Fort Bliss while others prepare for the energy buildup on the platforms in both locations. O'Connell walks over to the subspace radar console to center the ping of the antichamber on its display then raises her voice to get everyone's attention. "OK, when you complete your tasks notify me when you're ready to proceed to phase three!" One by one, she receives an answer from everyone then nods to Camille squatting nervously next to a device looking like a flattened beehive with a scorpion's tail. She hesitantly turns the spatial generator on. Instantly a green mist appears and sparkles on the lab's Dynalink Converter. A low-level rumble vibrates the air and slowly changes in frequency to an ear-splitting howl. O'Connell verifies the results on a display then flips a switch to synchronize the phasing platform at the Command Center and the one in the lab.

In seconds a huge ball of green energy engulfs the lab's Dynalink Converter causing the room to distort as it emits bands of light. As the energy reaches its apex, it suddenly turns translucent exposing the faint outline of the antichamber inside. A glittering black vortex surrounds it and begins to suck air out of the lab. For an instant, time stands still as a final band of light slows to a stop and intensifies. In the blink of an eye, it quickly reverses direction and disappears inside the vortex devouring the green energy and the antichamber. A powerful shockwave surges in and out of the lab then radiates throughout the surrounding network of caves. The massive discharge causes the platform and lights to shut off temporarily.

As emergency lights and equipment come back online, O'Connell quickly scans the subspace radar screen to see it devoid of any incoming distortion waves from the third transport center. She switches to another screen to find the storm residing in the Zone completely dissipated except for a residual pocket near the Cavern City Airport.

She grins then looks around the lab to find Camille staring at her. "We finally did it my friend! There are no more incoming distortion waves and the storm inside the Zone is gone. I think the Shadow Team just saved the world."

Camille walks over and gives O'Connell a big hug then steps back anxiously. "Do you think Ritan and Reckston made it back safe?"

O'Connell shrugs as her forehead wrinkles. "I'm not certain, but I double-checked the data. There is nothing to indicate they didn't. Now, I suggest you quit worrying, let's open up some of that champagne Hopper and Dell pilfered a while back just for this occasion."

Camille stares at her for a moment longer then smile. "Yeah! You know that sounds like a good idea. I'll be back shortly with a glass for you." She turns and leaves to prepare a celebration for everyone.

O'Connell watches her go as a troublesome thought crosses her mind. *Today we succeeded but as long as the world continues to use quark technology and creates more subspace distortions bubbles, our future will always be in jeopardy...*

DARK DAY, BRIGHT FUTURE

5/14/2037

With celebrations in full swing, a severe earthquake rocks Shadow Base to its core. The ground shakes so violently huge chunks of rocks crash to the floor. Desperate minutes pass before the ground stops moving. O'Connell finds herself sitting in darkness and is surprised to be alive then wonders how they underestimated the repercussions of the deflection process on the immediate vicinity. Somewhere off in the distance she hears a man scream but it stops abruptly.

She has little time to ponder who it could be with the rest of the cave ready to collapse at any moment. She reaches into her breast pocket for a penlight and turns it on. The light pierces the dark revealing tons of rocks littering the floor. Through heavy dust and scattered equipment, she spots Camille, Hopper, and Dell huddled together against the wall as well as other survivors spread throughout the lab. Most of her team is missing and possibly buried under the rubble. O'Connell tries not to dwell on it and shouts. "Everyone OK?" About eight or nine people respond.

Hopper coughs to clear his lungs then asks her a question. "How about you?"

"Yeah, I'm fine but look at my lab." She points her penlight around then at some survivors as they pick themselves up off the floor. "If any of you are seriously injured, let me know." She waits a few moments but no one responds then points her flashlight at an engineer named Ethan. "Can you look for the box of emergency lanterns? I think they're on a shelf under a workbench near you. If you find it, pass one out to everyone."

Ethan nods. "I'm on it."

"Thanks Ethan, tell everyone to team up with someone before they look for survivors. Also, have them put any food, water or supplies they find in the center of the lab so we can take it with us when we leave."

He nods then starts rummaging under the bench.

Dell's voice enters O'Connell's mind. *Faith is alive but unconscious near the south exit. Hopper is grabbing a lantern then heading over to her. As for the rest of the Shadow Team, I don't sense anyone else alive outside this room.*

O'Connell weaves between large jagged boulders to reach Dell and Camille against the far wall. "Thanks Dell, in a way it makes me feel better knowing we're not going to leave anyone down here buried alive."

Dell nods in agreement.

Hopper's voice sounds distant as he shouts out to them. "I found Faith, she's alive but unconscious!" A few minutes pass before they hear his voice again. "I think she'll be OK, we're coming back now!"

As the remaining members of the Shadow Team spread out to search the lab, their lanterns reveal a heavily damaged cavern. O'Connell stops in her tracks and scowls as she realizes they must have made a mistake and that the future may still be in danger.

She frantically searches through the rubble and finds a wooden box containing items from Reckston's raid on the BTC. She crouches down to remove the Dynalink phasing band and attaches it to her wrist then retrieves a small felt bag containing the flat-panel optic reader, data disks and vials. She stands then weaves around huge rocks to open a panel on the subspace radar console and ejects the

SOL. She carefully puts it in the bag with the items then returns to Dell and Camille.

Camille immediately puts her hand on top of the phasing band as O'Connell inspects it. "Whoa! I hope you're not planning to activate that right now. We're at the hypocenter between two of the largest distortion bubbles ever generated. If we try to phase out of here, we may find ourselves forever lost in subspace."

O'Connell presses her lips together then nods. "You're right Camille. If possible, we should try to use the emergency escape tunnel first. If we reach the surface, I think we'll be far enough away to use it then, agreed?"

Camille reaches out and squeezes her shoulder. "Okeydokey."

Faith has her arm around Hopper's shoulders as they approach and stop in front of the three women. O'Connell gently inspects her scalp then looks into her eyes with her flashlight. "How are you feeling Doc?"

Faith puts a hand to her forehead. "I have a headache but it's nothing to worry about."

Dell puts a supporting arm around Faith. "Please, let me help you. It's the least I can do since you saved my life." Faith smiles as she leans against Dell.

O'Connell looks around then raises her voice. "Listen up everyone! We need to leave before the rest of the cave collapses. Grab what you can from the pile of supplies you've collected. Hopper is going to guide us through the escape route so listen to any instructions he may have. I hate to say this but for now, we'll need to leave the dead behind."

She shines her flashlight on Hopper's face. "Are you ready?"

Hopper grimly nods, picks up some supplies then addresses the team. "The climb to the surface will be difficult and dangerous so keep your mind focused on the path in front of you, not on the ones who perished here today. One missed step could endanger yourself and others. Watch out for loose rocks and space yourselves out in case there is another cave-in. If you get into trouble, don't hesitate to ask for help. Alright everyone, let's go!"

The remaining members quietly follow Hopper out of the lab and into the dark tunnel ahead. Within minutes, the place is empty except for O'Connell who stands at the door. She lifts her lantern high in the air to take one last look around. With a sigh, she turns and leaves wondering if she'll ever see this place again. The light in the room quickly fades to black as she travels across the rock-strewn cave outside.

After a physically draining three-hour climb through unstable rocky tunnels, eleven grimy men and women of the Shadow Team exit via an escape hatch and into direct sunlight. The dark cloud hanging over their heads evaporates as they ecstatically hug each other, thankful to be alive and safe on the surface.

Nearby they see a dilapidated building probably built to house survivors like themselves. Bordering the structure is a field of colorful wild flowers and windblown grass. The sight and smell is overwhelming and instantly reminds Dell of a perfect day she visualized outside a cave months ago with Hopper. She probes her love's mind and senses his only concern right now is for everyone's safety. Understanding, she smiles as she realizes her dream of being a couple may still come true.

After a short rest Dell, Hopper, and O'Connell gather to discuss their options. During the tense conversation, O'Connell runs her fingers through her hair. "I know it sounds crazy but this can't wait! We need to explain to the President what quark technology will do to this world as soon as possible. If we don't, all our hard work may be wasted."

Hopper shakes his head then he rolls his eyes. "O'Connell, I agree with you but don't you think the President will be shocked to see so many *dead people* appear out of thin air. You forget you've been considered deceased longer than the rest of us. On top of that, you want to tell him continued use of quark phasing technology could possibly wipe out humanity and sterilize the planet? Come on, that's going to be one tough pill for anyone to swallow."

O'Connell's anger rises as Dell interrupts. "I think Hopper's right. If we all show up it will raise too many questions. I believe it will be better if you go alone since you're the most knowledgeable about the effects of quark technology and best qualified to make President Wellington understand. It may be difficult to persuade him to help but if you put some thought into it, I'm sure you can succeed. Personally, I don't think anyone would mind waiting here, it's been ages since most of us have been out in the open." She looks at Hopper and grins. "Sound like a plan?"

O'Connell's brow wrinkles as she ponders the idea. "I suppose you're right Dell. If the team won't mind staying here a few days then let's do it." All three nod in unison. O'Connell shrugs then turns to inform the remaining team members of their decision.

A loose circle forms around her as she addresses them one last time. Pain and sadness is still evident on many of their faces. "I know it's hard to believe we lost so many good friends after accomplishing such a great feat today but don't let this get you down. In time, we'll bounce back stronger than before. Right now, try to stay focused and understand our fight to save the world may not be over. I'll be talking with the President shortly to convince him the world needs to stop using quark technology. If he decides to help, maybe he'll provide accommodations as well. Once again, thank you all for agreeing to stay here for a couple of days. If you have any questions or needs, just ask Hopper or Dell since they are both highly trained survivalist.

She reaches into her pocket and takes out a small bag containing several items from the future then hands it to Camille. "Take care of these until I get back OK?" She touches the woman's lips to keep her from saying anything. "Our future may depend on it."

Camille gives her a pouty expression that changes into a grin.

O'Connell smiles back then turns around in a circle. "I promise to return with some supplies or to take you to a place to stay. I look forward to seeing you soon." She gives them a heart-felt wave then switches the Dynalink phasing band to run on internal power. Camille sadly waves back as a bright white light engulfs O'Connell's body and disappears.

The remaining team members find themselves staring at each other. Hopper finally breaks the silence. "I'm honored to be in the company of so many brilliant men and women. Today you took steps towards saving our world and gave humanity a future to look forward too. O'Connell really doesn't know how long it will take before quark technology will start having an effect on the environment, but to insure our future stays bright, I'm sure she'll find a way to convince the President to limit or eradicate its use. However, right now we need to change gears and focus on ourselves. Let's investigate that building over there. It looks like it will provide excellent shelter for the night. Later, we will do an inventory of our supplies and then after that...after that, we'll just play it by ear OK?" Hopper stops to look around the circle with genuine concern, his gaze finally falls on Dell who gives him a kind smile.

Camille's cheery voice finally breaks the solemn mood. "This sounds like camping to me. I can hardly wait to see the sunset." She runs off to inspect the building, the rest soon follow leaving only Dell and Hopper looking at each other.

With blue sky and a bright warm sun overhead, Dell's smile grows as she walks over and tenderly grasps Hopper's hand to lead him out into the field of colorful wild flowers and windblown grass. "Don't worry my love; they'll be alright for now. You know, I wouldn't mind seeing the sunset myself."

TROUBLE IN WASHINGTON

5/18/2037

President Wellington leans back in his chair as he looks around a large table full of high-ranking officers and leading scientists. McCloud and Colonel Barland sit next to him on his right. Wellington hides his irritation as he wonders to himself. *O'Connell, where are you? You should've been here a half hour ago.*

He leans over and presses a button on the conference table. "Helen! Has security notified you if my special guest arrived yet?" A light briefly appears and fades in the back of the room. Everyone turns to see a white-haired woman in a clean lab coat standing there holding several rolled charts. Conversations erupt all around the room as most of them recognize her.

With a sense of urgency, O'Connell walks to the front of the room as a man's voice comes over a speaker on the desk. "Mr. President, this is Corbin from security. We haven't detected any field activity within a five-kilometer radius. I'll notify you as soon as we see something."

Wellington scowls then presses the button again. "Corbin, my guest just arrived. I want no interruption until further notice. That is all."

Feelings vary around the room as O'Connell approaches the President then turns to face the assembly. Wellington raises his voice over the growing commotion so everyone can hear. "Everyone settle down. Quiet please! These have been extraordinary times and today is no exception. I would like to reintroduce a colleague of yours, Kathleen O'Connell.

He nods to her with a reassuring smile. "I know most of you are wondering how O'Connell is alive and well after being missing for over a year? Well, she and others have been secretly working on a project I created to discover the effects of quark technology on our environment and is here today to present their findings. Keep in mind everything discussed is to remain top secret until further notice." He gestures for O'Connell to begin.

O'Connell spreads out a chart on the table, immediately a map of the earth appears on the wall behind her with areas shaded in red. "I will be happy to answer your questions but first, let me share with you what we discovered." She takes out a laser pointer from her pocket then turns around and points to one of the shaded areas. "When the Zone first appeared in the southeast region of New Mexico, weather patterns changed drastically. A short time later, other areas started reporting the same phenomenon along with failing communications and a rise in the sterility rates of local livestock. If this trend continues unchecked, it will only be a matter of time before it affects humans as well as plant life.

So how could these effects from an explosion in the desert spread so quickly and without detection?" She pauses to look around, but no one responds.

"Surprisingly, the clues were in front of us all along. The answer lies in the physics of subspace distortion. Even before the arrival of an unknown enemy force inside the Zone, teams of scientists around the world were already experimenting with quark technology. Through our investigation, we discovered the enemy force also uses an advanced form of this same technology. My team has documented that when phase fields are generated, it distorts subspace and interacts with a newly discovered, but not fully understood, *ninth* dimension."

"Let me give you an example of what I'm talking about." She picks up an empty glass off the table. "Imagine this glass half filled with water to represent space and the other half with cooking oil to represent time. Regard the boundary area between the two as the present. Now if left undisturbed, the two liquids would naturally repel each other and coexist in harmony one on top of the other." She picks up her laser pointer and shines it through the glass. "In this state, a ray of light can easily pass through both mediums. Now consider this laser beam as the influence of a ninth dimension—I'll refer to it as Radiantnine from now on.

"Now imagine if the glass was shaken. Static bubbles would form between the two layers and cause the Radiantnine to scatter and distort in the middle preventing it from passing through. These bubbles are what we call 'subspace distortion.' If we continue to use quark technology, we will prevent the mixture from reverting to a separate, harmonious state. We can already see severe environmental tragedies occurring around the world as the result of Radiantnine colliding with these subspace distortion bubbles."

McCloud interrupts from the far side of the table. "Hold on right there O'Connell. Are you going to insinuate that quark technology is to *blame* for the strange weather? Do you expect us to stop using the world's greatest technological breakthrough because of that?"

O'Connell's face turns red with anger as she watches him casually discredit her research. She is already irritated that McCloud tried to snatch command of Bunker 24 from her before it blew up. It takes all her will power to keep her voice steady as she confronts him. "Just because we can do something doesn't mean we should! Look around you McCloud. Can't you see with your own eyes what's happening to our world? I'm telling you, if we continue to use this technology, humanity at some point will cease to exist. If you let me finish my presentation I will show you the proof!"

She points to rolled charts on the table as the room erupts into several arguments.

President Wellington holds up his hands in an attempt to restore order—but it is to no avail. He shakes his head then motions O'Connell to follow him to a private conference room in the back.

General Thoughts

Colonel Barland raises his eyebrows as he watches President Wellington and O'Connell leave. He covertly signals McCloud and two High Guards to follow him outside to the garden area.

When they arrive at the edge of a large fishpond, Barland locks eyes with McCloud. "O'Connell is definitely hiding something, how can she know so much? It's too coincidental to show up only four days after what happened at Command and the sudden disappearance of the storm inside the Zone."

McCloud nods in wholehearted agreement. "I also think this team must be working with the aliens. Did you notice how she arrived without setting off the spatial-detector alarms? And really now, the *ninth dimension?*" McCloud continues to think about it then realizes O'Connell's team must have a treasure trove of knowledge. His jealousy turns to excitement as a plan forms in his mind.

"You know, if O'Connell has acquired advanced technology, maybe we should create a reason for her to share it. O'Connell did say she's here to tell us to stop using quark technology. Well, let the world stop using it while we secretly manufacture additional phasing bands. As soon as everything is in place, you can rescue the General so he can fulfill his dream. At some point, I'll ask the President to see if O'Connell's team can help us capture a renegade General. That way we can glean information from them, while at the same time, sabotage their efforts."

Barland grins ear to ear then picks up a pebble and skips it on the water. "McCloud, I'm impressed! So we're going to play both sides of the fence. I like your plan already. It would be an honor to rescue the General. I've been itching to activate the High Guard and our growing subservient army for their true purpose anyway." He snickers then imitates General Pierce's voice. "To create world peace, one where there's no fighting between countries, just one man and his loyal army to keep them all in check." They both laugh again as they walk back to the meeting.

Shadow Plans

Frustration boils in O'Connell as she looks across the desk at President Wellington. "I thought I reached them. That bonehead McCloud and his friends, all they can think about are their own selfish wants. Don't they understand that the whole human race is at stake?"

Wellington nods. "I agree with you, but what did you expect when you showed up in front of everyone using your, ah...What did you call it? A Dynalink phasing band? When you arrived in my living quarters four days ago to tell me what you've been doing at this Shadow Base, I didn't believe you. When you told me about this Reckston person from the future, you got my interest. When you said Captain Phillips and Lieutenant Thompson were alive and well, you had my full attention. However, it wasn't until you *phased me* to their location to say hello that you made me a believer.

"By the way, kidnapping a President is a security violation to the highest degree, so please don't do that again." His face remains solemn as he looks her in the eye and continues. "Unfortunately, anything you say to my assembled staff today will probably go in one ear and out the other. Since we can't disclose most of the information you shared with me, let's give them some time to look at your data and try their own experiments. I'm sure they will see the danger of this technology and discontinue its use on their own. If not, I may have to make it an executive order."

A knock on the door interrupts their conversation. "Mr. President, your presence is being requested."

Wellington takes a small clock from his desk and places it on the table then answers in a loud voice, "I'll be there in two minutes." He stands up and pats O'Connell on the back. "I know you don't want to use your device any longer but I need you to phase your team to the safety of my ranch in Michigan. General Hamrick is already there and has prepared some accommodations for your team to rest and recuperate. Sound good?"

O'Connell nods her approval as he takes out a slip of paper from his pocket. "Here are the coordinates. I think you'll find everything to your liking. If they start getting antsy though, let Hamrick know. I'm sure we can come up with another project they can work on. Oh! By the way, why were you late for the meeting?"

O'Connell grimaces. "Just before I left, there was another big earthquake near our camp. I'm afraid Shadow Base might be under a mountain of rock by now."

Wellington frowns then shrugs. "I suppose it's just as well. It's one way to keep the location and its equipment hidden. I hate to imagine what would happen if some of those devices from the future got into the wrong hands. In addition, due to the knowledge your team acquired, under no circumstances should either of us disclose their identities. It could make them a target for competing rivalries or even worse, put them in harm's way." He shudders then taps his wrist. "It looks like it's time for me to answer my staff's questions now. I'm sure they're going to try to poke holes in our story. I look forward to seeing you and your team in Michigan as soon I get a chance. Good-bye for now."

O'Connell stands and shakes Wellington's extended hand. He gives her one last look of encouragement then turns and leaves. Several loud conversations rage in the background as the door opens and closes behind him. O'Connell sits back down and listens to the ticking clock on the desk wondering how much time do they really have?

PERFECT DAY

5/14/2037

After a day of countless aftershocks and a surprise visit from the President to say hi and deliver food, Dell and Hopper sit together with their backs against a tree to watch the sun slowly set. Hopper purses his lips then glances at Dell as if wanting to say something but remains quiet. He finally takes a deep breath then turns to ask a question. "Why have you always cared so much about me?"

His question surprises her but answers tenderly. "I was hoping you would ask me that someday." She pauses to collect her thoughts then continues bravely. "The day I rescued you from the Zone, I saw a man whose love for his wife had no bounds. I knew right then I was going to save you even if it killed me. The love you give Eileen is what I've been searching for my whole life." Tears start to flow down her cheeks as she tries to keep her composure. "When I awoke in the hover jet and saw you lying next to me, I wished you could love me the same way."

Crickets begin to chirp as the fiery ball of the sun touches the horizon. A look of anxiety spreads across Hopper's face as he unbuttons the pocket of his overalls and takes out Eileen's letter. Dell nervously watches as he removes it from the plastic then gazes to the skyline.

Hopper hesitantly leans against her. "For years I've kept this letter knowing it was Eileen's last gift to me. It keeps me going even in my darkest hour but I've come to realize I depend on *you* much the same way. From the beginning, you've supported, encouraged and allowed me to keep sane in this mixed-up world. With you by my side, I have the strength and courage to open it right now." With trembling hands, Hopper carefully unseals the flap and unfolds the faded sheet inside.

Dell tenses as he begins to read out loud.

Dear Lucas,

My love for you runs very deep. The night we met on the train, I knew you were my special man. Listening and consoling you in your moment of grief made me feel needed and loved. Until then, I felt alone, lost in a world of strangers. You planted a seed of hope in my heart that blossomed into a beautiful flower during that first early-morning sunrise. As the years pass, that precious moment has always shone brightly in my memory, but lately you seem distant and troubled. True love is hard to find. Please don't let your walls get between us. Keep what's important to you close and intimate. As the sun sets tonight, I hope you can open your heart to me as you once did and release your burdens. I promise to carry you through the night with love and compassion. Let tomorrow begin a new day for us with our bodies and souls as one.

From my heart to yours,
Eileen

Hopper barely finishes before uncontrollable sobs take his breath away. Dell rocks him gently back and forth. "It's OK my love. It's OK..." Slowly his sobs fade away, eventually the sound of chirping crickets fill the evening twilight once more. Hopper's face is wet and blushed when he finally looks into Dell's deep-blue eyes. He holds up the letter for her to see. "Somehow I've come full circle. Eileen gave me this to express her love and desire for a new start because she was concerned I was losing sight of what was important. Now, at this very moment, I feel like I'm in the same situation I was back then. Eileen's right you know...true love *is* hard to find."

Hopper shakes his head to clear his mind then takes a deep breath. "Dell, I do have feelings for you but I'm afraid to say—" He suddenly stops speaking. In his mind, the faces of Dell and Eileen merge as he puts the letter on the ground to let a gentle breeze blow it away.

With a renewed sense of hope and urgency, Hopper clears his throat and passionately embraces Dell. "I *do* love you! From this day forward I'll love you with all my heart and want us to share our lives together!" The intensity of his emotion towards her is utterly overwhelming.

Dell's heart flutters as her spirit takes on a life of its own as it leaves her body and flows into his. Never in her life has she experienced such a complete feeling of love. The sensation is like a drug coursing through her veins. Her eyes finally focus then tenderly lifts Hopper's head to look him in the eyes. "I now know dreams do come true. I will love you forever my darling."

That night the stars twinkle brightly in the sky above as the two of them laugh and cry while making love until the break of dawn. At sunrise, their naked bodies lay intertwined in the field of wild flowers and windblown grass.

As the sun continues to warm them, Dell begins to toss and turn in her sleep then mumbles to herself. Tears stream down her face as she suddenly sits up and reaches out to someone. She grasps the medallion tightly as the message from her father replays once more in her mind. Distraught with pain, she lifts it to the sky to view it in the early morning light.

A warm sensation begins to spread throughout her body as the device unlocks the final phases of her telepathic development. She looks around in awe as her thoughts expand like a cascading ripple out towards the horizon and beyond. The minds of thousands appear as glistening points of lights with her at its center. She forgets to breathe as future events start flashing through her mind. She finally takes a deep breath causing the images to fade away. In shock, she looks down and gently rubs her tummy realizing a new age has begun knowing twin daughters will soon be growing within her womb.

Gradually a smile spreads across her face as she quietly whispers to herself, "Yes Mother…my eyes are open now. I too look forward to the time when we will all be together again in mind, body and soul."

Feeling complete and truly at peace, she quietly lies back down next to her man and hugs him tightly. *My love, no matter what path we take in life, I know we have nothing to fear…"*

Hopper slowly wakes to see her smiling then notices her eyes are extremely bright and glistening with an intensity he's never seen before. As the sun continues to rise, they take the time to snuggle one last time then stand and dress. They walk hand in hand back through the field of wild flowers and windblown grass to the building in the distance…

PENDULUM OF TRUTH AND JUSTICE

9/11/2037

Pierce enters the back of the visitor's room with his hands and feet shackled wearing an orange jumpsuit. His face is unshaven and bears multiple bruises. He stops to glare at two guards as they push him down and into a seat. On the other side of a thick, shatterproof window sits his attorney, a beady-eyed man with white shoulder-length hair dressed in a gray pinstripe suit.

Pierce leans forward to whisper through several small perforated holes. His voice is tired and nervous. "Good to see you Mr. Garrett. Any news about my case?"

Garrett nods. "Your High Guards were cleared of wrongdoing and released back to active duty. With the help of Colonel Barland, I was able to peek at the board of inquiry's findings and it doesn't look good. I'm afraid they're going to throw the book at you. To them, it's an open-and-shut case and are recommending the death penalty for high treason. They're treating you just like a terrorist, stripping you of command and your constitutional rights. If you go through with your so-called trial, it will be nothing more than a sham. I'm afraid your days are numbered Mr. Pierce."

Pierce stands up but sits back down as the guards quickly ready their batons. He leans his head against the window trying to control his anger. "Mr. Garrett what the hell are you talking about? I was set up, I'm innocent!"

"Just relax Mr. Pierce. No need to get worked up. There's still one glimmer of hope here." He slides several sheets of paper through a slot under the glass. "Take a look at this, it's a new lie detector test called the Pendulum of Truth and Justice. It's some sort of fast-track justice system being initiated for extreme cases like yours. Because of your psychiatric test results and the case detective's findings, the prosecuting attorney says if you're willing to answer five of the Board's questions truthfully, the death penalty will be off the table and your sentence reduced to ten years minus time served. I'm told there's even a chance of early parole. Now, how does that sound?"

Pierce slowly shakes his head realizing it's too good to be true. "Hmm, sounds fishy to me! So what's the catch?"

Garrett looks away briefly as he clears his throat. "Ah, you see... if you're caught lying you basically become your own judge, jury, and executioner."

Pierce lets out his breath as he shakes his head in disbelief.

Garrett quickly continues. "I know it sounds crazy Mr. Pierce but if you say you're innocent then this shouldn't be an issue, right? However, if you consent to this I won't be allowed to defend you as your attorney while the test is in progress. That means your answers will be completely up to you. So read those papers to know what is required and understand the consequences of failure." Mr. Garrett taps on the glass to get Pierce's attention. "Think of it this way, you'll at least be *in charge* of your own destiny."

Pierce's eyes go out of focus as he remembers what *being in charge* meant to him. That's what he really wants right now: to be in charge. He glances at the menacing guards and sneers. *You fools will pay for what you did to me!*

He focuses his attention on Garrett. "Just tell that good-for-nothing prosecuting attorney I'll consent to the test. I know I won't fail so let's get it over with—the sooner, the better!"

9/18/2037

A young man wearing a white, long-sleeved shirt with a red silk tie walks around a dark stage separated by a heavy curtain. He enters the right-hand side and turns on a huge, glittering electronic reader board as if preparing for a game show. He picks up a small communication device and puts it in his ear as he motions a female assistant onstage. A cute woman with long brown hair wearing a gray dress and red belt approaches.

He eyes the woman's figure then addresses her. "Megan, I think we are ready to begin. Remember, all you have to do is reveal the questions at the appropriate time and bring me the evidence when I need it." He smiles then winks at her. "Got it?"

She blushes. "Yes, Jason."

He touches her nose then turns on his mic and addresses an under lit audience. His voice is cheerful but calculating. "Attention everyone. We are now ready to proceed. Let me start by welcoming all invited witnesses and an honored guest, President Wellington over a satellite link. My name is Jason Blackstone, I'm the prosecuting attorney who will be hosting tonight's special proceedings." He extends his hands out in front of him and shrugs. "Who said court has to be long and boring? Not anymore, it's my pleasure to share with you what our judicial system will become for our most despicable, hardened criminals.

"As you know, our current system is in chaos and can no longer support countless court hearings, endless appeals and long prison terms for criminals who have no desire to change or accept responsibility. It's a waste of valuable resources and it siphons hard-earned money from good citizens like you and me. From now on, our prisons will only be for those who have honestly repented, accepted blame, and most importantly, prove they are *willing* to reform."

Blackstone swings an arm to point to the left-hand side of the stage as a spotlight illuminates a large glass cell. "Take a good look ladies and gentlemen. There are no lawyers, a judge, or even jury members here tonight. Only a cell where a guilty man will be placed. He himself will be his own judge, jury, and maybe—just maybe—his own executioner.

Gasps are heard throughout the audience as he continues. "Tonight that man's own voice and body's reactions will decide his fate—not you, me, or anyone else. Let me be clear: there is no doubt about his hideous crimes, the most serious being the activation of an entire nuclear arsenal at Fort Bliss, Texas. For what ends? We're still not sure, but we have undisputable proof it happened.

"So, the focus is not on his crimes but on whether he deserves a second chance at life. Is he willing to reform from his evil ways? To find that out, he'll be wearing sophisticated metal bands around his arms, legs and neck that contain the revolutionary BRAVE technology—short for Biometric Rhythm Adapting Vector Enhancer. I won't go into detail about how it functions other than to say it will be virtually impossible for him to lie and get away with it.

"Our first participant has already waived his right to a traditional trial to prove he is remorseful and willing to reform by answering five preapproved questions by the Judicial Board. If answered truthfully, his life will be spared. If not, a collar around his neck containing a powerful euthanizing drug will terminate his life at the conclusion of the answer period. He glances at the audience and smirks. "Now, we wouldn't want that to happen, would we?

Blackstone approaches the large reader board which starts flashing PENDULUM OF TRUTH AND JUSTICE. Below the glittering words are five blank panels labeled one through five. He points to the first panel. "Now, it is important to stress that each question must be answered within five minutes." He crouches down then taps a stationary pendulum at the bottom of the display causing it to swing. "When this pendulum is calibrated to an individual, it will become a window to the subject's subconscious and oscillate in real time telling us whether their answers are truth or a lie. If more data is needed, it will continue to swing in a circle."

He stands again then continues. "Sophisticated collars attached to the individual limbs will collect hundreds of measurements every millisecond. That data will then be synced to a computer in here and processed in real-time. After each answered question, the result will be tabulated and the Pendulum of Truth and Justice will pass judgment. If the answer is true, the test will continue. If not, well…

He puts a hand over his earpiece and nods. "OK, I just got word that the Reformer is on his way. Is everyone ready for the show to begin?" He holds up a hand to his ear waiting for a response. Finally, someone starts clapping and the rest join in. He continues when the applause dies down, "Alright then!

He points to Megan who stands near a door at the rear of the stage. "Megan, please bring out Shadley Pierce. He's a sixty-two-year-old military man who until recently, was a General of our troops and the President's right-hand man. Everyone, stand up and give this potential Reformer a big round of applause." As Megan opens the door, a bruised and battered man in a blue jumpsuit enters, surrounded by eight security guards armed with batons.

Pierce's eyes widen when he sees an audience standing and clapping at him like he was some sort of gladiator going into battle. His face hardens as his breathing becomes short and rapid. *So this is how it's going to be. Strip me of command, take away my dignity and humiliate me in front of everyone. I promise even if I die today, I will rise up from the dead and destroy every one of you for mocking me.*

Batons prod him to the center of the stage then into the clear, shatterproof glass room where he is forced to lay out on a padded, horizontal table. The guards clasp metal bands around each of his limbs including one around his neck. When finished, the bands magnetically lock to the table restraining his movements.

The guards depart but a few seconds later Mr. Garrett enters and whispers in his ear. "Don't worry about a thing Mr. Pierce. Just answer the questions truthfully and try not to get caught up in any of Blackstone's games. I'm sure he'll try to make you talk longer than necessary, so use the techniques I taught you to keep yourself on track and your answers brief. After I leave, you'll be on your own so think before you speak. Stay calm and if you need support...I'll be sitting in the front row."

Garrett leans back to look at Pierce's bruised and unshaven face. "I believe in you Mr. Pierce, so hang in there just a while longer OK?" Pierce nods as Garrett squeezes his shoulder and leaves.

As the door closes behind him, the isolation is overwhelming. Pierce can hear his own heartbeat racing in his chest. After what seems like an eternity, his heart rate and breathing finally return to normal. Slowly the padded table tilts vertically permitting his feet to touch the ground. The magnetic force holding the metal bands instantly disengages allowing him to walk freely around his glass cell.

Pierce sees a young man in a white shirt and red tie approach then touch a communications device in his ear. The man's voice comes over an intercom in his cell. "My name is Jason Blackstone and I am your prosecuting attorney. It is good to see that you decided to wear the required blue uniform for this special occasion. Are you ready to prove you can be reformed?"

He doesn't wait for an answer as he inspects the metal bands through the glass. "Let me say, it's an honor to be talking to a god tonight. You have the power of life and death at your disposal—or more precisely, *your* life or death. By now, you should know lying is pointless. Anything you say or do will be used to determine your fate. But before we begin, I need to ask you three calibration questions first."

Blackstone looks at the audience and laughs. "And they don't count against the five I'll be asking you later." He turns his attention back to Pierce. "So tell me Reformer, what is your name?"

Pierce loses his focus as he imagines slitting Blackstone's throat with a rusty old dagger. Out of the corner of his eye, he sees Garrett quickly stand and sit. "Ah…my name is Shadley Pierce."

Blackstone looks on the other side of the curtain which prevents Pierce from seeing the results on the reader board. He watches the pendulum swing left and right signaling a truthful answer. "OK! So far so good. Reformer, is my tie yellow?"

Pierce rolls his eyes. "No."

Blackstone smirks as he checks the pendulum and nods. This time he continues to look at the pendulum as he asks his last calibration question. "Reformer, do you plan on telling the truth tonight?" Pierce pauses causing the pendulum swing in a large circle waiting for more information. It elongates then swings left to right as Pierce finally answers yes.

Blackstone smiles at Pierce then looks at the audience. "Ladies and gentlemen, I think we have a genuine Reformer with us tonight. With calibrations out of the way, we can proceed as planned. Reformer, prepare to answer the five questions the Judicial Board has chosen for you.

He glances at Megan who nods and waves as she tends the reader board. Blackstone waves back then approaches the edge of the stage to face the audience. His smile changes to a serious, grave expression. "Ladies and gentlemen, you are all required to remain silent throughout these proceedings and under no circumstance will an outburst be tolerated." He looks over his shoulder at Pierce. "Do you have any last words before we begin?"

Pierce clenches his teeth as he glances at Garrett in the audience who nonchalantly shakes his head back and forth. Pierce looks Blackstone straight in the eyes. "No. Let's just get this three-ring circus over with, the sooner the better." He turns and starts pacing nervously around his cell as he gathers his thoughts.

Blackstone walks back towards Pierce. "Reformer, before I ask the first question, I want you to understand that you'll have only five minutes to answer it. Before your time runs out, you'll need to clap your hands together once to indicate you are done so we can continue to the next question. If you fail to answer any of the questions in the allotted time or if your answer is a lie, your life will be terminated. Is that clear?"

Pierce takes a deep breath trying to control his anger and frustration. "Yes, it's clear."

"Before each question, I will present a scenario. Only after I say the words 'please explain' will the machine start recording and the countdown begin. Is that clear?"

Pierce glares at Blackstone. "It's clear Damn it!"

"Very good. Now, here is your first question. It is by far the simplest to answer. On the night of May fourteenth, 2037, shortly after your arrest, you said some very interesting things the Judicial Board would like clarification on."

He motions Megan to bring him an item from a nearby table. He takes a small silver tin from her hand then holds it high in the air for Pierce and the audience to see. "This item was retrieved from your uniform that night."

Blackstone brings it right up to the glass where Pierce is standing and opens it up to show a dozen or so white tablets inside. "Is this item yours?"

Pierce recognizes it as the tin Dr. Matthews gave him. "Yes. What of it?"

"Question number one is, what were the tablets you were taking that night? Please explain."

Megan rotates question number one over causing the countdown clock to activate.

Pierce laughs. "Is this some type of joke? I'm sure you analyzed them and know exactly what they are. I got them from Dr. Matthews, they're some sort of powerful relaxants and they put me to sleep every time."

Blackstone rubs his chin. "Really now? Are you sure about that? We had Dr. Matthews thoroughly questioned by some of our best and he only vaguely remembers giving you some advice in passing, let alone giving you these. You realize if you're still lying when your time is up, that collar around your neck will inject you with a deadly cocktail of drugs and kill you in seconds?"

Pierce's face turns red. "That quack is lying! He gave me that tin and those relaxants. I don't know what lame method you use to question people but I assure I can beat the truth out of him."

Blackstone struggles to contain his laughter then dabs his eyes. "Your own method to obtain the truth brings tears to my eyes, I got to give you credit for that. You sure seem adamant about this. So…is that your final answer?"

Pierce looks nervously at Garrett who re-assures him with a nod. Pierce sneers at Blackstone then claps his hands.

"OK Reformer. Let's see what the Pendulum of Truth and Justice has decided." Blackstone glances over and is shocked by the result. He scratches his head. "Amazing, how can this be? The pendulum is pointing to the word TRUTH. But on the night in question, you said you took pills from this tin containing a powerful relaxant. We tested your blood that night and found it free of drugs. The only thing this tin ever contained was common breath mints. Reformer, please explain to me how you can openly lie even now!"

Pierce can hear Garrett clearing his throat from the front row. He looks at Blackstone and smiles. "I answered your stupid question and I'm not required to explain any further." He claps his hands once more to make his point.

"Reformer, you seem so full of yourself tonight. Alright then, let's see how well you answer the next question. It's definitely harder than the last. This one is regarding events on the thirteenth and fourteenth of May. You said you saw Captain Lucas Phillips, and by your own admission he spoke to you then somehow tricked you into activating the nuclear arsenal at Fort Bliss. Now, the Board knows Captain Phillips and his squad died in the Zone on August third, 2036 when Thumper detonated. There is no possible way they could have survived that explosion. During the investigation, an unknown informant brought to our attention security footage showing you switching Captain Phillips' phasing band just before HM2 was about to begin. Maintenance records indicate that particular band was out of service. It's evident you wanted no one to escape the Zone even if the mission was a success. So question number two is, did you really see Captain Phillips and have a conversation with him? Please explain."

Megan smiles as she rotates question number two over causing the clock to reset and countdown again.

Pierce backs away from the front of his glass cage as he relives the horror of hearing the Captain's voice in his mind as he fell into the freezing depths of hell that night. Sweat beads on his forehead as he tries to think of how to respond then touches the collar around his neck. *Why did they pick that particular question? Out of all the events to have happened that day, it was the worst. Even if the Captain somehow survived and made all those things happen, there is no way to explain it without sounding crazy.*

"Reformer let me remind you that you have three minutes remaining to answer the question."

Pierce approaches the front of his cage again to see Garrett slowly extending both of his arms as if yawning. He nods slightly then turns his attention to Blackstone and notices his face flush and lips pressed together. Seeing his discomfort somehow makes him feel better. Pierce turns away and closes his eyes to gather his thoughts. He opens them again to find himself looking at the metal bands around his wrists.

Blackstone leans toward the glass, his voice more gentle than before. "Reformer, you have two minutes remaining. You're welcome to talk to me about it."

Pierce nods and takes a deep breath. "You're right. I should say something."

Blackstone breathes a sigh of relief. "Yes. Please tell me what's on your mind. In this case, something is better than nothing."

Pierce straightens his shoulders then stands as if waiting for a firing squad to shoot. "I know what I'm about to say will sound crazy but to be honest I really don't understand everything that happened that day."

Sweat begins to form on Blackstone's face as he quickly looks at the clock then to the pendulum swinging in circles. Despite the man's crimes, he doesn't want to see him executed with the President watching. With urgency clearly in his voice, he turns back to Pierce. "Reformer, one minute remains! Your running out of time…now tell me the truth! Did you really see Captain Phillips that day and have a conversation with him?"

Pierce remains silent, finally he speaks in a calm and thoughtful voice. "I don't see how it could have been possible, but yes. I saw him as clear as day then vanish right in front of me. Later that night, he spoke to me in my quarters but for some reason I couldn't see him. I cannot explain any further because I don't understand it myself."

A chime dings throughout the auditorium, indicating fifteen seconds remain before Pierce's time runs out. Blackstone hastily rushes his words out. "If that is your final answer, please clap your hands now!"

Pierce hides a smirk as he puts his hands together and then stretches his fingers as if he had all the time in the world. He finally claps his hands together with two seconds left on the clock.

Blackstone wipes perspiration from his forehead with his sleeve. "Well now Reformer, don't you think that was a little too close for comfort?" He doesn't wait for an answer as he turns to look at the reader board. "Let's see what the Pendulum of Truth and Justice has decided." Just like before the pendulum points to the word TRUTH.

"Amazing, Reformer! Two for two. I don't know how you can continue to lie with the BRAVE monitoring every bodily function." Blackstone scratches his head again then turns to the audience. "Doesn't it feel a little warm in here? Megan, can you please bring me some water?"

As Megan brings him a glass of water he pulls out a card from his shirt pocket and scans the next couple of questions. *Let's see what's next. Hmm…Codes, Famine War…Killing of thousands of civilians.* He quickly glances over at Pierce and shakes his head in disbelief. He puts the card back in his shirt as he takes a drink then hands the glass to Megan.

Blackstone approaches Pierce before speaking. "Reformer, to stay in accordance with regulations governing this proceeding, we must continue to the next question without delay. I wish you luck. You're going to need it." Blackstone turns and walks to the front of the stage once more. "Wow! Ladies and gentlemen that last questioning session was quite intense. But something tells me it's not over…oh no, not by a long shot. Three questions remain. Will he answer them truthfully? Or will he lie and die? Let's find out!

Blackstone swings his body around and points an accusing finger at Pierce. "Reformer, regarding events on May fourteenth, 2037. You somehow obtained two highly classified codes that are randomly generated every hour from two different locations. The layers of security surrounding them are astronomical but not only did you retrieve them, you also used them to activate Fort Bliss' entire nuclear arsenal bringing the entire nation to DEFCON One. Soon after, other nations around the world followed suit.

"You may not realize this but you brought humanity to the brink of an all-out nuclear war! I cannot stress enough how severe your crime is because it is beyond words. Now, we have indisputable proof of your guilt through eye witnesses, a digital thumbprint approving the activation from a computer terminal in your quarters, and camera footage of you ordering personnel in Command to perform very specific operations we still don't understand. Therefore, question number three is, how did you get those two fifteen-digit codes? Please explain."

Blackstone gestures Megan to rotate question number three over. As the clock begins the countdown, tension in the room rises as everyone waits for Pierce's next words.

Pierce holds his breath then lets out a nervous laugh. "Who thinks up these stupid questions?"

Blackstone grins at the crowd. "I suggest Reformer that instead of asking questions, you should be answering them. It's not like you have an abundance of time on your hands."

Pierce's anger begins to rise. "You think you're funny don't you, Mr. Prosecutor?"

Blackstone's expression changes to surprise. "Another question? Let me remind you that if you don't start talking I'll be the one having the last laugh tonight."

Out in the audience, Pierce sees Garrett covertly point his index and middle fingers at his own eyes. Pierce grunts and turns to

Blackstone. "You're right. I need to focus here. So how did I get those codes?"

Pierce shakes his head back and forth then hesitates. "Well…I don't have a straightforward answer to give you. You see, soon after entering my quarters, I took some relaxants from the tin you showed me earlier then washed it down with a shot of vodka. I must have then fallen asleep on the couch after that." Pierce breaks out in a heavy sweat as his breathing becomes labored. "And then…Well, I had this dream…where…I was going to hell."

Blackstone looks at the pendulum swinging in a circle then rolls his eyes, convinced Pierce has completely lost it. "Oh my! To *hell* you say? Then what happened next?"

Pierce walks around the glass cell a couple of times then clears his throat, forcing himself to speak. "Well, I then started having these visions and powers as a voice in my head told me to fulfill a fantasy of mine."

Blackstone turns to the audience and swirls a finger around his temple. "Voices? Fantasy? Really now, this is by far the most *amazing* story I've ever heard. But let me remind you Reformer, you have just over two minutes to tell the truth or you will execute yourself."

Pierce puts his hands on the glass wall in front of him as his mind goes back to that night to relive that terrifying moment. He is lost in thought as he searches for words to explain himself.

"Reformer, one minute remains. Please clarify your answer."

Pierce looks up sharply. "I am telling the truth damn it! My fantasy is to rule the world to issue in a golden age of peace. I'm sure everyone has thought about doing that at least once in their lives. Right? All I did was think about getting the codes and they just magically appeared on my computer screen. I activated the arsenal because I believed it was just a dream. It really did happen that way!"

Blackstone waves a hand in the air. "Rule the world? Magically appeared on the screen? Whoa! I think there may be some sort of oversight going on here." He turns to Megan. "This Reformer passed the psychiatric test, right?"

Megan walks toward Blackstone then stops. "I don't understand either. I was present when the test was performed. Results showed he is extremely arrogant, self-centered and has little value for life but sane enough for these proceedings."

They are both startled as a chime dings throughout the auditorium indicating only fifteen seconds remain. Blackstone hastily turns back to Pierce. "Reformer, quickly clap your hands if that's your final answer."

In a daze, Pierce claps his hands one time then leans against the table in his cell. His dream for world peace fades as he touches the collar around his neck and waits for judgment.

All eyes turn to the Pendulum of Truth and Justice to see it pointing to TRUTH. Immediately the audience bursts into a loud uproar. Blackstone covers his ear to listen to a voice over his communication device. "This is President Wellington. I've seen enough of this. Terminate this test now. No more questions! I am granting Shadley Pierce clemency. Please release him to be reevaluated for psychiatric treatment."

Blackstone looks at a camera and nods. "Understood Mr. President." He turns to the audience and waves both hands to get their attention. "Everyone settle down! Ladies and gentlemen, please be quiet!"

He waits a few moments for everyone to take their seats and become silent again. "What a wild night. Who could have guessed that outcome?"

He shakes his head in disbelief then walks over to Pierce waiting to receive his answer of life or death. "Reformer, you passed judgment by answering the truth but it's clear you need serious medical attention. As of this moment, your trial has been terminated by President Wellington himself. He granted you clemency so you can receive psychiatric treatment not a death penalty. I'm not sure how you made it this far but something must be wrong with our testing process." He motions for the guards. "Please remove this Reformer from the cell and take him to the infirmary at once."

Pierce stands up straight as the guards enter and remove the bands. As they prod him out of the room he looks back at Blackstone with a puzzled look on his face. "But I'm not crazy. I told the truth. I told the truth!"

Blackstone laughs as he waves good-bye. "Yes, I can see that." As Pierce exits the stage, he takes a deep breath and motions Megan to the door. "Megan, please bring out Roslyn Butterfield. She's a thirty-nine-year-old who until recently, was a Chief Petty Officer in the Navy. She is guilty of sabotaging the newly commissioned USS Seacrest, which recently sank off the coast of California killing all hands onboard. Everyone, stand up and give this potential Reformer a big round of applause..."

Over the next couple of months, dozens of tests are performed on Pierce. Psychotherapists are mystified as to why he believes the things he does. Hoping to cure his mental illness from a possible chemical imbalance, they give him mind-altering medications but it is to no avail. As a last ditch effort, they administer electroconvulsive treatments, but even then, he is unwilling to cooperate or change his story. Eventually, they deem him criminally insane and send him to a supermax security prison in Texas called the Pandora Complex to live out the remaining years of his life.

GENERAL ALARM

8/13/2038

On a cold misty morning, five shadowy figures in active camouflage quietly infiltrate the walls of the Pandora Complex. A hooded man with bushy eyebrows watches with amusement as searchlights shutoff throughout the supermax prison. His gaze shift from one location to another then kneels to plant a small proximity sensor near a heavily used walkway, prepared to kill unsuspecting guards and prisoners alike. As if connected by one mind, the group converges on several large, vertical pipes and force open a narrow access door then disappear inside. A few minutes later, a pitched gunfight breaks out several levels below.

An intense shootout startles Pierce awake as debris skitter across the floor and into his cell. He cautiously climbs out of bed and approaches his bars. "Who's there?"

Amid shards of shattered concrete and mangled bodies, the hooded man with bushy brows calmly approaches. "It's me, Colonel Barland with some of your loyal High Guards. We have come to set you free."

"Ah...You are all truly loyal soldiers. I knew you would come for me some day." He runs a hand though greasy unkempt hair as his anger rises. "What took you guys so long? The last eleven months have been pure humiliation."

Barland pulls back his hood then takes a Cuban cigar from his pocket and hands it to Pierce. He lights it before continuing. "Sir, we've not been sitting idle. McCloud and I have prepared for your return so you can finally fulfill your dream of world peace. We already shipped thousands of modified second-generation BRAVE devices out as gifts to government officials and other key personnel around the world. It is only a matter of time before it brainwashes their minds to become unsuspecting soldiers for us.

"Currently, the combined strength of our High Guard and subservient army is nearing ten thousand strong. Many of the BRAVE recipients have already given us access to top secret government information. Just this week we discovered some shocking news you may be interested in. We don't have all the details but we now know the aliens are humans from the future and that a group of scientists calling themselves the Shadow Team collaborated with them at a place called Shadow Base. Awhile back, President Wellington himself admitted to creating this team to discover the effects of quark technology on the environment, but we now believe that was just a cover story. What's even more shocking is that Captain Phillips and Lieutenant Thompson were saved by this group and are apparently alive and well." Barland stops and grins waiting for General Pierce's response.

Pierce's hands trembles as he takes a puff from his cigar then throws it on the floor. "So the President knew all of this before my trial? And that bastard Captain Phillips...he's really alive?" Pierce grips the bars of his cell and lets out a blood-curdling scream that echoes down long dark hallways. "So *all* of them are responsible for getting me stripped of command and sent to prison to be treated like a lunatic the rest of my life! I'm going to hunt down and torture the President and every member of this Shadow Team. As for the Captain...well, I'm going to reserve a special place in hell." Pierce's face contorts into pure rage as he remembers the man asking if there's a devil. He slowly nods then continues. "Then…I'm going to show him what a real devil can do!"

"Colonel Barland, get me the out of this cell…*Now*!"

Barland motions Pierce to stand back as he places a small black disk over the locking mechanism then touches some buttons on his phasing band. Immediately the disk and several inches of steel disappear allowing the door to swing open.

Four High Guards salute Pierce as he walks out into the hall. As he returns the salute, one of the prison guards moans. Pierce glares at the guard then takes Colonel Barland's pistol from his holster and chambers a round. "It looks like I have some unfinished business to settle before we go."

He crouches down as the guard's eyes flutter open and grow wide as he realizes a gun pressed against his head. Pierce leers as his voice becomes harsh. "I told you someday, you would regret beating me with your baton. You and everyone else who made my life miserable are now going to pay." The guard begins to pray but abruptly stops when the pistol discharges splattering blood on Pierce's face. He stands up then hands the gun back to Colonel Barland with a smug look on his face. "That's right, soon everyone will be on their knees begging and praying for peace just like this pathetic soul. I feel obligated now more than ever to initiate Peace Around the World!" Barland's face finally cracks a smile as Pierce begins to laugh. It starts out low but grows in intensity until it is echoing down the halls.

A brilliant, white light cuts the laughter short. The silence that follows is short lived as several alarms begin to blare throughout the Pandora Complex.

EPILOGUE

Since the Shadow Team eliminated most of the subspace distortion bubbles in and around the Zone, and an absolute ban placed on the devastating quark technology by the world council, Radiantnine passes freely once more through time and space. Weather patterns quickly return to normal around the world bringing bountiful harvests and healthy offspring in people and animals alike.

Only the demented souls of McCloud, General Pierce and Colonel Barland struggle to resolve some puzzling questions before continuing their quest for world peace. Where is Captain Phillips and the members of this Shadow Team? How are they going to find the location of Shadow Base? What technologies did they learn from the people of the future? As they hunt for the answers, they prepare for their most important goal of all...*revenge*.

Located somewhere deep within the Appalachian Mountain Range of Kentucky, an old abandon military bunker comes to life as thousands of High Guards upgrade equipment and fortify its defenses. The air inside is damp and cold but three men sitting at a sophisticated holographic table don't seem to care. A burly man dressed in a highly embellished blue uniform wearing an intricate silver PSI band on his head looks at a topographical map of the United States then quickly leans back in his chair. He says nothing for a moment as his facial expression changes from deep anger to almost a polite smile in less than ten seconds. He finally looks up and points a stubby finger at a grey haired man in a white lab coat quietly watching him. His outstretched arm exposes a shiny new BRAVE device on his wrist. "So, what you're saying McCloud is that President Wellington is currently hiding Hopper and the Shadow Team at his estate in Michigan?"

McCloud nods cautiously, "That is correct Lord Shadley. One of our new informants named Ethan says he's one of the original Shadow Team members and is currently helping build a lab to counter any subspace distortion bubbles that might be generated in the future..." He pauses to clear his throat then winks at Colonel Barland hiding a smirk, "and surprisingly enough, they're searching for you. Apparently the President is worried you're going to cause some trouble and wants you captured as soon as possible."

Pierce laughs then takes a cigar from his pocket and lights it. "Cause some trouble huh, is that all he's worried about? After playing me like a fool, humiliating me in front of the others and forcing me to prove my innocence, I'll make the word *trouble* sound insignificant after I exact my revenge on him, Captain Phillips and the Shadow Team!" He stops to calmly puff on his cigar then grins. "But why stop there? I'm a man of my words, as soon as were ready, every man, woman and child will know me as the Great Reformer. So gentlemen, let's stop bullshitting and continue our preparation for the most important goal of all... Peace Around the World!"

THE END

Thank you for reading *Storm on the Horizon: The Zone*

Send comments to stormonthehorizon@paulwintersbooks.com
Or visit my website at http://www.paulwintersbooks.com

Made in the USA
Columbia, SC
07 May 2021